The Montreal Cats

The Montreal Cats

Stories by Lois Braun

Turnstone Press

Turnstone Press gratefully acknowledges the assistance
of the Canada Council and the Manitoba Arts Council.

Cover art: Rae Harris

Design: Manuela Dias

This book was printed and bound in Canada by
Kromar Printing Ltd. for Turnstone Press.

Two stories have previously appeared in the
following publications: "Jumpers" in *Prairie Fire* and
"The Montreal Cats" in *Border Crossings*.

Canadian Cataloguing in Publication Data

Braun, Lois, 1949–

The Montreal cats

ISBN 0-88801-199-7

I. Title.

PS8553.R36M6 1995   C813'.54   C95-920201-3
PR9199.3.B73M6 1995

for Donny, who left us too soon

Table of Contents

The Montreal Cats

Lizzie stood on a thick plank bridge she'd laid across two oil drums, and washed the house. Beneath her the clumsy cats amused themselves in leaf piles she'd raked up earlier. A soprano climaxed inside Lizzie's transistor radio, the one she'd got from Jamin for Mother's Day years ago, and which now squatted on one of the drums. The Saturday afternoon opera was nearly over, tenors and bassos and sopranos climaxing all over the place, and as they did, Lizzie sang with them, every Saturday, trying to match their high notes and low notes, and the cats down below, whenever her voice bleated on those very high coloratura passages, froze in the middle of their leaf-pile diving and laid their ears back as flat as they could.

They had torsos shaped like nail kegs; their legs were stiff, stunted spindles poking out from the fur of their bellies. Sometimes if Lizzie called them when they were out in the yard, they would try to run to her. Their yellow eyes would stay faithfully on hers as they made their way across the lawn, lurching like two buffalo in a silent Wild West movie, or like the rocking horses William had carved one winter. Lizzie worried about these city cats, these Montreal cats, unused to exercise, defenceless in the open spaces of her farm, where an acre or two lay between the safety of the oil drums here and the granary sitting on blocks over there, under which they would creep when a strange vehicle sped up the long driveway leading to Lizzie's house, or when roaming dogs came around. They could not climb trees. And so she spent a good deal of time calling them and rounding them up and warning them.

The cats were not unattractive, despite their clumsy bodies. Manu, the male, was the colour of the dried elm leaves that surrounded the farmhouse in fall, and C-Sharp was as black and sleek as the piano key for which she was named and whose single, plaintive note she sang when she was hungry. Their faces were handsome, their eyes bright, and they had similar personalities, though Manu, who was older, was somewhat more complacent than C-Sharp and often wore his eyelids half-closed. They imitated each other; if Manu jumped onto the seat of a chair under the kitchen table to nap, C-Sharp would jump onto the seat of one of the other chairs. At night, they both slept on Jamin's bed in the abandoned attic room, but not cuddled together, and Manu always struggled up the steep staircase first. In the morning, Lizzie, from her bedroom next to the stairs, could hear them coming down—ka-THUNK, ka-THUNK, ka-THUNK, on the wood, one step at a time, front legs followed by hind legs, first C-Sharp, then Manu.

Listening to the opera on the cheap transistor was like looking through binoculars backwards; voices sounded like they were coming out of a deep, steel-clad well. Lizzie could not really hit those high notes. After all, she was a fiddle player, as William had been. She'd never been allowed to sing in the band. None of the women sang much, maybe one song per night.

Lizzie wiped the siding above her head with strong, broad strokes of the beach towel she'd pulled out of Jamin's closet, and wondered how she would get at the narrow strip that she could not reach between the towel and the eaves. The sun was weakening. Very soon she would have to throw out the dirty water in the metal bucket and drape the towel over the plank and gather up the cats and go in to prepare supper. She would have to solve the problem of the unwashed strip of house tomorrow, though tomorrow was Sunday. She thought the step-stool in the machine shop might just fit onto the width of the plank. But where had her stepladder gone? It had been missing for eight years, since William had got killed driving to Medicine Hat to play in a fiddle contest. Had he taken the stepladder with him to the grave? It did not make sense, but very little did. If Jamin were here, she could reach the strip of siding under the eaves. Her legs and arms were longer than Lizzie's, long like William's.

Even Jamin's beach towel was long. When Lizzie hung it over the plank, you could see how grimy it was, but it was still pumpkin-coloured, autumn-coloured, which was why Lizzie had chosen it for her October house-washing over the rags she'd fished out of the cellar. The towel had never been to Montreal. By then Jamin had finished her swimming days, finished with the dugout-diving and trips to Lake Minnewasta in the Pembina Hills. Perhaps, thought Lizzie, Jamin will remember how beautiful the summers are here and come home from Alaska to visit me and the cats. Perhaps she would even stay. Lizzie worried for a moment that maybe she should not have desecrated the towel so.

Whistling for the cats, Lizzie flung her wash-water out of the bucket across the limp October grass. C-Sharp and Manu cringed at the slap of water on the ground, but hobbled after her.

She made their supper first. One thing Jamin had done after coming home from Montreal with the cats under her arms, and before fleeing the prairie for Alaska, was to take the truck to Winnipeg to buy a big supply of cheap cat food from Victor Fox Foods. Lizzie kept the awkward bags in the cellar and scooped into one with a dipper every morning and evening. For herself she fixed cold, cooked chicken necks and boiled beets. The cats, having finished their meal, jumped up onto the sewing machine beside the kitchen door, first Manu, then C-Sharp, and watched Lizzie roll the neck bones around in her mouth as she loosened the meat with her tongue. Beet juice mingling with her saliva stained the bones and they came out red when she plucked them from between her front teeth.

"Don't give the cats bones, Ma," Jamin had instructed before heading off to work for some musher up north, training and feeding and grooming his sled dogs. "Especially chicken bones." And so Lizzie didn't. She tried to follow Jamin's directions about the cats exactly, so that if Jamin came back someday she would see that her mother had listened to her. Then maybe Jamin would stay home. Maybe she would forgive her mother for leaving a child alone in the Woody in front of the Queen's while she sat in the pub to watch William play his violin on stage. It had happened only a few times. But Lizzie was certain that was the reason Jamin did not love her. Why had Jamin still loved William, though? He was the one who travelled from town to town playing in the band. And yet it was Lizzie who got the blame for leaving Jamin in the car alone in the dark.

Sitting at the table by the window Lizzie saw a car's headlights in the dusk, coming up the driveway. Its approach was cautious as though it were trying to sneak up on her and C-Sharp and Manu. And so perhaps it was. People who knew Lizzie and had been at the farm once or twice usually roared up the driveway in a cloud of dust. She searched the gloaming for the car's identity. As it got nearer she could tell that it was a small car, decrepit, spotted with rust, one she had never seen before. "If they wanted to surprise me, they wouldn't have their lights on," said Lizzie to the cats. "Or maybe it isn't *they.* Maybe it's . . ."

She got up from the chair to cross to the other window, where she would be able to see the occupant of the car alight and walk up to her door. One person got out. A man. A stranger.

"I'm nearly out of gas and I need directions," he said when she opened the door. "Do you have gas? How far am I from town?"

He was younger than she'd expected, driving a junk-heap like that. Lizzie would have known he was not one of the locals, even if he hadn't asked for directions, because he did not have their accent.

"I only have diesel. All I drive is diesels," she told him.

He moved closer to her. She stepped back. "How far am I from town?" He had a dark brown beard, but he was handsome enough. And tall. Quite tall. Beside her the cats thumped to the floor, first C-Sharp, then Manu.

"Twelve miles," she said.

"I'm on *E* now."

"You might as well drive till it's empty. You'll at least be closer to town and who knows? You might run dry next to a farm that has regular gas, or at least purple."

"Purple?"

Lizzie relaxed a little. The way he said purple told her he was not hoping to steal her sock-money or violate her under the crescent moon that hung low in the northern sky. She held the door wide open. "Come inside," she said.

The man hesitated, but gave her a smile as he stepped across the sill, and she saw that he wore small rimless glasses. Perhaps he was older than she'd first thought. And he wore a tie woven from silver metallic threads. Lizzie imagined how the threads would glitter under the stage lights at the Queen's. She wanted the man's tie. How would she get it?

It was when he entered the kitchen that Lizzie noticed the cats. They were standing like book-ends at the archway leading to the unlit sitting room. Their hair was straight up and their backs were curved like the doorway itself. They stared at the stranger with owl's eyes. Lizzie suspected she had made a mistake.

The man heard the whining growls coming from the back of the cats' throats, and he glanced over at them there in the archway and laughed. "It must be my beard. Animals are often frightened by my beard."

Lizzie did not mention to him that she herself wore a beard every Saturday night, and the cats had never been frightened. Then she saw his eyes searching the kitchen and the darkness of the sitting room. He didn't look at the table, or the cupboards, or the pans and herb bundles hanging on the walls. He didn't look into the sitting room to see who might be sitting on the sofa. His eyes darted about in the low places—under the table, beside the stove—almost as though he expected to see more small animals.

She said, "You can telephone my neighbour, or a garage, if you like. Here are some numbers. My daughter wrote them down. I don't like telephones. My daughter did. Not any more, I fear. Or you can wait a while and go with me. I'll follow you. I have to go to town tonight."

First Manu, then C-Sharp slunk on their spindle legs further into the sitting room. They shone their eyes like flashlight beams onto the strange man.

"I'll go with you," he said. And he sat at the table while Lizzie ran water into the beet pot. Out of the corner of her eye she could see him taking quick glances into the sitting room. He seemed to be looking beyond the cats. Then his gaze fell on the pink-tinged vertebrae scattered on her plate, which she had not yet cleared from the table, and Lizzie thought she saw his own vertebrae stiffen and the pink fade from his cheeks.

He probably thinks I ate the chicken raw, thought Lizzie. Well, it was none of his business. She picked up the plate. No sound came from the dark sitting room. Lizzie scraped the bones into a bowl in the cupboard beneath the sink.

"Wouldn't your cats like those to chew on?" asked the man. "I used to have a cat."

"Did it die of chewing on bones?" asked Lizzie.

"It was stolen. By a friend."

"Either it wasn't stealing or he wasn't a friend."

The man looked again into the dark room. "It was stealing and it was a friend," he said. "Do you have any other— pets?" he asked at last.

Lizzie opened a cupboard door to put the clean plate away. A mirror hung on the inside of the door. She looked into it and saw that beet juice had darkened the corners of her mouth. "Yes—a big shepherd dog." William had trimmed his beard and moustache every Saturday night at that mirror. "He wasn't crouching out there on the lawn when you drove up? He likes to surprise visitors. I usually keep him tied up when I'm expecting company. Ah, well— maybe he was out after rabbits. He probably won't let you out of the house later." It was all a big fib, of course. She had no dog. The man's head twitched towards the door through which he had entered Lizzie's kitchen.

But there had been a third cat. Jamin had brought three cats from Montreal. He'd been a young, slender radical, accustomed to the alleys of an old city, too curious about what lay beyond the farm's boundaries, staying away some- times for days at a time, refusing to eat from the same dish as C-Sharp and Manu. One day while Lizzie was picking apples from the last live tree in the orchard, she'd seen him lying on the shoulder of the road with his eyes glued to a mourning dove eating gravel on the opposite shoulder. Way off, a glint of chrome beneath white dust rounded the wil- lows at the bend in the road near the Schwitteck farm. Lizzie knew she could not reach the cat in time to chase him away, and even if she tried she might scare him right into the vehicle's path. If she managed to shoo the bird away, the cat would probably run after it onto the road.

By then it was too late to try to slow down the vehicle. Lizzie saw the cat raise its hindquarters, ready to skim across the road towards the clumsy, witless dove. Lizzie ran. Halfway across the meadow, she stumbled on a mole-hill, fell face first, and skinned her elbows and wrenched her ankle. She heard the rumble of the truck and, still lying in the weeds, covered her eyes and waited. The tires dug into the gravel as the driver braked. When Lizzie looked up, the body of Jamin's cat lay in a lump in the centre of the road. The mourning dove's wings whistled above her head. Dust crept like a graveyard mist across the meadow, into the orchard.

Lizzie sent a note to Jamin. Jamin answered. "He was my favourite," she wrote. That was the last time Lizzie had heard from her. Lizzie believed that Jamin had said he was her favourite so she would have an excuse to stop writing. The man here in the kitchen seemed to know that there had been a third cat.

"You're not from around here," she commented.

"No."

"Where did you come from?"

"The city. "The city where he got the tie. "What do you want in town?"

He shrugged. "Friends."

"Better ones than that thief, I hope."

"You said you have a daughter?"

Lizzie hung up the dishtowel and turned to face him. She tried to find in his eyes the reason for Manu and C-Sharp being afraid of him. She was sure they knew him. "Will you do something for me? Take this basin down into the cellar and fill it with the pellets from the bag. Down there." She pointed to a narrow door beside the one that led to the sitting room. "Make yourself useful. There's the switch."

The man stared at the basin, which still had a few pellets in it from the cats' recent meal. Lizzie took his wrist and placed the basin in the palm of his hand.

When he reached the bottom of the stairs she hurried into the sitting room where she found C-Sharp and Manu crouching beside the chesterfield, ready to squeeze their hulks under it if the stranger came looking for them. Lizzie took them one on each hip past her bedroom, past the bathroom and up the ladder steps that disappeared into the ceiling. With her hands engaged by the bundles it was an awkward climb and she had to use her elbows to brace herself as she ascended to the attic room. Lizzie tossed the cats onto Jamin's bed and closed the trapdoor over her head on her way back down.

In Montreal Jamin had lived with a man with whom she constantly quarrelled. Jamin had always been a quarrelsome girl. And one time, on a visit home, she had been bruised and had held herself as if in pain. But she said,she had fallen. That was before William had died. Lizzie remembered thinking that her daughter was very unhappy with the man in Montreal. And there was something about the cats . . .

The man was not in the kitchen. He was taking a long time to do the task, as Lizzie had suspected. How had Jamin come by the three cats? Lizzie knew that Jamin had told her, but she had not listened carefully enough; all that mattered at that time was that Jamin was back, Jamin was home. Lizzie was sure one or even all the cats had belonged to this lover of Jamin's, but Lizzie did not believe Jamin had stolen them from him. And if she had, it was no doubt because he had been cruel to them, neglected them somehow. Now he was in her cellar looking for the third one, the dead one.

At last she saw the man's floating head framed by the cellar doorway. He came into the room holding the basin filled with reddish-brown pellets.

Lizzie took the basin from him and ran warm water over the pellets. Then she put the bowl on the floor next to the refrigerator. "Puss-puss-puss," she called. "My daughter's name is Benjamina and she doesn't live here any more." She looked for dismay in his expression, for a twitch on his face. But he just looked into the sitting room, waiting for the cats to come. "Doesn't live here any more?" he said with his back to Lizzie. "Moved to the city, eh? Didn't want to live at home."

"I must get ready to go to town now," said Lizzie.

In her bedroom Lizzie put on William's black shirt and his black suit. She left her door open, in case the stranger tried to snoop around while she got ready, and sure enough, there he was outside her bedroom. "May I use your facility?" he asked.

As she listened to a long and heavy deluge of water into her toilet bowl in the next room, Lizzie tied the beard around the back of her head. The beard was not too real-looking, but neither was it just a cheap Hallowe'en beard. She had made it herself from the hair of a long-dead, long-haired brown mongrel dog that had hung about the yard some years ago.

Ah, there it was—thinking of the stray dog had made Lizzie remember. The man Jamin had moved in with—what had his name been?—owned a cat. But he had not allowed Jamin to play with it or hold it on her lap. So she had gone and found two strays for herself from the alleys of Montreal, and had not let him touch them. Something like that. It must have been during a Christmas visit that Jamin had told the story, because Lizzie could smell turkey as she thought about it. Lizzie was certain her daughter had said she'd brought two cats to the Montreal apartment. And yet she had appeared on Lizzie's lawn, on her way up north, with *three* cats.

As Lizzie picked up the violin from beside the dresser, the bathroom door opened and up in the attic room C-Sharp sang her mournful note. Lizzie quickly plucked the strings of the violin.

The man glanced into the bedroom as he passed by. He fell back when he saw her. Now Lizzie could see the dismay in his eyes.

"What is going on?" he gasped.

"We play at the hotel every Saturday night," said Lizzie. "We are all women, four of us, and we are all dressed as men. All widows of musicians." Every Saturday night she became William for a few lime-lit hours on the stage at the Queen's.

"Your cats are locked in the attic," he accused. Her diversion with the violin strings had not worked.

"Nonsense. They're under my bed. Come and listen to us play tonight."

Before they left the house, Lizzie whistled out the screen door for the make-believe shepherd dog. She shrugged after waiting for a few moments, then held the door open for the stranger. "You know, a tie like yours would look nice with this suit," she said as they crossed the raked lawn.

They drove the twelve miles to town, he in his rusted car, she in her diesel truck, she following him along the dark gravel road. Lizzie could tell by his licence plate that his car was a rental, though he had led her to believe he lived in *her* city. "Rent-a-wreck," she chuckled through her beard.

He did not run out of gas. As Lizzie had suspected, he was not on *E*. However, he did pull into the Co-op gas station when they got to town. Lizzie waited for him.

The hotel pub was already blue with smoke and filled with a hundred lumpy bodies silhouetted against the lit-up stage when Lizzie and the man arrived. He fell in with the crowd and the drinking immediately, and Lizzie mounted the stage with her violin. The other women resolved from the smoke and, after the audience had clapped, began to play.

Lizzie kept her eye on the stranger, who moved around the pub talking to his make-believe friends. She also drank beer when a piece of music did not require her violin. She could not find him during the break, but when she got back on the stage for the second set, there he was beside the jukebox, looking at her.

"Yes, I see you, Raymond," she said to herself, for she had remembered his name.

Halfway through the set, Lizzie began to like him a little. His glasses and the tie sparkled in the glow of the jukebox, and he seemed to be smiling at her. He stood out in the crowd, being so tall. And Lizzie began to think she might be able to trust him after all. She could be wrong about the cats. Maybe if she invited him back to the farm tonight, or in the morning, he would wash the unreachable strip of siding under her eaves.

She became lost in the music. When the second set was over, the man was gone. They played the last set and he did not return to the pub.

Lizzie looked for the stranger in the parking lot, where many men were tipping up their bottles to their lips and telling jokes and puking on the cold concrete. But his car was not in its spot.

When Lizzie unlocked the door of her house, she scarcely looked at the pieces of glass glittering on the kitchen table and the floor beside it, scarcely felt the cold blowing past her curtains as she slouched into the sitting room, did not need to look up to see the black square of emptiness at the top of the ladder steps. She hardly noticed the silence.

Now Jamin would not come home for sure. Lizzie would never see her long legs and her long brown arms again. And who would wash the house way up there beneath the eaves? The room was getting chilly, but Lizzie, dressed in William's wool suit, did not feel it.

Perhaps she would not tell Jamin what had happened. And then when Jamin came home, Lizzie could tell her that the cats had simply disappeared. It would not exactly be a lie.

What a sight he must have been, tiptoeing around the yard, calling, searching for the third cat, *his* cat, watching over his shoulder for the big dog, running for his life to his wreck of a car with the fat bodies tucked under his arms and the spindle legs making dangling shadows in the moonlight.

But a square of white gleamed there on one of the flat rungs that led to Jamin's room, something that had not been there when she'd left.

A corner ripped off a road map, with writing on it: *She owed me something*. That was all. "He could at least have left me his tie," Lizzie said, to herself.

She sank onto the chesterfield, and tucked her violin under her beard and half-closed her eyes. Beneath a dark and silent attic she played C-sharp with her bow. Outside, the pumpkin-coloured towel fluttered on the thick plank bridge.

Toxic Wastes

"Can you hear that, Uncle Otto?"

"Yes, I can hear it." The radio was almost at full volume to make up for the sound of the wind blathering through Otto's side vent and Dale's open window. "That's Ray Charles."

TELL ME WHAT'D I SAY
TELL ME WHAT'D I SAY
TELL ME WHAT'D I SAY NOW. . . .

"We used to listen to that song in the old days," said the old man. Then he sang, too, in a high voice so delicate Dale cranked up his window halfway so he could catch the pure, papery tones coming from his great-uncle's throat: "SEE THE GIRL WITH THE DIAMOND RINGS, SHE KNOW HOW TO TWIST THAT THING, OH————"

Dale hooted and slammed his foot onto the accelerator. The dust trail lengthened behind them.

Uncle Otto stopped singing to ask, "How come you know it? How come you know the words to such old music?"

"My mom has a whole bunch of records and stuff!" Dale

shouted, trying to direct his voice towards the old man and
keep his eyes on the road at the same time. "Old rock-and-roll
and blues stuff. Me and my sister used to listen to it whenever
Mom and Dad were out for the evening." Used to. Dale had
tried it alone a few times, but it hadn't worked without
Nina's strap-shoes sliding and hopping on the flattened
living-room carpet.

Uncle Otto shook his head. His cap seemed not to move,
though, when his skull twisted inside it. "Can't really imagine people nowadays being interested in Ray Charles,
either," Otto cried. "You know this part? COME ON TWIST THAT
THING, COME ON TWIST THAT THING, KEEP A-TWISTIN' THAT
THING. . . ."

They sped past chained dogs, roving dogs, a woman
holding a hoe in her garden, girls lying in a row on beach
towels on a scorched lawn, slinking cats, and sparrow hawks
on hydro wires. Dale did not have his driver's license yet.
But he had a learner's permit. His mother had wanted the
trash heap behind the guest house cleaned up before the rest
of the summer relatives began to arrive, and everyone had
been occupied except Dale and Uncle Otto. With the back of
the pick-up piled with floes of styrofoam, old asphalt shingles, and waving streamers of plastic, the two had set off for
the dump ten kilometres away.

The main reason Dale had wanted to haul the trash was
that he'd hoped his mother would let him go by himself. It
was all side-road driving, not much chance of running into
cops. He could extend his trip a little, stop and talk to the girls
sunbathing on farm lawns. Then his mom had made him take
Uncle Otto along. Such a joke—Uncle Otto hadn't driven for
years. What use would he be? What could possibly go wrong,
anyway? "Do you think I'm suddenly going to forget how to
drive, in the middle of driving?" Dale had whispered to his
mother as they closed the tailgate. Uncle Otto was already
climbing into the passenger seat. Of course, they needn't

have whispered, the old man was so deaf. Still, a chance to drive was a chance to drive.

And then Uncle Otto had begun beating time on his knee to the rock-and-roll pounding out of the truck radio, and Dale had cranked up the bass and the volume and the speedometer. And Uncle Otto had smiled.

"So you and your sister used to dance to Ray Charles," Uncle Otto said in the middle of the song. "I didn't see her this morning. . . ."

Dale slowed down at an intersection of lonely dirt roads. "She's gone, Uncle Otto."

"Gone?"

"She went east."

"East?"

One minute a sister who danced with him in girlish shoes, a girl with bitten fingernails, the next a brittle, secretive rebel with a cold diamond on her nostril.

Dale's fingers clutched the wheel a little harder. "She went with a guy."

Uncle Otto looked straight ahead. "Oh. Well, then. She'll be having fun," he said as though Nina had decided to take a ride on a ferris wheel.

"I don't think she's coming back."

"Everybody comes back."

One of the styrofoam pieces flipped off the pile on the back and wafted onto the shoulder of the gravel road. Dale watched it in the mirror, but Uncle Otto kept on warbling. "MAKE ME FEEL ALL RIGHT, WELL I FEEL ALL RIGHT NOW. . . ."

As they bounced over the swells at intersections, as the tires spit stones against the bottom of the chassis, Dale realized someone new had slipped into the seat beside him. A hitchhiker he'd picked up along the way. It reminded Dale of the legends his friends liked to tell about passengers appearing mystically in the back seats of cars on freeways, passengers who looked like Jesus, or like somebody who'd died recently in a highway accident. This man looked like Uncle Otto, was deaf like Uncle Otto, but had a life unknown to Dale. The man sitting on the tattered seat now could remember the words to Ray Charles songs, could dance with his fingertips the way he once might have danced with his whole body. And when Dale glanced at the old man from time to time, he noticed other new things: the outline of coins in the man's pants pocket; a warp in the zipper of his jacket; the jacket itself, covering those bony leathered arms even as the sun beat down; one thick black hair among the grey ones frosting his chin, one black hair crying out for its youth.

Dale didn't know how Uncle Otto had spent the last eighty years, except that he'd been a farmer, and that when he was—how old?—middle-aged?—he'd listened to rock-and-roll, to Ray Charles.

Dale let up on the accelerator and turned down the radio, wanting to say something about it, something important, ask a question maybe. Dale turned to the old man. Just then, Uncle Otto lifted his hand to his mouth. Glistening pink gums slithered across his lower lip and a graceful curve of teeth. He held the dentures for a few moments, while his tongue searched the real gums inside his mouth. "Raspberry seeds," he hissed. "In the jam, at lunch. Damn raspberry seeds. Seeds in everything. They find all the foods they can that have big, hard seeds, and that's what we get." He stuffed the plate, too large for his collapsing jaw, back into his mouth.

They turned onto a connecting road that led to the municipal nuisance grounds. Here more sparrow hawks interrupted the clean, even sways of hydro line. There were always more preying birds around the dump. The rise of it appeared a kilometre ahead, and in the centre of it, volcano-like, a billow of whitish smoke.

But something new had been added. "What's all this?" cried Uncle Otto as the truck neared the approach road to the grounds.

"What've they done?" Dale echoed.

More than one object presided over the narrow entrance today, where there used to be just a driveway. Three things: a broad, steel-link gate, about eight feet high, attached to thick steel posts; an old brown station wagon, almost too long to fit on the bit of gravel between the road and the gate; and beside the gate an enormous sign, a billboard really, that leered down at two women perched on the hood of the car.

Dale pulled over to the side of the road. The women turned and fixed their gaze on the faces of the boy and the man in the cab of the truck.

Uncle Otto peered through the dusty windshield at the sign. "What's it all about?"

NO DEAD ANIMALS	NO SCAVENGING
8-FOOT WOOD PRODUCTS MAX	SEPARATE YOUR WASTES

BY-LAWS #1346-3 & 1012

And below the billboard, another smaller sign, nailed onto the larger one:

POSITIVELY NO DUMPING
OF DEAD ANIMALS
BY ORDER

Dale read the instructions loud enough for his uncle to hear.

Uncle Otto pointed to the gate. "Look, it's padlocked!"

"They've got hours now. 'Tuesday to Friday 8 A.M. to 9 P.M. Monday and Saturday 8 A.M. to noon. Closed Sundays.' "

"Damned council!" said Uncle Otto. "They never used to have hours, or gates, or by-law numbers."

It was true. You used to be able to go in any time, day or night. Dale knew guys who shot rats at the dump at midnight. He suddenly remembered where he'd seen the two

women before; they used to work at the dry-cleaners before
it shut down.

"What day is it?" asked Uncle Otto. He rolled down his
window, as if that would help him understand the signs, even
make them go away.

"Monday. 3:15."

Uncle Otto said, "Let's go get some dead animals. We can
lay 'em right in front of that Berlin Wall of theirs."

One of the women—the blonde one with the wide mouth
and full lips—slid off the hood of the station wagon and came
towards them.

Uncle Otto jerked his thumb over his shoulder. "Didn't
we see a dead skunk on the road back there?"

The woman went to Uncle Otto's window. "Now they
got rules," she said with a sweep of her arm in the direction
of the dumpsite.

Dale nearly laughed out loud. *Now they got ROOLS.* Her
lips were coloured a bright pink.

"Me and Suzy aren't exactly in the mood to go home and
unload all this junk and then load it up again in the morning,
just to follow these *orders* of theirs, you know? I mean, I'm
taking a bunch of women to a baby shower tonight, you
know? I don't plan on having them sit on top of a pile of toxic
wastes in the back of my Chevy."

Uncle Otto had his hand cupped around his ear. He
looked at Dale. "What's she yapping about?" he whispered.

But the woman touched the old man on the shoulder. "I
said, I think this stinks!"

"Stinks! Let's go get that dead skunk!"

"Did you check the lock?" asked Dale.

"Check it? Suzy practically put a crowbar to it. See, they
got this scummy new caretaker. Sort of a dumplord, you
might say. He sure is enjoying twitchin' his ass in everybody's
face!" She shouted for the benefit of Uncle Otto. "Hey, that's
good music you're listening to."

Uncle Otto nodded. "Fats Domino."

"Right on!" The woman thrust a rigid thumb through the open window.

Dale saw cardboard boxes tacked up in the back of the wagon, and he wondered what the woman meant by toxic wastes. Then his eyes followed the barbed-wire fence that stretched out along the ditch on either side of the gate. It looked to him like the fence ended in the shelterbelt of a nearby farm. If he were alone, he would go through the ditch at the point where the willows met that fence, and . . .

"You know, me and Suzy—my name's Loretta, by the way—we were thinkin' "—she gestured towards the willow shelterbelt—"we were thinkin' we might sort of go in anyhow, if we can find an opening. I don't think the people who live on that farm can see what's goin' on from the house. . . ."

Uncle Otto cupped his ear.

"She wants to sneak in!" Dale explained.

"That's the stuff!" Uncle Otto slapped his thigh. "That's the stuff!"

Dale stared at the padlock and at the heavy chain that tied the two halves of the gate together. What would happen if they were caught? Who patrolled here? Getting scolded by the dumplord was one thing, but if the cops showed up . . .

The other woman approached the truck. Her hair was dyed a purply colour and stood straight up on her head. She came to Dale's window. "So what's up, Loretta?" she called through the cab, past Dale's doubts and Uncle Otto's devil-may-care.

Loretta shrugged. "Well, follow us," she said, "if you're interested. I like your guts, sweetie!" she said to Uncle Otto, whereupon he leaned forward and twisted the volume knob on the radio.

"I'M WALKIN', YES INDEED, I'M TALKIN', BOUT YOU AND ME. . . ."

The station wagon jiggled down onto the ditchbank that

ran parallel with the fence and continued on through the tall grasses towards the last fencepole partially hidden among the cascading leaves of the willows. A meadowlark flew up as they passed her nest, and lit on a post near the gate.

Dale looked at his uncle. "Well?"

"Go," said Uncle Otto.

But still Dale did not follow the bent grasses left in the wake of the low-slung station wagon. He worried about getting caught. Not for himself, so much, but for his great-uncle and all his ancestors before him who had had lives unknown to him.

Uncle Otto flapped his bony hand toward the stickshift. "Go, go, go," he muttered, as though the deed were as simple as skirting a puddle on the road.

They dipped down into the bent grasses and stole along the fence-line to the willows. The women had already made it through an opening at the end and were on their way back on the other side of the fence. As the vehicles met and passed, Suzy and Loretta made faces at Dale and Otto and waved both hands, which sparkled with rings and bracelets.

It was easy. So easy with Fats Domino and meadowlarks and sunshine, and the two ex-dry-cleaning ladies, and an old man with young guts.

At the head of the trail leading into the heart of the volcano a burnt-out mattress frame rusted quietly among virile weeds. Pools of stagnant liquid bordered the driveway. It was probably water, but the weather had been dry for some time, and Dale shivered at the thought of what else the liquid might be. Another wooden sign, a small one: "SEPARATE YOUR WASTES!" Here and there other bits of renegade trash poked up above the pigweed. Dale tried to keep his eye on the road and on the bumper of the car ahead.

At the centre, between mounds of landfill, they discovered surprising orderliness: small fenced-off sections labelled TIRES and STEEL and CONCRETE and CHEMICAL PAILS;

a brand-new corrugated-steel shed, wired to a hydro pole several metres away; a white wood-frame biffy; and, radiating from the centre, more trails leading to various pits.

"This is too neat to be a dump!" cried Uncle Otto.

The largest pit, in which smouldering fires sent up ribbons of smoke that joined together to form the volcano cloud everyone saw from the road, was near the shed, and Suzy and Loretta had already parked beside it and were opening the back of the station wagon. The smell of rot and smoke nearly strangled Dale, but his uncle seemed not to notice. "Close your window, Uncle Otto!" Dale yelled as he rolled up his own.

"Why? You'll have to get out in it anyhow!"

Suzy and Loretta, too, seemed unmindful of the foul air. They pointed and laughed at the rubble, and motioned to Dale to get out of the cab. He stepped out and was assaulted by a tornado of ash. He brushed at the air in front of his face. For a moment, he stared into the pit, and at the objects still untouched by fire: juice tins, bottles and jugs and jars, fragments of insulation, even window frames, and, at the very bottom, that shimmering, glassy liquid.

At the side of the oblong pit, a small yellow bulldozer squatted behind the curtain of smoke and fumes.

The women began to pull cartons from the back of the car and stack them on the ground. All the cartons were the same and looked as if they had never been opened.

"What are you dumping, anyway?" Dale asked in a strangled voice.

"Well, see, you probably didn't know it, but Suzy and me are hairdressers. Last year we bought a whole batch of cheap hair rinse. We got a bargain on a volume order. And it was natural, see."

"Yeah, natural," said Suzy. "Natural is big. We found out just how natural this stuff is."

"Not only was it crap to start with—left a coating of lard

on your hair—but after we'd had it on the shelf for a couple of months it started to turn colour." Loretta ripped the flap off one of the cartons. "See this pretty shade of green? Kinda the colour of boiled snot, wouldn't you say? It started off white."

Dale screwed up his face and coughed. "Why didn't you send it back?"

Loretta continued unloading the flat boxes. "Sweetie, we phoned and wrote letters and even told the government about it. But the crummy little business that brewed this stuff went belly-up almost the minute after we placed our volume order. We have to wait in line to lay our complaint and get our share of the settlement. Hah!" With great effort she tossed one of the cartons into the pit. It landed on the gently sloped bank and did not even break open.

"If we'd come during proper hours," said Suzy, "the master of ceremonies would probably have made us put it back there in that pen with those chemical pails."

"Naw," Loretta drawled, "it's too pure in there. Those pails have all been triple-rinsed. Didn't you read the sign? This dump is very clean."

Dale heard the truck door click shut. Uncle Otto approached them, his body curved like a piece of short, bent wire.

"Are you gonna pour it out on the ground or what?" Dale asked.

"Well," said Loretta. She place the last carton on top of the skewed and slammed the tailgate closed. "Why don't we ask the dump spirits what to do?"

"Get that stuff off the back, Dale!" shouted Uncle Otto. "Let's go! Too many flies here!"

Dale began to pull shingles and styrofoam and plastic off the truck box, but Loretta went to the driver's door of the station wagon and reached in with her long pink fingernails. She stuck her arm in up to her shoulder, and when she withdrew it, rock-and-roll followed. Breezes peppered with ash and smoke lifted her heavy blonde hair and the sun reflected off her glossy mouth. "I think we should do a dump dance!" she yelled at them. "To let the dump spirits know we need a sign telling us what to do with the deadly hair rinse!"

But though Uncle Otto could hear the beat of the Elvis Presley song, he could not hear what Loretta had said. Dale wondered what his uncle must be thinking, seeing the two women jiving around the pillar of hair-rinse boxes. As he climbed onto the back of the truck, Dale imagined what life must be like, being able to hear only the things that are shouted at you, only the thing other people want you to hear, and none of the gentle sounds of the world, birds and breezes and refrigerator motors. And yet what difference would it really make, not knowing what was in the stack of boxes, not knowing that Loretta had invented a reason for the scornful dance? What it all came down to was the bodies, the beat, the warmth of the sun, the stink, the ash in the breaths you took.

And then, when Dale next looked up from his task, there were Loretta and Uncle Otto jiving among the flies and smoke, and Suzy twirling by herself. Dale could hear Loretta's voice above the radio. "DON'T BE CROOL—TO A HEART THAT'S TROO. . . " Uncle Otto bounced at the end of her supple arms like a stick on a short rubber band.

With one final heave, Dale emptied the truck. The last bits of shingle tumbled down the slope, styrofoam flew the wrong way, plastic bags soared and got caught in distant chicken-wire fencing. Dale leaped from the tailgate and slammed it shut. "BABY IF I MADE YOU MAD—FOR SOMETHING I MIGHT HAVE SAID. . . " He wanted to dance, too, wanted to jive with Loretta the way he'd done with Nina. . . .

But a noise greater than Elvis stopped everyone in mid-frolic, before Dale could imitate his sister's strap-shoes in the ash and dirt, before he had a chance to circle the idol with his Uncle Otto.

Way off at the side of the pit, at the short arc of the oval, the bulldozer began to move. Dale whirled around and stared at the building he assumed was the headquarters of the dumplord, and saw what they had all missed when they'd arrived just minutes ago: a pick-up truck parked behind the steel structure. But perhaps the person operating the bulldozer was not the dumplord. Dale watched the yellow machine. It prowled at the edge of the pit behind the clouds of smoke and heat waves and flies and cinders. He could not tell who was at the controls.

Get Uncle Otto out! Get him away! Dale tugged at the old man's arm. To his dismay, his uncle used his free arm to wave with, to wave at the bulldozer operator. "C'mon, Uncle Otto! We're breaking the law!"

"What?"

"We better scram!" Loretta cried. And she gave the pillar a shove. The boxes scattered down the incline. Dale noticed that the name of Suzy and Loretta's salon was stamped on every carton: SU-RETTA'S CUTS N DO'S. *Su-retta's* was in small fancy lettering, the rest in large block letters.

"We have to leave right away!" Dale shouted again. "We're breaking the law!"

"Not me! I'm not breaking any law! Nobody asked me if I wanted to have hours at the dump! My dump!" The old man walked towards the bulldozer.

Hearing that, Suzy and Loretta stopped in their tracks, just stood by the open car doors, probably shocked by the old man's nerve. It dawned on Dale, too, that maybe there was something legitimate about his uncle's complaint. Dale had thought at first that Uncle Otto was too far gone to know what he was doing, taking on the dumplord. But if he still owned land in the municipality, shouldn't he have some say in the operation of the dump?

The could have escaped. The dozer moved slowly, almost clumsily, along the edge of the pit. What had the dumplord seen, what had he heard? Did he have their license-plate numbers? Why didn't they flee?

But then the bulldozer came to a halt, and the driver slithered down from the cab. He came to the front of the machine and watched them.

Dale gawked at the man. "That's Keyhole Kenny! Kenny Slimp. He was in grade twelve when I started grade nine."

Kenny Slimp was the skinniest guy Dale had ever seen. He'd tied the arms of his shirt around his middle and was naked from the waist up. The top half of his body seemed disproportionately long and snake-like, and his high forehead and blond hair have him the appearance of being bald. He looked to Dale like an albino weasel rearing up on its hind legs. Dale wasn't sure why he was called Keyhole. He'd heard different stories. Someone had said Kenny Slimp was so thin he could slither through a keyhole. Somebody else had told him Kenny Slimp liked to watch his sisters through the keyholes of the upstairs bedrooms in the old house his family lived in, watch them undress at bedtime, watch them get ready for their weekly baths. Dale had imagined huge keyholes, what a naked girl would look like framed in one. He'd never have done that to Nina.

"Did somebody rub a lamp without telling us?" commented Loretta, a little too loudly.

"I can't believe he runs this place," said Dale. Kenny Slimp had a high school diploma. "Maybe he's just working here for the summer."

"How did he get in?" Loretta wondered out loud.

Slipped through the keyhole in the padlock, thought Dale, truck and all.

Uncle Otto meanwhile had walked right up to Kenny and was now berating him for not opening the gate, shouting to be heard above the clatter of the idling bulldozer engine. Dale ambled towards the pair, unsure whom to rescue. Flies landed on Kenny's bare torso. Dale imagined them chewing on the pale skin. Kenny slapped at the flies languidly with long-fingered hands.

"I own this dump!" said Uncle Otto. "My land is just a couple of miles from here and I still pay taxes on it!"

Keyhole Kenny Slimp looked past Dale and the old man at Suzy and Loretta, who still hovered near their station wagon. Then he spat on the ground and said, "I know who you all are."

"What?" Uncle Otto replied.

Trying to conceal his panic from the women, Dale said, "We thought if you were here it would be okay to dump."

"You broke in. It's against the rules."

ROOLS echoed in Dale's head. "We're leaving."

"I could fine you," said Kenny.

"What?"

From behind him, Dale heard Loretta snort. "Probably gets a percentage. Ask him."

Suddenly Kenny began to cough. He coughed long and hard, making gagging noises, and leaned against the caterpillar tracks of the bulldozer to support himself as he doubled over with the spasms that shot through his narrow body. When he stopped, he said, "Damn flies!"

Uncle Otto wagged a finger at the thin face. "I'll be talking to the council about this!" Then he lurched back to the truck.

Kenny straightened up, undid the shirtsleeves tied at his waist and began to slither into his shirt.

Dale said, "Look, I'm sorry about this. I guess we shouldn't have done it. It's just kind of new to us. . . ."

Again Kenny spat into the ash. "Everybody's sneaking in here. I come here and find stuff in the wrong place all the time. This time I finally caught somebody."

"How much is the fine?" Even above the noise of the bulldozer, Dale heard the station wagon doors slam.

"Not enough!" Kenny shouted. "Not enough!"

"Are you going to open the gate for us?"

"Hah! Go back the way you came!"

Suddenly Dale wanted to embarrass him, wanted to ask him about the naked sister he used to spy on, maybe still did. Maybe Kenny still lived at home with his parents and bedroomsful of Slimp sisters that he watched through old gaping keyholes. But with Loretta and Suzy driving away, the insult would have been powerless, a secret shared only between the combatants. Dale turned and walked toward the pick-up truck and Uncle Otto.

As he got into the cab, he heard Kenny yelling, "What's in those boxes?"

Dale started the truck. He leaned out the window as he rode past Kenny on the way to the approach road. "Boiled snot!" he shouted.

When they got to the gate, the station wagon was already on the other side of the fence. This time the good-bye waves from the two women were limp, spiritless. Any by the time Dale had reached the place where the beach towels were spread out on the farmyard lawn, the girls still spread out on top of them, Uncle Otto was asleep in his corner, his cap askew, mouth open, lips folded inward. Dale drove more slowly than he had earlier, and the radio was silent. The landscape had not changed. Even the bicycles were still in the ditch. When Dale recognized the shape the willows and poplars and maples gave his farm, he wished he'd thought of taking a different route home. Perhaps it wasn't too late.

He turned towards the ditch and angled down its steep bank. Uncle Otto's body swivelled on the fake leather seat, and his eyes popped open. He said nothing, but Dale could tell he did not know where they were. "Shortcut!" Dale yelled. His voice bounced in rhythm with the pick-up truck.

Once through the ditch, they found a grassy strip between two large fields of mustard. Dale stepped on the accelerator and turned up the radio. This time Uncle Otto did not sing. He only stared at the blur of yellow that reached far out to the horizon.

It wasn't a shortcut that Dale sought. He only wanted a different way home. Something to mask the bad taste Kenny Slimp had left in his mouth. Something to amuse Uncle Otto. Dale was not ready to go home.

Nevertheless, he made the truck go faster and faster. Uncle Otto's arm shot out suddenly. Dale felt the thin fingers claw his right arm. He stood up on the brake pedal. Too late. The pick-up lurched and twisted and lurched again. Metal struck metal, shoulders met doorframes, heads cracked against ceiling, chins against steering wheel and greasy dashboard.

They'd hit a rut, a drain that ran across both fields to carry the run-off after a downpour. Disguised by a thick growth of quack-grass and thistle, it was almost invisible at this time of year. But Dale knew the drain was there; it had been there all his life, and he'd driven through it with his father, gently, cautiously, many times.

And Dale knew he'd hit the brake too hard, turned the wheels too sharp. They wouldn't have gotten knocked around so bad if his reaction hadn't been so adolescent.

The truck stopped, finally. Uncle Otto sat tilted in his seat like a crash test dummy.

"Uncle! Are you okay? Are you okay?" Dale shouted at the top of his voice. He reached out and touched the old man's arm.

"Are you okay?" the papery voice came back at him.

Dale couldn't tell if Uncle Otto was merely echoing him in some sort of brain-damaged haze, or if he was clear-headed enough to be concerned about his partner.

"Let's get out!" Dale said. He needed to see if his great-uncle could still walk straight, think straight, see straight.

The boy and the man circled the truck, pretending to look for external signs of the accident. Both rubbed sore spots on their bodies, and finally Otto said, "You might have bent the chassis. Your dad will know."

Dale hammered the hood of the truck with his fist. How many more crimes would he commit before the day was over? The council would call his father and demand the dump fine, the truck would be a write-off, his great-uncle would eventually succumb to injuries incurred from his grand-nephew's reckless driving.

"How does the motor sound?"

"It's all right, I think," Dale replied. He couldn't tell his father. "Uncle Otto, could you —could you drive a little way down the trail here? I'll watch and see if everything is working right."

And that's what they did. Dale stood at the open door and helped the old man relearn the controls. The truck moved at a snail's pace along the track. Dale walked alongside at first, then ran on ahead to see if anything looked loose or cock-eyed. Then he let the truck pass. He saw Uncle Otto sitting erect in the driver's seat and making jerky little adjustment to the steering wheel. Dale watched from the rear. His uncle had seen the drain before he had. Or did he remember it from some earlier time, from decades ago, when he might have ridden here with Dale's grandfather? Or perhaps he just knew that drains cut across all fields everywhere.

It seemed to him all at once that the truck was speeding up. "Whoa! Whooooa!" He began to run.

Uncle Otto did not slow down right away. But he squeezed the brake before Dale caught up, and had shifted into neutral by the time Dale arrived at the open window.

"Do you miss your sister?" he said as he slid over to make room for Dale.

Dale stared at his great-uncle. He shrugged. "Yeah, I guess so." Uncle Otto had said Nina would come back. Everybody comes back, he'd said. Dale knew that if Nina did come home, nothing would be the same. He'd already changed in a small way, and he realized for the first time that small changes can be very big changes.

Uncle Otto pointed to the dials on the dash. "I think we lost the radio. Couldn't get any music when I was driving." Just the radio, then. For now, anyway—just the radio.

"I could have had those women," said Uncle Otto as they started off again. "They were fine women. And they wanted me. I could tell." His shoulders lifted with a sigh. And when they fell, he seemed to have shrunk to half the size he'd been when driving the truck only moments ago.

The drive along the fallow strip between the mustard fields took a moment and forever. At a place in the track where fewer weeds grew, a gopher poked its head up out of its burrow. Normally, Dale would have sped up and tried to hit it. But he kept a slow, steady speed, and remembered what Uncle Otto had said about laying the body of a dead animal at the dumplord's gate, and how the idea had amused him. But now he felt sorry for the dead cats and skunks they'd encountered on the dirt roads on the way to the dump, sorry that no one laid them to proper rest, sorry that they had to rot unpitied on merciless gravel because the dump had gotten too pure.

How had Keyhole Kenny gotten in and still managed to lock the gate from the outside?

Dale turned to his great-uncle. "Where exactly is your land, anyway?" He didn't feel like going home yet. Maybe they could take a run up to Uncle Otto's land and see how the tenant's crops were doing. Uncle Otto would probably appreciate that.

"What?"

"Let's go look at your land!"

"What land?"

Dale stared at the shrivelled face, the one black hair in the frosty chin.

"I sold my land twenty years ago," the old man said in his thin voice. "I haven't owned anything for a long, long time."

How will I know what's true, Dale wanted to ask. How can I know what's TROO? How can I know who you are if you've forgotten yourself? How can I know who Nina will be when she returns, who I will be? If she'd been with him today they would have laughed through everything, like Suzy and Loretta had laughed.

Dale gazed into his rearview mirror. The grassy strip looked smooth and straight and pure, as though nothing had ever happened there and never would. Virgin, like the woolly living-room carpet in his parents' house. Dale couldn't see the drain any more. But he knew exactly where it was.

Tattoo

"Why would she be *late?* Is she a late sort of person, Ingrid? Do you think this would be all right with her, to get started like this even though she's not here? All right. All right. You know her best. Did I tell you I took Freddy to Magda's grave yesterday?"

Belle Luther's fluttering paralyzed the others at the dinner table, the ones who were not late: Stefan Luther, Belle's step-nephew; Ingrid, his wife; their teenaged children, Kris and Fran; and Belle's second husband, Freddy, who was eighty-six and had recently become uncommonly fixated on his first wife, who was dead. It was August, and they were assembled at Stefan and Ingrid's farm for a routine family meal, except that Ingrid's niece, Libby June, was late, because of a tattoo, although the family did not yet know the reason. Stefan and Ingrid's youngest child had already been fed. They could hear him playing trucks on the front porch.

"Now then," Belle said at last, and the diners came to life. Round the table from hand to hand went Ingrid's slow-baked pork slabs slathered in sweet ketchup and hot mustard and

sugar and butter; her mashed potatoes stirred up with horse-
radish and sauerkraut; early corn, cooked on the cob, with
kernels glowing like pearls through an envelope of steam;
last year's red beet pickles; popovers flecked with caraway
seeds and threads of old cheddar; tomato slices, yellow-pink
and still warm from the garden sun. And Belle Luther's
ever-present wild portulaca and sorrel salad.

Annabelle Luther had arrived at the farm at a quarter to
six dressed in an oversized T-shirt with a picture of Beethoven
on the front, and a long red cotton skirt. She'd begun to fret
about Libby June at 5:55. Ingrid phoned Libby June's house
in town, but no one had answered. Libby June usually finished up at the chiropractor's at 5:30. Finally Ingrid suggested
that they all sit down to supper. "She's probably on her way.
Sometimes they go overtime at the clinic."

"Where he could have picked up _mud_ I don't know, but
I certainly did not want it in my car," Belle continued. "He
hobbled over to the plot carrying a geranium stalk. I held
onto his elbow, I was right at his side the _whole time_. He put
the geranium stalk down on Magda's grave and we walked
along and looked at all the other ones in that row. He likes
the headstones with the little carved lambs, you know. Those
are where _babies_ are buried. He gets all weepy thinking about
the dead babies, but they're his favourites. Except, of course,
for Bishop Funk's monument. He's in total _awe_ of that one.

"We get back to the car and I notice him pawing the grass
with his right shoe, kind of feeble-like, because he can't really
stand on one foot. And then he leans on the car and scrapes
some more, and I go and look and here he's got this sticky
clump of _mud_ in the instep of his shoe. I don't know whose
idea it was to buy runners for him—was it yours, Stefan?—
but runners have treads, and getting mud in an instep is bad
enough, but when the mud is in a _tread_ in the instep, well, all
you can do is find a stick. Maybe we should put a wet
dishcloth beside him."

Uncle Freddy's chin was patterned with red sauce. Though he could hear little of Belle's monologue, he did see her deep-set eyes fixed on his chin. He searched his lap for his napkin, but the napkin had slid to the floor beneath the dining-room table almost as soon as he had put it there. Kris grasped it with the toes of his own runners, pulled it forward, and handed it back to Uncle Freddy, who smiled at Kris and croaked a thank you, but replaced the napkin in his lap without remembering to wipe his chin. (He did think of it later, but by then the sauce had begun to stick to his bristles.)

"So I looked under the trees for a fat twig, and then I took it back to the car and told him to brace himself with both hands against the car while I lifted his foot and tried to *gouge* the mud out of those damn treads."

"What the hell are you yapping about, Belle?" Uncle Freddy shouted suddenly. "I haven't seen anyone else open his mouth the whole time we've been sitting here."

"I'm telling them about our visit to the cemetery today," Belle shouted back. "About the geranium and the mud on your runner."

"Aunt Belle," Fran said, with only a little scorn in her voice, "runners don't have insteps. Unless I don't know what an instep is."

"These do."

"They won't let me be buried there," Freddy lamented. "Full, they say. I don't know where to go. Shouldn't a man be buried beside his wife?"

Stefan put his hands on the old man's shoulder. "You were Magda's second husband. She didn't know the graveyard would get filled up before you died. You don't really want to be buried next to her first husband anyway, do you?" He'd explained it all to his uncle many times before.

But Uncle Freddy shook his head and said, "Where will I rest?"

"Belle has a nice spot for you and her in the new cemetery."

"Then I got him to sit on the car seat with his feet sticking out and I worked away at that mud with that twig, which, I may not have mentioned, kept *breaking*, and him telling me to forget it, let's get out of here. . . ."

"Did he get any mud in your car?" asked Kris.

"In the end, no, he didn't, hallelujah. But where did he *get* the mud, I'd like to know. Where did you get the mud, Freddy?"

He tried to shush her with a wave of his fork.

Belle leaned over to Ingrid. "Libby June should have been here by now."

"Yeah, call the cops, Mom," said Fran under her breath.

"What's that?" queried Uncle Freddy though a mouthful of potatoes.

"Libby June!" hollered Belle. To Ingrid, "Have you heard from her brother yet? When is he coming?"

Ingrid speared a beet from the Depression glass bowl Stefan had bought for her at an auction sale the previous fall, and gazed at the pool of magenta blood forming on the whiteness of her china plate. "Donny Jame," she began. She cleared her throat. "I think we're all asking ourselves, deep down, if we're ready to . . . deal with . . . him." Though Ingrid's eyes were still in the spreading puddle of beet juice, she could feel the sidelong glances of her family biting her like cornered birds. "All of us except Libby June, of course."

Thirteen years earlier, Ingrid's older sister had shown up at the farm with two children. She'd been married to a trucker and had been living in British Columbia for ten years. During that time, the two sisters had scarcely seen each other. Natalie was a rebel. She'd run away with the trucker when she was seventeen and, except for birthday and Christmas cards, had no contact with her family.

But then one day, there she was, knocking on the Luthers'

kitchen door, the two children, Libby June and Donny Jame, standing behind her on the veranda.

"I'm done with B.C., Ingie. Bob and me haven't been together since *he* was two." She pointed with her cigarette at the boy. "I'm going up north and I'm taking Donny Jame with me. He's not—smart. There's something wrong with his development. He'll be okay up there with me. But Libby June, she needs to keep up with school and have opportunities, and I don't know when I'll be settled and have enough money to raise them both properly."

Ingrid had only been able to stare at the lusty, handsome woman who was her sister, but was so unlike her, Ingrid. She stared at the copper loops and rings and bands Natalie wore in her ears, on her arms, her fingers, and at her copper-coloured hair, and at the white sweatshirt with the ragged armholes where the sleeves had been cut away, and at the copper-coloured tendrils peeking out from Natalie's under-arms.

Ingrid did not know at the time what Natalie meant by *not smart*. Donny had stood shy and quiet on the veranda and watched the Luthers' golden retriever puppy chase grass-hoppers on the lawn, while the sisters talked in the kitchen. His eyes were dull, not the way a four-year-old's should be when watching a dog, and he did not try to play with it. Years later, Ingrid remembered his eyes and wondered if he'd been beaten.

And before she knew it, she was left standing on the veranda holding Libby June's hand, while Natalie and Donny slipped away in a Toyota truck with a shell over its box, before Ingrid even had a chance to talk to Stefan. Fran was three at the time, Kris only one year old. Libby June did not cry or call after her mother. Ingrid had stood on the porch trying to hold all those tears back, tears for Natalie and Donny Jame, and for herself, being so bewildered at the turn of events, but mostly for Libby June, who was taking it so bravely, having obviously been well informed about her mother's plan; Libby June, serenely waving to the shrinking box of the Toyota as it sped down the long driveway.

The story of Libby June was legend in the Luther family. They both loved and hated Natalie for what she had done. Libby June's father, a stranger to them, they only hated.

Natalie had not come back for her daughter. She'd meant to, hundreds of times, but her return got delayed, either by the Luthers, because it did not take them very long at all to love Libby June, or by Natalie herself, whose splendid schemes seemed forever to be falling through.

Of Libby June's younger brother the Luthers heard little. Until about a year ago. Donny Jame was in trouble with the law up in Whitehorse—drugs, theft, vagrancy. The authorities said he needed a different environment.

Natalie decided to send him to stay with Libby June, because she had turned out to be the most stable of the three. Natalie would follow as soon as she could. He was to arrive on a bus in a week's time.

"Well, there's no question," Annabelle Luther cried. "There's no question that you'll love him. You'll all *have* to. We must keep him tight at our bosom. Tight at our bosom. I've only met Natalie once or twice, but I don't know if she ever had one. Not that it's her fault. . . . For goodness sake, Ingrid, eat. Life goes on."

"I'm fine, Aunt Belle." (No one believed her.)

"He's not a monster. He won't consume us with fire."

"I should have kept him here with us in the first place."

"Don't look back, dear." Belle started filling Ingrid's plate. "You can't live on beet pickles."

"Aunty"—it was Fran—"what exactly do you mean by *bosom?*" She stared at the front of her great-aunt's T-shirt.

Belle looked down at her chest and noticed a small spot of barbecue sauce at her cleavage, between Beethoven's piercing eyes. "By bosom I mean—" She wrapped her napkin around her forefinger and dipped it into her water glass. Her finger disappeared between her breasts as she tried to dab away the sticky stain.

"Belle, if you stretch the cloth like that when it's wet, you'll have a dent there forever."

"A *dent?*"

"A dimple in the material. Here. . . ." Ingrid half-stood and raised the shoulders of Belle's T-shirt so the spot was higher, just under her collarbone. "Now wipe it. I don't think plain water will do it."

"By bosom I mean belonging. Donny Jame's problem was he didn't have enough family up there."

Kris, trying not to watch the goings-on at his great-aunt's breast, said, "What makes you think we'll be enough bosom for him?" I mean, it sounds to me like he's got, like, mental stuff."

"Keep him busy and keep him at your bosom, I say."

Ingrid looked across the table at Stefan. He was spreading a thick layer of butter in the hollow of a popover he'd split with his short-fingered hands. When he looked back at her, Ingrid roller her eyes up into her head. He copied her, then pushed the entire popover-half into his mouth and chewed it, his eyeballs still hidden beneath his lids.

"Muh, look at your shirt," said Fran.

"Oh, for Pete's sake," Ingrid muttered. "Why don't I just get us all brushes? We can paint each other with that blasted sauce. . . ."

"Libby June must have forgotten," said Belle. "More salad, anyone?" Beethoven, wet between the eyes, dared them to say no.

They had just finished their wedges of saskatoon pie when the kitchen door latch squeaked and Libby June appeared at the dining-room entrance with the Luthers' cat riding on her shoulder. Libby June didn't walk to her place at the table right away, simply stood there, as though she'd forgotten where she was, as though unaware of the cat fawning against the side of her head, whispering hoarse sweet-nothings into her ear.

Ingrid got out of her chair and faced her niece. "What's wrong?"

Libby June looked nothing at all like her mother, Natalie. Nor did she resemble her father, whom no one had ever met. But they knew she didn't look like her father because she looked so much like Fran. Their faces echoed photographs of grandparents and distant cousins, photographs Ingrid kept in precious albums under her bed—elegant faces, skin faintly olive-toned, eyes brown and keen.

The cat sprang to the step-stool beside the dining-room door. "I'm sorry," murmured Libby June. "I'm late. It's . . ."

Ingrid led her to the empty chair beside Fran. "Is something wrong?" Libby June was still in her uniform.

"Not exactly."

"Do you want to eat?"

"Not now."

"Coffee," said Belle.

"She doesn't drink coffee," Fran replied.

"Of course not," Belle remembered.

"I got ready for work this morning." (They could all tell from the way she didn't look at them that something was or had been very wrong indeed.) "I put a banana and some cashews into my lunch bag. I left the door unlocked for the electrician. I put my trash at the curb before I left." (They scoffed mentally at the idea of Libby June's trash; she recycled practically everything.) "And I went to work. Does that sound normal? Do those sound like normal things for a person to do?" (Perhaps it would be a joke after all.)

"Everything at work is normal. I put on my white dress in Dr. Dewey's lavatory (he calls it a *lavatory*), and wash my hands, and go to the reception area, and people start to come in and walk up to my window and ask for Dr. Dewey. Some of them have appointments, some don't. Some wait, some don't. One woman says she has a dislocated toe, a boy and his mother come in to see if the doctor can fix the boy's growing pains, one man says he's put his back out swinging his grandchild up in the air. Grandchildren can be real killers, says the lady with the dislocated toe." (Here Annabelle shook her head and clucked her tongue.) "I fill out their forms, take their five dollars, make out receipts. Dr. Dewey pops in and out of his examining room and smiles over his half-glasses at the people in the waiting room. They like it when he smiles at them ahead of time; it makes them feel that they might be next, or at least that they'll have a painless session at the end of their waiting.

"Late in the morning we have a little break. No one is waiting and the next appointment isn't for a while yet. Dr. Dewey goes into his office to sign forms and look at his mail and have tea. (Coffee is too strong on his breath when he's treating patients. He only eats garlic on Fridays or Saturdays.) I sit by the window at the back, in the kitchenette, and drink tomato juice from a glass. He calls me into his office to discuss the plans to redecorate the waiting room and the reception area. 'I want real art on the wall,' he says. 'Where do I find some?' His wife phones."

"Now what are *you* yapping about?" Uncle Freddy cried.

"Shhh, let her finish, I'll explain it later." Stefan spoke directly into the old man's ear.

Freddy disengaged himself from his chair. "I gotta go."

"When I leave his office I see that there are two people waiting . . ."

Annabelle Luther got up and floated around the table in her red skirt, collecting empty serving platters and vegetable bowls.

". . . two old men, who may have come together in a car, I'm not sure. One rubs his elbow, the other his lower back. By noon the doctor has done them, and he goes home for lunch and I eat a banana . . ."

"I wish she would get past the banana and get on with it," Belle said to Kris as she scooped up his fork and knife."

". . . and catch up on the forms and the filing and the bookkeeping. The afternoon goes much the same, *except* for this: at four o'clock Dr. Dewy says, 'I'm hungry for doughnuts. Why don't you go over to the bakery in the mall and bring us each a couple?' ."

Libby June paused. Her eyes seemed to be focused in Ingrid's plate, where saskatoon berries lay scattered among crumbs of pale gold crust. The others followed her gaze to the plate, half expecting to see insects crawling out of the pie.

"I wouldn't mind a doughnut," she went on, "and no one is waiting, so I go across the street to the mall and buy two chocolate-glazed and two peanut-sprinkled doughnuts. And when I get back . . ."

Libby June leaned forward and reached for her napkin, which still lay butterflied in its plastic ring at the head of her plate. She held onto its ends and began to tug it this way and that. "When I get back I can hear men's voices in the examining room. Someone came in while I was gone. It's happened before; I just catch them when they come out.

"The phone rings. It's Webber, the electrician. He wants to know how many new outlets I want in my bedroom."

Belle Luther, still milling about the table, whispered to Ingrid, "The *electrician* made her late?"

"The phone rings a second time. It's Dr. Dewey's wife again. Just then, Dr. Dewey comes out of the examining room. I don't know why he came out. Maybe he's going to do an ultrasound treatment. Maybe he's out of gel. And I say, 'It's Delores. Do you want to talk to her now?' I expect him to say

no, but he says yes, he'll quickly take it in his office. If he'd
said no, if he's said, 'I'll call her back,' the way he normally
does, well, I don't know . . .

"He goes to his office. But he forgets to close the examining room door. I pass the door on my way to the kitchenette
to put the doughnuts away. His patient is sitting on the
examining table stripped to the waist. The men hardly ever
put a gown on. He could have put the gown on, but he didn't.
I try not to look as I reach in to pull the door closed; Dr. Dewey
believes in discretion. I mean, what's to see on a man? Most
of them like to show off their bodies. But still, I try to be
discreet. But out of the corner of my eye I can see that there
is something unusual about this patient's body, and I can't
help but glance at him."

Ingrid and Belle and Kris and Fran and Stefan leaned
forward slightly.

"I just—glance up from the doorknob, you know? I
shouldn't have. You shouldn't look at the patients when
they're stripped. But that's why I had to close the door. In
case somebody came into the waiting room. You can see a bit
of the examining room from the waiting area.

"It was meant to be, I guess. I was meant to look at the
man, to look at his chest."

The napkin lay in shreds. Stefan and Ingrid sipped coffee,
Kris frowned and drummed impatiently on his place mat
with Uncle Freddy's abandoned teaspoon, Fran's eyes glittered, challenging the young woman who was part cousin,
part sister, to deliver a meaningful conclusion to her long
story.

"I wonder now if I would have recognized him when he
came to pay at the end, or he me. I don't think so. I don't think
so. And I wonder why my mother never told me.

"He had something written on his chest. After the first
glance, I closed the door. But I opened it again and looked
again, because I couldn't believe it. On his chest in dark blue

lettering—fancy dark blue writing—'LIBBY JUNE,' and below that, 'DONNY JAME.' "

"Oh my god," said Ingrid. "Bob?"

Libby June nodded. "My father. Bob."

"I close the door again. I mean, you don't just walk up to a half-naked man and say, 'I think you're my father.' I go back to my desk and start to type. There is someone else in the waiting room now, and I have to keep my hands and my face under control. So I type furiously. I make a list of all the patients that have been in today, plus the ones I can remember from yesterday and the day before. I type the names of all of you and all the people on my street, and I even make up different kinds of doughnuts: marshmallow-glaze-toasted-coconut-sprinkled, and so on. You know, whatever comes into my head. The whole time I'm thinking, What do I do when he comes out, when I'm face to face with him?"

Libby June looked at each of them, into their eyes, as she said: "You see, I was not happy to see him. At first. Not happy at all to see the man who left us and never came back, as though we were nothing more than a pair of stray cats. Joy was not what I felt at finding my father for the first time in fifteen years. The vibes were bad. And yet here he was, with our names scrawled across his pecs as if we were the most important things in the world to him."

Ingrid could not meet Libby June's eyes. She dabbed at the corners of her mouth with a balled-up serviette, though the saskatoon juice was long gone.

Stefan finally spoke. "He probably had it done when Donny was a baby, before they—your parents—had their troubles."

"Or maybe," put in Kris, "he had your name done first, and then added your brother's when he was born."

Libby June tilted her face up. "Uncle Stefan, I don't look like my mother, do I?"

Ingrid wondered, Why doesn't she ask me? I knew Natalie best.

"Only a little," was all he said.

Fran said, "You don't have a name tag on your uniform. He would never have know."

Kris waved the teaspoon at Libby June. "Tell us what he did when you told him."

"What makes you think I told him?"

Ingrid's napkin froze in mid-air. "You mean you. . . ?"

Uncle Freddy had gone out onto the porch to play trucks with Coy. Every so often his stooped body doddered past the dining-room window, which looked into the porch. Every so often he laughed. Coy made truck noises in the back of his throat.

"I didn't look right at him when he finally came out. But it was weird to hear him say his name, *Bob Hollis*. And he said his neck and shoulder were shot from long-distance driving. He's still a trucker. And I wanted to say, My whole life is shot because of your long distance. I kept my eyes down and didn't say any more than I had to."

"Your life is not shot," breathed Ingrid.

"He left, and I took the next patient in before Dr. Dewey even said he was ready for her, and then I ran outside and saw Bob walking towards the mall, and I ran after him and I said . . ."

"Did you tell him right there in front of the mall?"

"I told him I knew his wife Natalie and would he meet me in a few minutes to talk about her. He was very excited about that and said sure and I said I would be at Marie's in a few minutes, and I pointed it out to him, and he said, 'Oh yeah, I remember Nat talking about that place. Mall's new, though, isn't it?'

"I ask Dr. Dewey if I can leave early, and of course he knows something is up, but I don't explain, and he says okay and I go to Marie's. Between Dr. Dewey's and Marie's Cafe I

have to decide what to do. If I don't tell him right away I can't
tell him at all. I can't just interrogate him and then at the end
say, 'Oh, by the way, I'm your daughter—you know, the one
whose name you have tattooed on your chest?' He would
feel totally . . ."

"Hoodwinked," Belle offered.

"He'd seemed so excited when he heard I knew Natalie.
That's what made me decide to tell him straight out."

Belle gasped and clasped her hands over her wet spot.
"But what are we doing to do with *him?*"

"Poke him with sharp sticks?" suggested Fran.

Uncle Freddy appeared at the window. He wagged his finger
at them. "What a pathetic bunch you are!" they heard
through the glass. "Pathetic!"

"So you told him over a coffee at Marie's Cafe?" marvelled Kris. "What did he say?"

"The first thing he said was, 'There must be a God. I never
thought I'd see you again.' And he cried. A little. And then
of course he asked if Donny James was here, too. And then I
told him the story of how my mom left me here, and how I
stayed and stayed, and about Donny Jame and Mom in
Whitehorse, and he said, 'So it was Whitehorse.' And you
know what he said then?"

Libby June looked only at Ingrid now. "He said, 'I tried
so hard to find you after your mom left me. I phoned Ingrid,
many times, but she always told me the same thing: they all
went up north, and they don't want to see you.' He had no
idea when he came to town today, to visit an old buddy, by
the way, that I lived here, have lived here almost my whole
life. So, it turns out my mother ran out on him, not the other
way 'round, as I was led to believe."

Everyone was silent as they absorbed Libby June's story.

At last Fran said, "I guess we'll forget about the sticks,
then?"

Ingrid stood straight up, her body stiff. "He was a drunk!" she shouted at all of them. "He beat Donny Jame! I'm sure he did! If you would have seen him that day—the look on his sweet, sad face, those terrified little brown eyes. . . ."

The others shrank from her momentarily, from her sudden stature and from her lie.

But then Libby June and Stefan both touched Ingrid at the same time. Libby June took her hand. Stefan pulled on her arm so that she sat down again.

"Yes, you're right," Libby June continued, "he was a drunk. But so was my mother."

"Libby June!" Ingrid cried, nearly leaping to her feet a second time.

"They were both alcoholics, Aunt Ingrid! After I was born, they were poor, and they started drinking, and when my mother was pregnant with Donny Jame, she was drinking, and that's why he's the way he is, not because my father beat him!"

"You believe that?"

The wheels of Coy's trucks running along rough wood sent a shudder through the house walls. Freddy Luther pranced by the window once more. In the dining room they heard his high-pitched cackle.

"My father hasn't had a drink for years," Libby June went on. "I don't know about my mother. Anyway, here's something else he said: he said, he gave up trying to find us because he finally had to accept that losing us was punishment for the drinking. 'Maybe my sentence is over now,' he said.

"As it turned out, Dr. Dewey had already told him in the examining room that he had a receptionist named Libby June. It's not that common a name, so he—Bob—had been suspicious when he came out."

"He didn't say anything! Ask you anything!"

Libby June shook her head. "No. He decided to leave it. He confessed later that at that moment, he got scared it might be me, and he didn't know what to do. By the time I'd chased after him, he said he was regretting not having asked me who I was. And he was relieved to see me coming at him." She looked into her lap. "I've never told Dr. Dewey my brother's name. He didn't really think, when he saw the tattoo, that there was any relation."

Ingrid leaned forward. "What does he want? What does he want, Libby June? A pound of my flesh? Natalie did not want him in her life. She told me to tell him those things."

"Do we have to keep him tight at our bosom, too?" said Fran.

Belle went out to the porch to tell Freddy. The others could hear her shouting at him in short sentences. She did not mention the tattoo.

In the dining room, things loosened up a little. Stefan and Kris and Fran stretched and backed up their chairs away from the table. Only Ingrid and Libby June remained hunched over their place mats. Libby June kept her hand on Ingrid's and talked about her new memories. Belle came back into the house with Freddy and Coy. Uncle Freddy patted Libby June on the head. "So your dad's here. My, my," was all he said. Kris wanted to know how Bob looked. Stefan asked where he lived and who he trucked for, and whether or not he'd remarried. "My parents aren't divorced, Uncle Stefan. You know what the best part is? Next month he's coming back here to stay with me and Donny Jame. You don't have to worry any more."

"How do you know that's the best part?" demanded Ingrid. "You don't know anything about him. He might be dangerous. He might want—I don't know—your money, or something."

Libby June laughed long and hard. "What money? Maybe you're thinking he'll go after *your* money."

"Stop it," said Stefan in his quiet way.

"Aunt Ingrid. Uncle Stefan. I've met him. I've talked to him. I've seen my father. And what I didn't tell you was that, even though I said I'd had those bad vibes at first, certain other feeling came back. Good feeling. Some good memories that I've never had before. He told me about the house we lived in at White Rock, and about the ocean and such. And little pictures that I've kept under lock and key in my brain for fifteen years suddenly popped into my head. But the main thing was his voice. It was my father's voice, even if he used to be a drunk. And maybe, yes, maybe hurtful things will happen again. But he can't hurt me. My mother can't hurt me. Only you—all of you could hurt me now. You understand?"

"Well," said Belle, from her original spot at the table.

"Could be interesting," chirped Fran.

Kris found a saskatoon on his father's place mat. "Sort of scary, though." He put the berry in his mouth. "Sort of mixed up."

From the bathroom beyond the kitchen they heard Uncle Freddy flush the toilet. Coy meandered towards the closed bathroom door to wait for his playmate, and Libby June smiled a soft, secret sort of smile that indicated neither fear nor confusion.

"Well," said Belle again, "we'll just start fresh. We'll just start fresh from wherever we're all at." And they found themselves believing her, what with Beethoven glaring at them from between her pillowy bosoms.

"I have to go finish cutting the barley," said Stefan. "Good crop, the barley, this year."

"I guess I'll finish greasing the fittings," said Kris.

But neither Stefan nor Kris got up from the table.

Aunt Belle put a plateful of oven-warmed food in front of Libby June. "I took Freddy to the old cemetery today. He wanted to take a geranium to Magda's grave. But he picked up some mud somewhere and I had to try to *gouge* it out of the treads in those runners of his. . . . Stick kept breaking. . . ."

Fran, who tended to be dreamy after eating, propped her chin up on her elbow and her foot on the edge of her chair seat, and slowly drifted away from the group.

Except for Libby June, and perhaps for Ingrid, who brushed imaginary crumbs from the place mats, they found it easy to forget about Bob. And they did.

Until they heard the sluggish barking of the old dog, the same one Donny Jame had watched romping on the lawn nearly fifteen years ago, now much slowed down, and who did little on the lawn except sleep, if the sun was out.

"Somebody must be on the driveway," said Kris.

"That'll be him," responded Libby June.

"Donny Jame?" gasped Ingrid.

"Bob. My father. He wants to meet you all. I told him I'd better come ahead of him to prepare you."

"What will we do?"

Ingrid sat rigid in her chair and peered past them through a distant window, hoping to catch a glimpse of him before he saw her.

"Can I ask to see his tattoo?" said Fran.

They heard his footstep on the porch, his knock at the door.

Cowboy Time

Oliver has always felt like a cowboy when he rides the Massey, a cowboy with his trusty horse. Spinning along the hard-packed dirt road to Havelland, sunset fading on his right, stars resolving overhead, lit-up farmhouses sliding by on his left, Oliver could be a cowboy riding on the range, despite the noise of the tractor engine. Ear protectors hang from the seat frame, but Oliver doesn't wear them on these short jaunts; the village is only three miles away. He is used to the noise. Most times, when he takes these summer-evening rides to the repair shop, Oliver feels a kind of cowboy peace, like a weld between heaven and earth.

Tonight, though, he finds himself caving into a slump over the steering wheel. More than once he must tell himself to straighten up, to keep his cowboy cool.

They don't make tractors like this Massey any more—flat, backless seat, enormous upright muffler that blares and smokes when the engine turns over, poorly fendered rear tires that leave the driver mud-splattered on rainy days.

What's more, it is difficult to mount—almost impossible when an implement is hitched to the back.

He bounces over a stretch of washboard next to the Berg farm. Jim Berg is just getting out of his Ranger. They salute each other as Oliver passes. A patchwork cat sticks its head out from among the grasses and weeds beside the road. For some reason, the cat makes Oliver think of a dress Marion used to wear, a funny patch-worky housedress that she kept on a hook at the back door, so she could slip into it quickly after shucking her sweat-soaked gardening clothes. He hasn't seen that dress for a long time. What has happened to it? She wasn't wearing it when he found her last night.

At the edge of the village, the Havelland store is still open. Oliver sees the blue-white of fluorescent lights through its grimy windows. The store, framed by rickety maple trees, is little more than a shack, will probably close down for good soon. Abe Lowen hasn't the money to rebuild. Once it or he collapses, the country store will be dead.

Oliver leaves the Massey idling next to a pair of ancient, gasless bowsers, out of which small trees magically grow, and buys a pack of White Owls from Abe's grandson, whom everyone calls Duck and whose mother worked in the store until she drowned a few years ago.

Oliver searches the narrow aisles. "Where's your grandpa?"

"Haying ditches with my dad."

Oliver shakes his head. "You're old enough to do that. Why don't you trade with him?"

"Yeah, I'd like to," says Duck. "But he likes haying too, I guess."

Oliver puts the money on the counter and wags the slender box at the boy. "One of these days I want to see you in those ditches and your grandpa here where he belongs. You tell your dad I said so. Keep the change."

Oliver hauls himself up onto the tractor once more. His

chest tightens. Little pains pierce his breastbone. He struggles into the seat and puts on hand on the gearshift. With his other fist he presses on the centre of his chest and sits very still for a moment. Slowly, still crouched over the steering wheel, Oliver turns his head towards the sagging store. From behind the till, and behind the dirty bright window, Duck's eyes are steady on Oliver, two brown, dark eyes, curious, not quite worried, gazing through a film of dust and cobwebs and tree sap. And even though Oliver is consumed with pain, he remembers the boy's mother, who drowned in the Red River.

Oliver loves the repair shop. He loves the noise and dust, the fantastic machines and tools scattered like toys, the violence of twisted metal, the cool beauty of finished pieces near the big double doors at the back. And in the corner where the welding is done, graceful, sporadic fountains of fire. The floor is so littered with tailings and gum wrappers and sunflower shells and discarded screws and bolts and washers, Oliver's eyes are always drawn to it, as though some treasure will reveal itself if only he looks long and hard enough. British America Oil drums, with handles welded on them, serve as trash cans, but Oliver can never figure out what they are used for when all the trash appears to be on the floor.

The man-door, where the customers enter the shop, leads to the order desk, and beyond that, the parts room. Despite being the place where quieter, headier business is done, this section is no less chaotic. The walls are papered with calendars, advertising posters, charts, pin-up girls, flyers, even crayon drawings done by children, all veneered with a mist of grease and the various dusts that float endlessly through the whole shop. The order desk itself is strewn with more papers, more hardware, empty drink bottles, half-filled coffee cups. Behind the desk, dust-coated filing cabinets, as well as parts cabinets that have spilled out of the parts room, line two short walls, and between those walls the Doctor transforms the chaos into harmony.

Bernie Krahn's father started the repair business thirty years ago. The father is dead now, but the sign out front still bears his name: D.R. KRAHN—WELDING—REPAIRS OF ALL KINDS. Because of his initials, people called him Doctor, and Bernie inherited the title when he took over the business.

The Doctor and his partner Frank wear matching denim baseball caps, matching navy overalls, and have their names emblazoned on white patches on their chests. The two men stay amazingly clean. But the caps, they are usually turned around on the welders' heads, so the brims keep out of the way of the welding masks. For Oliver, Bernie and Frank are a pair of mischievous backyard boys who like to tinker. He can never figure out, as he studies the drawings on the walls, whose children have made them. It is impossible to him that either men could have children. Oliver imagines his own son wearing a baseball cap backwards.

The Doctor stands behind the order desk, bent over a worksheet. With one hand he pencils numbers into a column, with the other he fidgets with a drive shaft a customer has brought in. Someone stuck a banner on the front of the counter that says, AL CAPONE NEVER SLEPT HERE. The letters are formed in fake bullet holes. Havelland, being only two miles from the U.S. border, is rumoured to have been a smuggling headquarters during Prohibition.

"Your mower's done," Bernie mutters without looking up.

"I thought you were going to put a new cover on here." Oliver runs his finger along cracks in the plexiglass on top of the counter, where customers drop the machine parts they want fixed.

"It's still right there around that corner. I just have to cut it to fit. Maybe I'll get to it at Christmas."

Oliver sits in his favourite spot, a swivel chair fashioned from the bucket seat of a '63 Mustang, flanked on one side by a large aluminum percolator and on the other by an apple-green soft-drink machine. "Got any Jamaica Dry?"

Her dress was wet up to the waist. She was half in the pond. Up to her waist in the pond.

"What are you doing mowing?" Bernie yawns. "Thought this was your fishing week."

Without getting up, Oliver puts his fifty cents in the slot and pulls out an icy cold bottle. "I'm not gonna go fishing this year, I guess." The shop is quiet. No lathes running, no compressors. "Where's Frank?"

The Doctor straightens up and sticks the pencil behind his ear. "He's been gone all day. Went to buy a headstone for his dad. Old Rolly hasn't had a headstone for almost a year."

Oliver watches as Bernie opens a file drawer and pushes the worksheet into a folder. A dusty brown telephone rings on another, smaller desk. Bernie grunts into the receiver for a few seconds, than hangs up and pours himself coffee.

"What do you mean, not fishing? Long as I've know you, this is your fishing week. Even when it rained. 'Fish bite great in the rain,' you always said."

It's my wife. It's Marion. . . . "Well, I can't really. Not this year."

Bernie twists the styrofoam cup on the cracked plexiglass. Plastic, styrofoam, artificial flavouring—maybe that's what's gone wrong between us, Oliver thinks to himself. Maybe that's what's gone wrong with the world. With Frank gone, the place is quieter than Oliver ever imagined it could be. "How can you manage without him?" he says out loud. "Busy time of year, isn't it?"

"Always busy. Any time of year." Bernie tips the cup to his mouth. "Poor old Rolly. First they couldn't decide where to bury him. And then they didn't know what to say on his headstone. I guess Frank's been confused most of his life."

"He's not from around here, is he?"

"He grew up east of here in the bush, close to Moosehorn Lake. His dad had cattle up there. Thing is, they never really were father and son. See, Frank's mother, Toots Darychuk, and this Rolly Gzowski had a fling about fifty years ago, and the result was Frank. Toots and Rolly never got married. Toots lived in town with the boy and her father, and Rolly lived on his farm. Frank didn't even know who his father was when he was a child. He says he found out gradually through mental telepathy. His mother didn't ever actually sit him down and tell him.

"Rolly always had an interest in the boy. Showed him a lot of affection and so on. But there was nothing more between the mother and father, so it seemed. After Frank got married, Toots got married to some guy in Ontario and moved away. Frank and Rolly stayed in the bush and lived practically side by side. Frank was a welder and Rolly a cattle farmer, and they had this kind of thing going between them."

"Thing?"

"Never discussed that they were father and son, never said more than a few words to each other at once. But every time it stormed in winter, Rolly would automatically show up at Frank's with his snowblower. And when Rolly got old, Frank blew his snow for him."

Was that all it took? Oliver wondered at the simplicity of it: no talking, just doing, being.

"About five years ago, Toots got cancer, and since her husband had already died, Frank moved his mother back down to live with him and his wife. By this time Rolly was pretty decrepit himself—arthritis, Parkinson's. . . .

"Well, Toots was in and out of the hospital. You know how it goes. And then all of a sudden one day Rolly shows up at the hospital. Now, have you ever seen him? I've seen him. You got to picture this guy: big schnozz, big pointy chin, long white hair, kind of folds all over his face, like his skin was made out of loose cloth."

Loose cloth, clinging to her legs, sucked tight around her legs and hips . . .

"He kind of looked like one of those Muppet characters. Used to be a big fat guy, Frank says, but by this time he was gone frail, except for his face; all the fat stayed in there. He walked slow and all stooped over, knees were shot."

In front of Oliver, on the wall, a Snap-On Tools pin-up girl in a red bikini, standing beside a red Mack Truck, grins at him, mocking Rolly's deformity.

"So he shows up at the hospital and tells Toots he's gonna take her home to his place to look after her. Frank doesn't know what to make of it. He's pretty sure Toots won't ever get out of that hospital again, so he just kind of ignores it. But every day he visits his mom she tells him about how Rolly has these big plans.

"Finally Frank confronts Rolly and tells him Toots is too weak to leave hospital and he should get it out of his head that he can take her home.

"Now, apparently Rolly always visited Toots over supper hour, when he was sure no one else would be there. So what he does is, he starts eating her meals for her, so that the nurses will think she's getting better. Must have quickly shovelled it down when the orderlies weren't looking. Very unselfish of him, considering what hospital food is like.

"Only Frank doesn't quite see it that way. When he finds out his dad—so-called dad—is scarfing down his mom's nourishment, he calls Rolly a parasite and a freeloader and whatnot, and has the hospital ban him from visiting her during mealtimes.

"Sure enough, Toots up and dies, Frank gets a job here and moves his family to Havelland, and Rolly stays in the bush and pines. Yep, just pines, is how Frank put it. So Frank does the right thing and gets him into the old folks' home in Granton, and five years later he dies."

The father dies! The father dies! The mother dies. . . .

Oliver can see that Bernie is watching him carefully. He tries to hide behind the Jamaica Dry.

"What's wrong?" Bernie asks finally. "You don't look good." Oliver clears his throat and takes another swig of the soda. "It's my wife. Marion. I found her—in the pond last night. Managed to get her out." Oliver shrugs. "Go on."

But Bernie is perfectly still now. His eyes are round, the bottom edge of the baseball cap sharp against his forehead.

"Go on," says Oliver again. "I want to hear the rest."

But the Doctor's voice is a monotone. "Hardly any more to tell. Frank has it all planned to bury Rolly here in the Havelland cemetery. Then the day before the funeral, Frank's looking through Rolly's papers and finds a certificate saying that he and Toots got married shortly before she died. Got some JP of something from out of town, pulled the curtain around the hospital bed and got hitched."

So simple, so simple. . . .

Bernie smiles a half-smile and picks up the drive shaft again. "Something, eh? How your soul hangs onto old feelings like that. Some people think their lives are over when their bodies start to give out. Can you just see those two? A stick-lady and a puppet, behind a hospital curtain, still in love after all those years, patting each other, making vows. . . ." The Doctor leans forward and leers at Oliver. "Maybe even some hanky-panky. Who knows?"

Oliver stares at a crevice in the concrete floor. How would he and Marion ever get to that place again? He pictures her, sedated on the sofa in a darkened sitting room, wrapped in velour, arm flung up over her forehead to ward off despair. "Must have been a shmozzle trying to figure out where to bury everybody, what with her having that other husband in Ontario," he observes.

The telephone rings again. Oliver clutches at his chest.

"So," says Bernie after he's hung up the phone. "How did your wife fall in the pond?"

Oliver runs his fingertips across the ribs of the empty drink bottle. He says nothing. Bernie the Doctor says nothing, just looks at Oliver with those backyard-boy's eyes. And all at once Oliver realizes the shop isn't dead quiet, the way he'd thought earlier. He can hear very loud sounds now, two roaring, unbroken sounds: an exhaust fan mounted on the ceiling of the workshop, and blood, or perhaps misery, rushing in his ears.

Oliver shuffles his feet on the cement. "You know what happened to my boy."

Bernie nods slowly. "Ran away. A couple of years ago."

"His picture's been on milk cartons in Toronto."

Bernie keeps nodding. "What was his name again?"

"His name is Benny. Marion, uh, she—well, she's gotten it into her head lately that he drowned in our pond. That he never ran away, but drowned in our dugout."

"Is there any chance. . . ?"

"No, no," Oliver scoffs. "Cops have caught up with him a few times. But he always gets away on 'em again. Next year he'll be eighteen, and they won't have to look for him any more." Oliver takes a deep breath. "He was the only one we had."

Suddenly Oliver remembers the White Owls. He takes them out of his pocket. "She says we should have dragged the pond. Somehow she's put the blame back on ourselves for his being gone."

The two men search for matches. Duck has forgotten to give Oliver the book of matches he was due. Bernie finds some under a box of Stir Stix.

"In her mind, we'll get him back if we free him from the bottom of the dugout. It's real twisted. Like, he's dead at the bottom of the pond, but if we find him he'll be alive for us again. She can believe that, but can't accept that he really is alive, drifting from city to city alone, without us."

Bernie puckers a silent whistle. "So she didn't fall in." He pulls an old chrome kitchen chair around the order desk and sits down. "Why do you think he left?"

Oliver continues to stare at the crack in the floor. Ashes drop among the debris. "I think we talked too much and didn't just let him be, let *us* be. That's how it is with an only child, an only son. We both talked too much at him. . . ."

"You should have taken him fishing. . . ."

"Never did. But—it's way more. It's just the way he was. We both blamed ourselves for a long time. But everybody who tried to help us—the police, counsellors, our friends— told us we'd been good parents, we'd done what we could. It's just the way the boy was. Marion seemed okay with it after while. For a long time, actually." Oliver blows a stream of smoke through the corner of his mouth. "And now lately it's been this pond business."

"Quite something," Bernie muses. "He's out there dodging bullets, doing a fine job, probably. Taking care of himself in some fashion. And here you are, you and your wife, taking it full in the chest. Gutshot, as it were."

Lights flash through the man-door. A car slides across the yard and gleams under the mercury-vapour lamp. The car stops and a woman the same height and thinness as Marion steps out the driver's door.

Oliver leans forward in the Mustang seat. she's come to look for him! She want to find him! She needs him!

He takes the cigarillo from his mouth. His mouth begins to curve into a smile.

The Doctor rises from the chrome chair.

And then it isn't Marion. The woman in the doorway is wearing jeans and a T-shirt. Her hair is a little like Marion's, but this woman has long earrings sprouting out of hers. Marion never wears jewellery or make-up. Marion has beautiful long dresses with flowers on them. . . .

"I'm looking for Frank. Is he back yet?"

Frank's wife! Would she have the answer?

As Bernie and the woman chat, Oliver listens to the fan and the blood roaring through his head. He looks at Frank's wife, and the Snap-On Tools pin-up girl, and he thinks about Toots Darychuk, and old Rolly, her forever lover. And he thinks about Marion screaming and fighting when he tried to pull her out of the mud and weeds.

He clears his throat and feels the burn of the tobacco. "So," he begins. "Quite something, what Rolly did for Toots." He looks at neither of the other two. One of them will answer.

Bernie says nothing, but keeps his eyes on the woman. At last she turns to Oliver. Her earrings dance. Her glossy red lips part. "What Rolly did for Toots?" She laughs, and Oliver can see her small beasts jiggling under the T-shirt. "Biggest pain in the ass around. What a doorknob." She glances at Bernie. He smiles. The line of his smile matches the line on the forehead made by the backwards baseball cap.

"Frank's wife Ginger," says Bernie after he hears her car door close.

"Ginger."

Rings of smoke appear in slow procession from Bernie's O-shaped mouth. He straddles the chrome chair. "One thing I know—you can tell Marion for me," says the welder. "Once you've eaten yourself up with self-blame, you can't get yourself back again. Trying to understand makes you go all wormy and mushy, like a tree full of termites. I can fix almost anything made of metal. I can weld and patch and solder. But you can't fix a rotten tree. That's why I'm a metalworker and not a woodworker." He rotates the drive shaft between the fingertips of both hands. "We can't keep everybody safe. Life isn't that way. Never was, never will be."

"I don't know what to do." Oliver pronounces each word separately, as though picking them randomly from a list. "I don't know how to help her. I'm her husband!"

"All you can really do is keep her away from the pond."

The two men puff on their cigars, Bernie more vigorously than Oliver, who feels the burn deep down in his chest. The exhaust fan in the workshop falls silent suddenly. Everything is quiet now. There is not even a breeze outside to rattle the loose bits of metal on the machinery in the yard.

"She used to pray," Oliver remembers. "Prayed all the time. She doesn't do that any more. Are you religious?"

"If you mean," replies the welder, "do I think God punishes us with crap like this because we've been bad or don't have enough faith, the answer is no, I don't. If you mean, do I believe we can make bad things go away by praying and believing, no I don't. Faith helps you get through it, makes you believe enough in the good things about life to go on living after you've had the shit kicked out of you. I believe there are good things in life. I just don't believe in a perfect world."

Oliver nods. He drains the last of the Jamaica Dry down his tobacco-seared throat. "Not ever?" he rasps. "Not ever. . .?" The drive shaft the Doctor has been waving suddenly strikes him hard in the chest. Pain shoots through his ribs. He hears the bottle hit the cement.

But Bernie isn't holding the drive shaft. There it is on the counter, beside a sheet of white paper, paper as white as angel wings.

Oliver feels himself falling forward. He digs his fist into his heart.

A roaring, a rushing, like wind. And cold. And a stone under his head. Someone pressing on him, hovering over him. Perhaps an angel with whom he will need to wrestle.

But lips are pressing on his lips. He can't breathe. A spasm begins to rise in his chest, and his body clenches to meet it. The pressing stops.

They'd been the welder's lips. Oliver sees the Doctor's stark face suspended above his own, its eyes dark and round beneath the crinkled band of the baseball cap. And behind the eyes, behind the welder, AL CAPONE NEVER, in dark, round bullet holes.

"Geez. . . ," Oliver hears him say.

Oliver lifts his head and tries to speak, though he has no idea what words will come out.

The Doctor gets to his feet. "I'm calling an ambulance."

"Why? Why?"

"Geez, Oliver. You . . ."

"No!" Oliver sits up. He can still feel the tightness in his chest. "No. I'm all right now."

"I'll get some water. And then I'm calling the ambulance."

"No! No. . . ." Oliver tries to get up and Bernie helps him into the carless bucket seat. "I feel fine. I'll take the mower home now."

"Oh no. Then I'll call your wife."

Oliver clamps his fingers onto the Doctor's forearm. "No you won't, Doc."

"Right. Of course not our wife. Your sister. Lives in Rosefield, doesn't she?"

Try to find my son. . . . "You won't ever tell anyone. Not anyone. Not ever. I get these spells sometimes. It's nothing." He tightens his grip on Bernie's arm. "Got it? I don't need any water."

"I thought you were dead! I gave you mouth-to-mouth."

Oliver notices that the Doctor is pale, scared, truly scared. "You wouldn't have had to. But—thanks." He smooths back his hair.

Bernie picks Oliver's cap up off the floor and dusts it off. "You can't drive. I'll give you a lift home and you can pick up the mower when—when you're feeling better." He puts the cap on Oliver's head and pats it down. "Maybe you were dead. Do you remember anything? Tunnels, stuff like that?"

"Yes, I do remember something. Sort of like a dream. I had this vision."

Bernie just stares at Oliver.

"This vision—Al Capone *did* sleep here. And I'm taking my mower home."

Oliver looks around the room. Everything looks different, feels different, like a place he's never been in. The light is too bright, the furnishings seem to have been misplaced. The pin-up girl's smile has turned fiendish.

"You're crazy!"

"I have to go!" *I have to keep her away from the pond. I have to take care of her. It's all I can do....*

"Wait!"

Oliver feels the Doctor's hands slapping the back of his shirt and pants.

"You got half the floor stuck to your clothes," says Bernie.

The two men walk out into the illuminated repair yard. Bernie gets onto the tractor first and backs it up to the mower. Together the men connect the two machines. When they are finished the phone rings. "Wait!" Bernie cries. He runs towards the man-door, and Oliver doesn't know whom he's told to wait.

Oliver gazes for a moment at the idling tractor. He will have to climb up slowly. He needs to get home now. He wants to be there more than ever before. And he wants to get there in the roofless compartment of his Massey, so he can look up and see the stars and the nearly full moon, and feel the night air in his lungs.

Because he did have a vision lying back there on the cement floor of the repair shop. Before he mistook the welder for an angel. Marion, strolling in the dark towards the pond, her flowered dress flowing behind her like a bride's train, her arms stretched out, loving, joyful arms. In the vision she was laughing, not worm-eaten and mushy the way the Doctor had said. And coming out of the reeds and small trees around the pond, the figure of a boy, still fourteen, still sweet and unspoiled, still the Benny they dreamed of, though he'd never been.

Through the open man-door, Oliver sees the Doctor talking on the telephone, the receiver curved around his speckled jaw.

Oliver lifts his eyes to the seat of the Massey. He reaches up to pull down on the brim of his cap, to tighten it on his head for the climb, and for the ride home. But his hand finds only empty space. The brim is not there.

The Havelland store is closed. One bulb still burns somewhere in the back, behind the crowded aisles. No lights at all show at Jim Berg's farm any more. The grasses are motionless beside the road, and no cat's eyes shine from the ditches or the fields. The blare and clatter of the engine fades, though the ear protectors still dangle from the seat.

Oliver tries to sit tall, to become the cowboy again, riding the range, heading home under the stars, the feet of his trusty horse stepping surely and steadily on the earth below. But the stars and the moon are gone. Perhaps clouds have moved in, Oliver thinks as he strains to see, through the utter darkness, some sign of Marion.

Burial Games

I don't remember the falling of the snow that winter. I don't remember the storms, or that the sky was layered day after day with mutinous cloud. Uncle talks about it sometimes, and old weathermen still mention it on television. But I remember certain things clearly about that winter: my near-death; a frightened young woman who became our teacher and then not our teacher; and another woman, a stranger who in one brief encounter invaded my soul. And I do recall the mountains and valleys and cliffs of snow that formed along the shelterbelts and on the south sides of buildings. On the schoolyard. Beside the teacher's house. It's just the actual falling of the snow I have no memory of.

Abie told us about the teacher in August while we tried to shoot gophers with our clumsy homemade bows and arrows. His father was a school trustee. "She's only eighteen, and it'll be her first job," he said as the arrows wobbled and the gophers laughed. Gaspard Delorme, whom we called Casper, and who would be going into the eighth grade in September, stared at Abie and sputtered, "Just eighteen!

She's almost my age," after which we showed him no mercy. Abie also told us her name: Lena Pieper. So by the time we started school, we were already armed with a healthy arsenal of nicknames for our enemy: Leaper Pieper, Pieper Leaper, Lena the Leaper, Leaping Lena. And when we were in an eloquent mood, Leaping Lena the Laughing Hyena. None of which had anything to do with what she was like. We just trusted to God that eventually she would, with our help, live up to one of the names—leap away from something, laugh funny, or, at the very least, peep.

My mother always referred to Abie and Casper and me as The Trinity. "So did The Trinity catch anything at the creek this morning?" "The Trinity's been riding the calves to death again!" Abie was Mennonite, Casper was French, and I, Scottish. I'm not sure just who was the Father, who the Son, and who the Holy Ghost in our trio, though I suspect the Ghost would have been Casper, not only because of his name but also because he was the one Catholic amongst the Protestants. Abie probably would have been the Father, since the Mennonites had taken charge of the morals of the community. That left me as the Son, the only Scottish lad for a hundred miles. Casper should have been the Father, being a lot older. But he didn't think or act older than we did. There were no boys his age nearby, just girls, of whom he was deathly afraid. So he hung around with Abie and me and gave us a very warped education about sex, in between fishing and whittling arrows.

My great-grandfather arrived in Nova Scotia in 1890 to farm, though his original occupation had been farrier. For some reason he had a hard time making a go of farming, and there were enough farriers in Nova Scotia for the number of horses. One night while he was in Halifax buying supplies, he met a fellow Scotsman in a pub, who told him that he should move to southern Manitoba where there was lots of decent farmland to be found and precious few farriers.

"Those Mennonites don't have any real sense about horses," the man said in the dark tavern over a heavy mug of dark ale. "They treat them like cows."

Great-grandfather packed up his family and moved to the Red River Valley, to a homestead that lay between the Mennonites and the Frenchmen, and became a farrier for both of them as well as a good farmer. His children found mates among the Scots north of Winnipeg

Most of the students at my school, built at the edge of a slough no good for farming, were Mennonite. The French usually sent their children to French towns for their education, no matter how far they had to go. The Mennonite kids, and a couple of Frenchies like Casper Delorme, and me, got along fairly well together. And though the girls were determined to like the new teacher (after so hating the male teacher we'd had the previous year, whom we boys idolized), it didn't take her long to disappoint them.

Like a nervous calf she was, with large brown eyes that rolled to the corners of their sockets and showed a rim of panicky red blood vessels whenever she came up against a tricky situation, which was several times a day. And her ears seemed to pull back. If she had been the one to save me that winter morning, I could have forgiven her those things. But she wasn't the one. She was hiding in the teacherage when it happened, and missed her one chance at redemption.

We didn't dare tell our parents that Miss Pieper spent her recesses and all noon hour in her little house. We swore Abie to secrecy. If the school board found out, she would be reprimanded, and that would be the end of our freedom.

We passed our carefree autumn playing various forms of baseball, gambling with cards under the willows, doing stunts up in the maple trees, and playing red rover with the girls. Sometimes we smoked rolled-up toilet paper, or real cigarettes, stolen by Casper from his dad. I don't specifically remember doing those things that particular fall, but I know for sure they were part of my boyhood, and those early fall days still are, in my mind, some of the best days of my life. And then, on a Saturday early in November, my father died. The moment of his death remains large and swollen in my mind.

I remember us walking across the yard together, me a little behind him, for he always moved with a long stride when he was working. We were on our way to adjust the tarps covering our hay bales. A wicked wind the night before had ripped the tarps from their moorings, and the forecast was for rain and sleet and snow. The sky was already darkening, though it was only mid-afternoon. I had on my cap, with the flaps over my ears, and probably gloves and a pair of wellingtons. The cattle in the near pasture were already edging towards the shed.

About halfway across the open space in the centre of the yard, my father stopped and turned to me, and pointed behind me to the eastern horizon. He started to say something: "Always look out for the tricky . . ." At least that's what I thought he said. He never finished the sentence, and I turned, too, to see what was so tricky, and perhaps even frightening enough to stop his words.

I saw nothing. The prairie was as blank as essay paper. And when I spun around to ask him to help me pick out the tricky-whatever, he was already on the ground, dead, and I think I knew it right away, because I didn't even try to shake him to consciousness, just ran for dear life to the house, in case the tricky-whatever that had killed him would get me, too.

We had the funeral in the Mennonite church two miles down the road But the minister came from St. Andrews, which was many miles away, down river. We went to St. Andrews for services at Christmas and Easter, and the minister had visited us once or twice. The funeral itself is blurred now. I remember seeing Abie with his parents in one of the pews as my sisters and my mother and I followed the coffin out of the sanctuary.

When we got to the cemetery, though, a fear clutched me that I won't forget. The cemetery was right beside the school. Of course I'd always known that, always known we recited our times-tables next to a graveyard. We were strictly forbidden to leave the school grounds, and especially forbidden to play in the graveyard. But after hours, Abie and Casper and some of the others and I prowled among the stones and markers, and sometimes we even went there at night, usually around Hallowe'en, to play hide-and-scare in the shadows.

But we hadn't ever thought about the spent lives the granite gravestones represented, even though my very own grandparents and great-grandparents lay beneath the sod where we played. As my uncles and some other men from the community shovelled dirt into my father's grave, my heart nearly stopped, and when my mother placed flowers on top of the mound I felt my father suffocating down below, felt his panic.

They said he'd had a heart attack. No autopsy was done. Now, I know it could have been a stroke or an aneurysm; mother said he'd complained of a headache after breakfast.

It didn't matter. We shuffled out of the cemetery to a waiting car, stunned that a solitary man, connected to so many things—to the cows in the pasture, to the big barn my grandfather had built, to the fields that stretched flat and wide to the horizons, to the trees whose branches he lopped when they got in the way, to the tractors he drove, to my mother, to his children, and even to the cats to whom he carried supper scraps on his way to the barn in the evenings —that all those connections could be so suddenly and finally severed, like snapped cables with their ends hopelessly frayed.

I went back to school the very next day, even though my mother said I could stay home, because I wanted to be near my father, perhaps even to visit the grave during the noon hour. Surely Miss Pieper would let me go, if I went alone. But when twelve o'clock came and she put on her coat to go to her little house, the words wouldn't come. I didn't know how to phrase my question. Casper and Abie and all the kids were quiet and distant that day, and I could imagine that distance growing if they heard me ask. Nor could I bring myself to sneak away; someone would notice, and it would get whispered around.

So I didn't visit Father's grave by myself. For a few weeks my family went Sundays, to the place where the funeral director had poked a temporary steel marker into the earth; but after the first heavy snowfall at the end of November, we stopped, and my mother said we would have a stone put up in spring. Over the next few months the frequent storms changed the cemetery's terrain regularly, but I always knew where my father's grave was.

And no one would reveal to me what my father had been trying to warn me about as he perished in the brittle grass between the house and the big barn my grandfather had built.

They tell me much of the snow fell in December and early January. Winds and brief blizzards herded it into sheltered spots and shaped it into magnificent peaks and cliffs. There was a lull in the weather during the dead-cold days of late January, and then an encore in February when the air became moist and warmish.

How did I spend those months? No doubt my friends and I were very creative with the snow. Images flit in and out of my memory. The scorn we held for The Leaper was pervasive. She never smiled.

And what did I do while the snow came down and the north winds scuttled and banged around our house? Our windows were often shuttered in winter. I must not have seen the snow, must have gotten used to the noise of wind. My bachelor uncles looked after the cattle, my sisters fed the cats.

The day the lady came to the cemetery could have been during the late-January interlude, or it could have been early in spring, after the snowfalls had stopped. I've tried to figure out when it was; the snow was still fresh and fluffy, which would indicate January. But I'm certain that a week or two later the weather was pleasant, mild like mid-March, in which case the snow would have started to decay and blacken. And the snow was fresh. Of that there is no doubt. Perhaps it makes no difference when it was.

Abie and Casper and I were atop a drift near the toilets, probably the highest drift, or the Matterhornish mountain Abie's dad had made with his front-end loader when clearing the schoolyard driveway. I don't know if it was recess or lunch hour. The girls weren't around. Winter was a boys' season; the girls, especially the older ones, usually spent recesses inside "helping" Miss Pieper for a few minutes, though she always skidded on bare shoes along the slippery shovelled path to her house halfway through the break. Was she different when she was alone with the girls? Did she laugh with them, chatter about clothes and Nancy Drew and the March of Dimes? She always seemed the same when we came in at the end of recess, stomping our big rubber feet in the foyer and laughing loudly at nothing. But I began to wish I could sneak up and put my ear to the door, or climb a ladder to the high dormer windows on one side of the school where I could spy on the secret girlish recesses without being seen.

A blue and white Chevy drove past the school from the east, slinking along the ice-coated gravel. It stopped on the side of the road where the approach to the cemetery had been before the heavy winter concealed it. The car kept running and no one got out for a time. And then, as we watched from our lookout tower, the driver's door opened and a woman appeared, wearing a fur hat and a thick coat with fur trim. In her hand she held a clumsy bunch of flowers and ribbon. For a while she just looked into the graveyard, where only the tops of the stones and markers showed above a sea of white. Then she waded in, up to her thighs in snow.

I'd never seen her before, but I somehow knew what she was there for. How would she find the thin steel that marked my father's grave?

The handbell sounded at the schoolhouse, Abie and Casper dropped away and the sounds of the playing children faded. I could not take my eyes off the lady in the fur hat and the fur-trimmed coat staggering through the snow.

Someone must have given her clear instructions where he was buried. She headed right for the spot, though not without difficulty. Her hat fell off her head. She picked it up and clutched it in her hand. I could see now that she was older than I had first thought. A stray breeze lifted her hair off her forehead.

When she got to the place where my father lay, she dug about a bit to find the marker. I could have shown her exactly where it was.

Finally, she put the flowers down. I knew she hadn't found the marker because she kept casting about, as though measuring distances with her eye. Then she just stood for a while. Before she left, she anchored the bouquet as best she could in the snow. I could tell by their stiffness that the flowers were plastic.

She never saw me, didn't look in my direction.

I didn't tell my mother about it right away. I 'm not sure how long I waited—a week, perhaps. The woman had disturbed me. No, not the woman herself, but the fact that I had been so certain as soon as I saw her that she would search for my father's grave. I spilled it out one night while Mother and I were finishing the ice cream we'd made in a bucket of snow earlier in the evening. I told her about the lady in the cemetery, described her looks and her movements and the flowers she'd laid in the snowdrift. I did not tell her the rest, did not tell I'd felt very deeply that, if I'd had a chance to talk with the woman, we would have gotten on well. I had liked her from that great distance. I wondered if she was the tricky-whatever my father had begun to tell me about, too late.

My mother's face hardly changed. She kept her eyes on her ice cream. I watched her tongue flick into the corners of her mouth after each suck on the spoon, but she gave me nothing from her eyes.

When I'd finished my story, my great revelation, my partial confession, she said: "You need not worry about it. Your father had a bit of a life before he married me. She was a fairly harmless ghost. I doubt you'll see her again."

I didn't understand quite what she meant at the time. She gave me nothing from her eyes. But within me a yearning for my father sprang forth suddenly and gnawed at my heart, because now I missed not only him and all the attachments he'd had in my lifetime, but also the attachments he'd had in the past. My father had lived before I was born.

A wind came up during the night.

In the morning when I got to school I climbed the highest snowbank and looked into the graveyard. Its landscape had changed once more. The bouquet was missing from my father's resting-place, or at least, it was a bouquet no longer. Its parts lay scattered among the drifts and tombstones. A bit of ribbon and a stem of plastic leaves had gotten caught in the fence that separated the cemetery from the schoolyard. A lingering breeze from the northwest played at the ribbon and plastic, and together they made a ticking-clicking noise against the fencepost, an uneven, intermittent sound I could hear even when I was inside the school listening to The Leaper giving us instructions in her high, nervous voice.

Days passed. Suddenly another fresh blanket of snow obscured the old landscape and transformed our playground yet again. The weather had come from the south this time, creating sculptures in new places. The clicking plastic persisted.

The day of the new snow—a warmish, spring-feeling day —Abie and I saw two younger boys building a fort among a cluster of snowdrifts between the teacherage and the grave- yard. They had a shovel, which they took turns using, to hollow out and shape their tunnels and walls. We challenged their occupation of the area and the fight was on. We wrestled with them in the white, yielding dunes. Casper—where was he that day? I have a mental picture of him standing near some grade eight girls in the shadow of the school. Maybe it was that winter that puberty finally awakened in him. At any rate, he was not with Abie and me.

One of the younger boys got hurt—not badly hurt. His arm might have got twisted, or his throat a little bruised in my stranglehold. He went off to nurse his wound. Only one challenger remained—Pete Reimer, who was a year younger than me and two years younger than Abie. Having estab- lished our dominance of the hill, we gave Pete a final push backward into the snow and then fell beside him, breathing hard and grunting like proper warriors. But the whole time, I could hear the clicking of the plastic leaves against the fencepost. No one had yet bothered to disentangle the piece of bouquet from the wire.

Then I spied the shovel stuck into the drift a few feet away. I glanced at Abie and Pete, and then at the endless blue of the sky above us, and I shouted, "Now you're our slave! Bury us! All the way!"

Abie sat up. "Bury us, slave! Shovel us all the way under!"

"Shovel us under all the way!" Abie and I sang together.

Pete Reimer's family's farm was not far from mine. Al- though Abie was my school friend and a frequent summer friend, when we could ride our bikes to each other's house, Pete was a friend, too, especially in winter, on weekends, when we could meet halfway between our farms to sled or skate on the creek. He wasn't a pal, though, because he had moved into the community well after Abie and Casper and I had formed our trinity, and because he was *two* years younger than Abie, and *ages* younger than Casper. Pete really was a slave in a sense, the way I controlled our relationship, allowing him in only when it suited me, forcing him to be obedient to my whims. He envied The Trinity deeply. He always did what we told him.

Abie and I nestled into natural cavities between the drifts. I remember a feeling of contentment, of satisfaction at having made a good decision, a good plan. I remember listening to the lazy tapping of the fake leaf in the breeze.

Pete started on Abie first. Abie lay with his arms straight at his sides and his eyes closed and cried one last time, "All the way under!" I crossed my wrists on my chest—my father's hands had been folded on his waist—and stared into the clear sky and waited.

It took Pete a while to cover Abie completely. Pete was already puffing by the time he got to me. As the first shovelsful of now-heavy snow plopped onto my wool parka, I turned to look at the mound he had finished. To my surprise and delight, Abie had not kept both arms at his side; one mittenless hand poked up above the surface, its fingers straight and rigid like a fake hand on a stick, as though some discarded puppet lay there instead of Abie. I remember pulling the fur of my hood closer around my face to keep the stinging needles of ice away from my skin. Pete toiled steadily with his shovel, and I gave him his final instructions: to make sure the toes of my boots were covered. It seemed important at the time. When he got to my head, I couldn't help but shield my face with my gloves. The sharp clicking of the plastic leaves against the fence post faded gently away.

And as the darkness grew around me, I imagined being engulfed with green, leafy vines. I felt warm and drowsy and contented, and thought it would not be such a bad thing to stay cocooned there forever.

Pete did not cease his labours once he'd done me. Caught up in his special assignment, he continued with his shovel, filling in the space between Abie and me with more snow, and then the spaces between the mounds our bodies formed and the natural drifts beside us, and then smoothing everything over carefully, so that we were, except for Abie's hand, invisible. Obliterated.

Pete told me years later that he had watched Abie's fingers slowly curl, watched them turn white at the tips and knuckles, and had wondered if he was all right. He said he looked around a bit to see if Abie's mitten might be lying somewhere, so that he could slip it on the protruding hand, but realized it had gotten buried along with everything else. It didn't occur to him at the time, though it did later, that he could have put his own mitten on Abie's hand. Mostly, Pete just sat back and admired his masterpiece, while Abie and I slipped into unconsciousness.

And what visions did I have as I rested in that soft tomb, next to my father's hard and cold one? I wish I could say my spirit floated away to some spot in the blue sky where it looked down on the wonderful white scene below like an omniscient hawk, or that I had a conversation with angels, or talked with my father. But nothing like that happened to me. Maybe the tiny air pocket that I formed over my face with my hands before Pete shovelled snow onto my head prevented me from drifting that far.

What did happen was this: from within the shade of the schoolhouse, Casper cast a casual eye over the place where Abie and Pete and I had been playing. And all he saw was Pete patting down the snow with the back of the shovel blade. But before he turned back to the silly conversation he'd been having with the tall girls, Casper spied Abie's frozen hand. With a shout he bounded along the path that led between the drifts and then across the rolling hills of snow to the smooth valley where our bodies lay concealed. Casper told the story well in the days to come. It became a legend that survived until the day the school closed for good.

He began to scoop and scrape away the snow, all the while yelling at the top of his voice, "How long have they been under? How long? How long have they been like this?"

But Pete, stunned by the sudden flurry of panic (for by then children from all over the yard were rushing to the site), could only stare at Casper, protecting the guilty shovel in the crook of his arm. Where a moment ago all had been peace and serenity, now was pandemonium. Others joined in the frantic disinterment.

And then Miss Pieper appeared around the corner of the teacherage. Casper said she was on her way to the schoolhouse, unaware that the excitement might somehow connect with her. But she paused when fragments of conversation carried by the crisp winter air reached her calf-ish ears.

All at once she waded on high-heeled open-toed shoes into the soft dunes ("as though she'd never seen snow before," said Casper), not quite leaping, but straddling the snow wide-legged. She sank to her ankles. As she came she called out to the children in their brown parkas, who were scattered around the drifts like hungry sparrows, "What's going on here? What's happening? What have you done?"

I was oblivious to her approach, but opened my eyes just as she got to me. If it hadn't been for Casper and the others shaking and slapping me and telling me I could have died, I wouldn't have known anything was amiss. My coma had been painless.

The Leaper stood over me, her coat open, her feet buried in snow, her lipstick freshly applied, her eyes wide with terror, and as I gazed up at her I found myself wanting her to save me, to become my angel, to lean over and kiss me back to life. I was prepared to fall in love with her, the way a ten-year-old loves, adoring a beautiful, unobtainable mother.

She smiled! It lasted only the briefest moment. She said, "You're all right," for by then Abie had begun to gasp and wheeze beside me.

And then her face changed as she realized that what had happened had been dangerous, and that she would be held responsible if word got out. The smile remained—the curve of her mouth—but it took on a cruel twist as her eyes narrowed and her ears pulled back.

"You're all right then. Silly games! Aren't you funny, boys!" She turned to the rest of the children, among them my own teary sisters. "Everything's fine! It's time for class!"

She started back through the snowdrifts. "Better not play that game again! No more burials. No more burial games. . . ."

I watched her footless legs trudge away. It was a hard lesson I'd learned. She hadn't even bothered to help Abie and me out of our graves. I had mistaken her for someone else.

Abie warned me, despite his frostbitten fingertips, that telling anybody outside of school what had happened would mean the end of our freedom. My sisters looked up to me for some reason, especially now that I'd been resurrected, and I had no trouble engaging them in conspiracy, though deep inside I felt hollow, and weary of my contempt for Miss Pieper. I wanted to tell my mother everything.

I didn't have to, of course. The story was out by the time I had changed to my flannel pyjamas that night. My mother gave me the hug I had craved since stepping into the back porch, with my empty lunch pail rattling against the newel post as I kicked off my boots. Abie's father showed up to apologize on behalf of Miss Pieper and the school board, and by Easter Leaping Lena had been replaced by a retired gentleman, Mr. Schulz, who told us long stories about The War and about exotic foreign cultures and his boyhood as a missionary's son. For the rest of the winter we played broomball on a rectangle of hard, flat snow in the middle of the schoolyard, and when spring came, our Mr. Schulz organized the entire school (except for the very smallest children) into two seven-man baseball teams, which he coached with great enthusiasm. He was the pitcher for both teams. No one spoke of Miss Pieper again.

By the time summer came and it was time to stalk gophers, The Trinity had collapsed. Casper began hanging around with a grade niner who had a '49 Pontiac his father allowed him to drive around the fields and farmyards. Sometimes we saw them cruising along back lanes with French girls in the car. Pete Reimer, the younger-than-us Pete who had shovelled us all the way under, took Casper's place. But we never thought of ourselves as a trinity after that.

A few days after my near-death, on a Saturday, I walked down the road from our farm to the cemetery, about a mile and a half. Someone had cleared the cemetery driveway of snow and cut a wide path into the yard. I did not have to fight my way in like the strange woman had. Even the snowdrifts that remained were hard now; I could walk right over them to the place where the plastic leaves clung to the wire. After I'd untangled the holly-like leaves I went to my father's grave, intending to stick them into the snow there. But shining through the hard gauze of ice and snow was a bit of pink, and when I broke away the gauze I saw that it was a plastic rosebud. I plucked it out and joined it with the stem of leaves, and took them both home. For years I kept them in a secret place in my room.

When I became an adult and began to bond with the memory of my father as a man, the need to learn the identity of the woman who visited his grave that long-ago afternoon deepened. But by then my mother herself had died and her brothers—my bachelor uncles—said they knew little of my father's private life before he married. And there is no one else to ask.

I don't know where the pink rosebud is any more; I've moved about quite a bit. But I am back now, back in the house where I lived as a child, and every day I walk across the same open space where my father died while my back was turned.

And I never cross the yard without thinking about his last words to me, about his warning. I believe now that he was speaking about the east wind. Because since I've come back, I've noticed how rare an east wind is on the prairie, and how, when it comes, there are sounds around the house you never hear otherwise, rattles and creaks in places that don't normally rattle and creak, as though ghosts are trying to get in. And with the ghosts comes unsettled, sometimes treacherous weather. Just before my father died we'd had squalls and sleet, and the winds had ripped the tarps off the hay bales. But I attend to other things that might be treacherous as well, always looking for all the tricky-whatevers my father would have taught me about had he lived.

We've not had snow again like we did the eleventh winter of my life. It's as though Miss Pieper took it with her when she disappeared early that spring. I feel sorry for her now, and wish we would have one of those chance meetings, and so I could apologize, so I could find out if, when she walked away from our school that last time, she walked into a springtime of her own, or if she still carries winter in her soul.

The Laughter of Women

"What about Syl and Ag? They have to be at the head table, too, don't they?"

"Where will they be sitting at the church? Not in the front pew, I'm sure."

"Then they don't sit at the head table. Everybody who's up front in any way at the church sits at the head table, and everybody else be damned, I think."

"Rae doesn't like Syl and Ag."

"They were her foster parents for six years!"

"She's says they were just in it for the money."

"Then why did she invite them? Or did they invite themselves?"

"Have you ever met them? They're sweet as can be. I saw them at her graduation."

"I was at Rae's grad! How come I never saw them?"

"*She* never said they were in it for the money. *You* said they were in it for the money. She just never felt very close to them because they had a whole pile of other foster kids."

"Proves my point."

"Hush. Let's figure out where to put Samantha first. Does the book say anything about birth mothers?"

The women lay scattered like abandoned dolls among the relics of their girlhood. The basement rec room of the Friesen house had never been purged of childhood, since the children had never quit coming. Once the youngest sister had grown up, the older ones had begun bringing babies home. Eight-track tapes and grimy Barbies were jumbled together with teething rings, dress-up hats, and xylophones. The upright piano their mother had guarded obsessively for fifteen years now stood battered and tuneless against warped panelling. She'd had it appraised after the last piano lesson resounded through the stairwell, before it had gone to pot, and discovered that it was worth little more than the easy chair in the corner near the stereo, or the hide-a-bed that had serviced countless slumber parties. Now she watched her grandchildren gnaw on its varnished edges. "It's only good for memories," she said. "Might as well let them make their mark on it for posterity." Two small windows, at ceiling height, partly grown over with vines on the outside, did little to provide natural light. A third one, facing west, admitted a few dirty rays late in the afternoon.

The babies were asleep upstairs, in quiet, characterless rooms, redecorated after the trickling out of the daughters had finally ebbed. The daughters were sisters this afternoon: Monica, who'd flown in from St. Paul, would fly back, and then drive up for the wedding with her beloved Leonard; Bri (for Sabrina), dreamy and lithe and dark-eyed, as though her name had formed her; Cookie, who, despite her name, tended to brood and slump in remote corners with a strong cigarette burning between her fingers; Wendy, a blonde beauty as a child, much favoured by aunts and uncles and teachers, but haunted-looking and wary as an adult—except when pregnant, which was often; and Dianne, the watchful one, the protector, the sister who, as the oldest, carried everyone else's anxieties in her handbag. Rae Jean, of course, was not present, having booked her day with mysterious errands. "I've booked my day," she'd chirped at them as she'd swung her handbag back and forth around her body late that morning.

Rae Jean was the only one of the sisters who'd been adopted. Chronologically, she and Cookie were twins, but they were nowhere close in any other kind of age.

Somewhere on the floor among the remaining five was The Book, the brides' bible. And though no one openly confessed to believing in The Book, and the meeting had begun with scorn and giggles and guffaws over the prissy, pompous rules set within its gilded covers, at least two of the sisters had used it in secret at their nuptials, and all were now finding themselves addicted to it. "This darn thing's like a chocolate bar," said Dianne at one point. "If you take one little bite of some piece of advice or other, you pretty well have to peel back the wrapper and eat the whole thing."

"I already checked," said Monica. "The book is obviously out of date. There's nothing in it about birth mothers, or ex-foster parents, or ex-mothers-in-law, or any other modern situations. Just this section on 'Your Own Special Circumstances.' "

"What does it say?"

"Rae Jean once told me Agnes wears a bag of peas behind her panties in the morning," said Bri.

"Oh, well, then, let's cross her off the list," cried Wendy. She reached for the little notepad on which Rae had reluctantly jotted down bits and pieces of wedding plans. "We wouldn't want to invite anyone who packs vegetables in her underwear!"

"Could prove useful at the head table," growled Cookie through smoke.

The truth was, the sisters did not quite know where to put even themselves at Rae Jean's funny little wedding. Fifty guests, three tables, and a jumble of friends and 'relatives' from Rae Jean's jumbled life. Her funny little life, as Monica put it. Given up for adoption by a fifteen-year-old mother, taken from her first adoptive parents when she was three because they fed her milk-bones for lunch and coffee whitener mixed with warm water, given to Sylvester and Agnes Hiebert for six years, where she was the youngest of eight foster kids who drudged away on the Hieberts' watermelon-and-pumpkin farm. Found by Margaret Friesen at an adoption fair at the Convention Centre (Margaret was serving as a volunteer for the Children's Aid Society one winter; homeless children were paraded on a runway like fashion models), whisked back to the Friesen home and plunked among the five daughters like a stray mongrel. And mongrel she'd remained. Until Samantha had come back into her life.

Samantha had hardly changed since she was fifteen, it seemed. Now thirty-eight, she'd had no more children, though she'd been married twice in her twenties, and lived out of a backpack. Her chestnut hair was "styled in a bristle-brush factory," as Monica put it, and her body had remained taut and slender. She could have been her daughter's sister. The two were distinctly out of place among the voluptuous Friesen girls, with their Dutch-Russian ancestry. Samantha introduced Rae Jean to a whole raft of creepy relatives and an assortment of backpacker friends, most of them intellectual drifters who dreamed of purity and guiltlessness. Rae Jean blossomed for a while, and the sisters, during that period, felt they and their parents were the misfits, the mongrels. But Samantha moved on, to some purer place, and Rae Jean responded by getting engaged to Tyrone, a second cousin of the Friesen girls. He was nothing like Samantha. Monica once suggested that it was Rae Jean's retaliation against Samantha for abandoning her for the second time.

"Why would Agnes Hiebert wear frozen peas in her panties?" mused Dianne. "Sounds sort of kinky."

"I think it was lower back trouble. She woke up in pain every morning."

"These notes aren't much help," said Wendy as she paged back and forth in the spiral-bound scribbler. "Listen to this: 'Flowers—do we need them?' 'Dress—buy.' 'Definitely no place cards at the brunch!' "

"Oh, well, something definite anyway," muttered Cookie.

Bri shook her finger at Cookie. "Look, you're the bridesmaid. Why don't you show some leadership here?"

Cookie shrank further into her cave between the bookshelf and the piano. "Get me out of this, girls."

At once the women broke into laughter. They rolled on the rug and held their stomachs and let the tears flow freely. It was a joke they had shared many times since Rae Jean had announced her choice of bridesmaid. "My twin, my alter ego," she'd called Cookie.

Something in their centre slowly sucked the mirth from the circle of women, drained it away into a vortex formed by Wendy and the little notebook she held. The smile on Wendy's face faded, her shape, moulded though it was by the beanbag chair, stiffened, her eyes darkened. The movement of the pages in her hands became rhythmic, almost robotic. One by one, the sisters turned motionless and expressionless, and fixed their own eyes on the notebook.

"What's wrong, Wen?"

"She wants napkins made from recycled paper?" suggested Dianne.

Wendy drew the scribbler closer to her face. "She's written something in the margins."

"Don't we all?" said Bri.

"It's the same thing each time."

"Don't we all?" echoed Monica.

"In four or five places, I think." Wendy leaned forward, and the others leaned toward her. "Listen. 'Coffin board, heavy stone.' " Thin paper rustled in the basement air. " 'Coffin board, heavy stone.' 'Coffin board, heavy stone.' "

Coffin board, heavy stone. The words formed on five pairs of lips.

"Must be the wrong notebook," breathed Cookie, the bridesmaid.

On their knees they waddled up to the beanbag chair. "She's written it very small and very faint," observed Dianne.

"-ly," added Monica. "Faint*ly.*"

Wendy dropped the notebook in her lap. "That makes it all the more frightening. It's like it's coming out of her subconscious or something."

Monica took the notebook from Wendy's lap and searched its pages, as though hoping to find clues, other phrases written in small, faint lettering in the margins of Rae Jean's funny little life.

Cookie sank back into her niche against the wavy panel boards. "Maybe we should check The Book. Under 'Your Own Special Circumstances.' "

"We shouldn't have looked at it." Bri snatched the scribbler away from Monica and closed it abruptly. "Did she give us permission to look at it? Anybody? Did she?"

"Am I dumb or what?" cried Monica. "What does 'coffin board, heavy stone' mean, anyway? You all act as though it's really significant or something. Pardon me if I don't catch on."

No one spoke for a moment. Upstairs, floorboards creaked as their mother tiptoed from bedroom to bedroom in crocheted slippers, keeping vigilance over the sleeping babies. The women downstairs slumped into a gloom of doubt.

"Well," said Cookie finally, "it just doesn't sound like she's real happy about the wedding."

"Well, I got *that!*" Monica shot Cookie a sarcastic look.

"That's all," said Dianne. "That's all."

"Mom's up," she added. "Maybe she knows what's going on."

"I think . . . ," began Sabrina. "I think she's just heard that somewhere one day, and wrote it down. Heard it from that geek Samantha introduced her to at the nature centre, the guy that makes soap and writes that science fiction stuff. You know how funny things stick in your mind."

"But it doesn't make sense," Wendy replied. "If it was scrawled all over one page, maybe. But these are scattered. You can tell she wrote them on different days. See? The pens are different, the handwriting is a little different, as if she were sitting in different positions. It really stuck in her head."

Cookie pulled a forty-five from a turquoise record rack squatting on the floor next to the stereo. The records had gotten wet one spring when the sewer had backed up during a torrential rain, and most still bore a white waterline across their middles. Cookie put the record on the turntable nevertheless, and thumbed at the knobs and dials.

"She's written out the guest list about twelve times," Wendy continued, having plucked the notebook from Bri's grasp. "And I don't see Samantha's name on it once."

"Oh, it must be on there once."

"And Tyrone's name isn't ever mentioned anywhere."

"Serves him right for having a name like Tyrone."

Monica sat and gazed at Cookie, who'd curled up in front of a stereo speaker. "Cookie, why are you playing 'Hats off to Larry'?"

Cookie's whole body shrugged. "Because it was there?"

Dianne was the only one of the sisters who'd ever actually bought forty-fives as a young girl. It was their parents who'd liked rock-and-roll in the sixties. They used to have parties in the rec room on Hallowe'en and Valentine's Day and on anniversaries. Toys and furniture were flung aside, and everyone would dance, including the little girls, on the shoes of the men, held in their father's arms, or swung gently by their hands by the pretty ladies who were their mother's friends. No one had dance parties any more. But all the sisters harboured a private yearning for them.

"Mom told me 'Hats off to Larry' was her favourite song once," Cookie added.

"She told me her favourite song was 'Woolly Bully'!"

"That was later."

Another silence hovered over the frayed tune labouring beneath the needle of the record player. Within it, within the two or three minutes it took for the phonograph needle to travel across the diameter of 'Hats off to Larry,' each of the sisters reflected on her own doubts and secrets, all the unspoken fears and regrets that had come and passed, the jealousies, the private anger.

Bri had married Monica's first boyfriend. She'd married him because stealing him would have seemed frivolous if she hadn't. Bri didn't care much for her husband. She'd only taken him from Monica because it was all she could do. Bri's sisters were better at everything than she was. As she moved from adolescence into adulthood, she'd needed to make her mark, and so became a master of seduction.

Monica, in response to her sister's treachery, had latched onto a wealthy accountant from St. Paul, Minnesota, and, though she believed she truly loved him, despised herself for her obsession with him, her possessive, fawning love. They'd had one baby, and then, when Monica became pregnant with the second, Leonard had cajoled her into having an abortion. Monica knew Leonard's only reason was that he was too self-centred to endure another demanding soul in his life.

And there was Wendy, three children already, the oldest only four. Monica envied her so. What Monica did not know was that Wendy had to stay pregnant; unpregnant, she was terrified of food. When cornered into situations where eating was inevitable, she always managed to find a place and a time to vomit undetected. Pregnancy allowed her to eat and be rosy and roly-poly. Nurturing a fetus was acceptable. No—wonderful. Unpregnant, Wendy did not exist. She was pregnant now, though she had not yet told her sisters.

And Dianne. Her siblings' conscience, their protector. The one who calmed them and led them and warned them. Her suffering came from deep within, unnamed, unrecognized, perhaps biological, chemical in nature, but powerful nevertheless. She had no close friends. She seemed even to keep a wall between her two children and herself. No one knew why, least of all Dianne.

Cookie was unmarried. She'd had many men and, despite her cynicism and brooding manner, was probably the happiest of the sisters.

Any of the others could have inscribed those words in the margins of Rae Jean's wedding journal. The different colours of ink and the variations in penmanship could very well be the proof of the sisters' ghostly writings.

And yet each knew little of the others' interior lives. Even Dianne dealt mainly with exteriors—physical illness, quarrels, traditional conflicts between husbands and wives. Together, in the comfortable rubble of the rec room, listening to 'Hats off to Larry,' they were, appropriately, exteriors.

Cookie swung the phonograph arm from the centre to the edge of the record and started the song again. But Dianne's voice rose above it. "Has Rae said anything to any of you?"

"Not me. . . ."

"I don't think so. . . ."

Bri said nothing, but shook her head.

"Let's just forget it, okay?" said Wendy. "If there's a problem she'll have to deal with it somehow. We told her we would look things over, get it organized for her. Let's just do it."

"She didn't ask us to."

"We offered, she . . ."

". . .didn't say no."

"She seemed to be having trouble with the seating plan. . . ."

Cookie slipped the forty-five into its space in the rack. "Let's nail that down, then: all those iffy mothers and such around the outside. Her real family—us—at the head table. Current friends and our relatives at the side—"

"But no place cards," interrupted Dianne.

"How many does that come to?"

They tallied up the numbers, estimated the no-shows, drew diagrams of the little banquet room at the neighbourhood restaurant where Rae Jean and Tyrone had decided to hold the reception. They were quick and methodical. No arguments broke out. Everyone agreed. And yet, each held something back, something tight within. Hesitation hung over their circle of agreeability like a pale, capricious smog.

"I have to say it," said Wendy at last. "I wish she wasn't marrying Tyrone. I think it's a mistake."

"Aw, Wendy. . . ."

"Well, it's true. He's so icky and sweet. She's going to get sick of that after a while."

"She's a bit icky and sweet herself."

"That makes it worse! I mean, what will their children be like?"

"He's a lot better than that first guy she went with."

"She went from one extreme to the other."

Rae Jean's first boyfriend, a nineteen-year-old kid named Amos she met at one of Samantha's picnics, had been a biker aspiring to get into the local chapter of a motorcycle gang. None of Rae's family ever met him, but Rae's wide-eyed descriptions of his shaved head, his tattoos, his chains and boots had been most entertaining for the other sisters during the spasmodic courtship. He took her to the gang's clubhouse one night for a party. She'd been so terrified the whole evening, she sent Amos a note the next morning, on flowery lavender stationery, ending the relationship. For weeks after, though, she lived in fear that he and some of his cronies would get even by abducting her or bombing her house. "Don't worry," Cookie had told her. "He's probably figured out you two weren't exactly a match."

Monica was snarling now. "I'm sick of worrying about every little thing that happens in dear little Rae Jean's dear little life!" Monica always had been the one to break down the quickest. Though never with Leonard. Just with her own family. She fumbled with her shoes and straightened her skirt. "I don't want to worry about *her* coffin boards and heavy stones. We all have our own to contend with."

And with that, the sisters heard the back door at the head of the basement steps snap shut. Rae Jean was home.

"Are you sure you don't want place cards?" Wendy hollered up the stairs.

Wendy's baby cried out from one of the upstairs rooms. Then silence. The sisters sat like stone.

Finally, "Wha-aat?"

"We're just done, Rae!"

"Oh. . . ? What?"

The women exchanged glances. "Better see what the kids are doing," muttered Dianne. She rolled her head on her shoulders and flexed her ankles.

Rae's misshapen loafers, appeared and hesitated on one of the upper steps. Above them her knees jiggled slightly for a moment, as if she were doing something above her head with her arms. Another step down, another, then a pause, one foot lower than the other, only the shabby shoes and the navy tights visible to the women waiting below. Then they saw the coat, unbuttoned, agape, and then Rae's eyes, round and bright against the gloomy stairwell.

"You what?" she said.

Last, they saw her hair. When she'd left late that morning, it had been a soft chestnut nest, a full but gentle swirl that fell over Rae Jean's temples and ears and brow, that all the sisters agreed looked much better than the butch cut she'd worn for so long. Now her hair was clenched in tight curls at the top of her head, perched there like angry newborn eels, coiled to strike. Her eyebrows arched high above her round eyes, as though pulled up by the taut curls.

"You went and got a perm. . . ."

"No place cards. We read it in your notebook. . . ." Monica and Bri spoke at the same time.

Then they saw the tears in Rae Jean's eyes.

"What's wrong?" said Dianne, who was nearest to her.

Rae Jean looked at Dianne. She seemed to be trembling. "Get it off me!" she wailed. "I hate it!"

Above them, a duet began to play, their mother's voice a soothing harmony beneath the chorus of waking children. How familiar it was to the five, how deftly it nudged memories in their collective mind. Rae Jean had never heard any of her mothers croon and coo to her when as a little girl she awoke from sleep, morning or afternoon. She was an alien, an orphan, a waif in their midst, someone to look after, even love, but never a part of the tentacled creature called the Friesen family, even though they knew all her secrets and few of one another's.

Behind Rae, Monica raised her eyes to the brown-stained ceiling and threw up her hands. She mounted the stairs to tend her whimpering daughter.

Wendy patted Rae Jean's hand. "You mean the perm? Don't worry, the wedding is a week and a half away still. It will have—flattened out by then. Kind of—let go a little."

"Ty will hate it!" The latest thing, calling him *Ty*. "I got it cut, too. . . ."

"Mummy?" A hoarse half-whisper at the top of the stairwell, a voice that could have been any one of the sisters' children. But Wendy, having made a consoling comment, took it to be one of hers and followed Monica.

On the coffee table that had nicked legs and peeling varnish lay the wedding bible and the spiral-bound notebook. Someone had closed them both and stacked them, and placed the pen on top. Bri drifted back there and sat down gingerly on the table beside the books. Cookie lay on her side in front of the stereo, her head supported by one elbow. She wore a cheshire smile, and Sabrina wondered if Cookie was laughing at Rae Jean's hair or at some more private irony. "Rae, come look," said Bri. She jerked her head at the notebook. "We drew this little map. We figured everything out."

Rae Jean shrugged off her coat and tossed it onto the bar. Without her coat, Dianne thought, Rae's hair looked less severe. She was wearing a pink sweater. She looked soft.

Bri picked up the notebook and wagged it at her. Cookie remained motionless on the floor.

"A map? Of what?" said Rae Jean as she took the notebook from Bri's elegant fingers with her stubby ones. "Oh, this dumb thing. I haven't written in it for weeks, months. . . ."

Dianne raised her eyebrows at Bri.

"Check the back page," Bri continued. "See? We made your seating plan: coffin boards at the head table, heavy stones along the side . . ."

Cookie made a choking sound. "Sabrina!"

Dianne stiffened and looked at her watch.

But Rae's attention was fully on the diagram and she seemed not to have heard.

Dianne, however, eyed her sister Sabrina with a wariness summoned from an earlier time. Bri had turned snakish, like the very curls on Rae's head. Dianne noticed it in her smirk and in the arching and stretching of her arms and legs and spine.

"Sure, I guess that'll be okay, Bri," said Rae. "Whatever." She plucked at her hair and tossed the notebook onto the table.

Dianne lunged at Rae and pinned her arms to her sides. "Don't worry about your hair!"

Then Dianne hugged Rae Jean hard and said, "It does look a little silly right now. It's happened to all of us. Remember when I got my eyebrows dyed? Do you remember that? I looked like Zorro. Look at Rae, Cookie. What does she look like to you?"

Cookie straightened up and crossed her ankles. "Well, I'd say she looks something like—hats off to Larry, he was untroo-oo-oo. . . ."

Rae Jean wrapped her head in her arms. "Do-ooon't," she whined from behind her elbows.

But between them Dianne could see her mouth parted in laughter. "Yep, you could hold an iron hat up with those coils, Sis."

Cookie and Dianne and Rae Jean laughed some more. But Sabrina climbed the stairs heavily, as though she had been the brunt of a cruel joke.

When Rae lowered her arms, tears once again spurted from between her half-closed eyelids. "Bri . . ." She sucked the word in. "Bri—she. . . She slept with Tyrone!"

Despite the rising hubbub upstairs, everything was instantly silent and still down below. The three remaining sisters looked like pieces in a sculpture garden, frozen in lifelike poses: Cookie bent forward in a sitting position on the floor, one hand on her knee, the other clutching at a twist of rug; Dianne leaning towards Rae, her hands on her hips, eyes squinty, brow slightly furrowed; and Rae Jean, S-shaped, a death's grimace on her wet face, embracing herself as though she were very cold or trying to keep herself from falling.

And then the lithe Sabrina's heavy tread on the steps began to echo like thunder in the cavernous rec room, though her voice could already be heard in the kitchen above. Dianne's gaze shifted to the little spiral-bound notebook lying on the coffee table where Rae Jean had thrown it only a moment ago.

"This really stinks."
    "Want a gas mask?"
    "Where would we get a gas mask?"
    "Grandpa's brother brought one home from the war. I think Dad still has it somewhere."
    "I can stand it. As long as it fixes this mess."
Rae sat on the peach-coloured vinyl seat of a faux-brass boudoir chair one of the girls had gotten for Christmas a long time ago. As Cookie pulled the comb over and over again, slowly, through Rae Jean's damp kinky locks, the vapours of the perming solution stung her nostrils. She tried not to inhale.
    Rae glowered at her reflection in the vanity mirror. "How long do you think it will take?"
    "As long as it takes."
    Earlier, Cookie had run up the basement stairs, two at a time, and commanded the women and children in the kitchen, "Don't one of you go downstairs until I say so. Not one of you!" She had not looked directly at Bri, had not even noticed if Bri were there. Then Cookie had grabbed her jacket from the entryway hook and run to the drugstore four blocks away. When she'd returned, breathless and red-faced, she'd had a quick smoke and then locked herself and Rae Jean into the basement bathroom.
    "I can't fix the whole mess," Cookie continued. "Some things you have to do for yourself." She squeezed the last of the thin yellow solution onto Rae's hair where it was the most dense and kept stroking the liquid through. At the same time, she held the ends of the hair taut with the fingertips of her other hand.
    "Is it working?"
    "It's dissolving the comb."

"Just don't light up in here."

"Thank god for the fan."

The mirror was clouded, and cracked across one corner. Yet if any of the sisters had been asked to describe the vanity mirror in the basement bathroom, none would have remembered it that way. It was the mirror where they'd first put lipstick on their childish mouths, where they'd checked the redness of a cheek after being slapped in a siblings' spat, where they'd examined their bodies for blemishes, tan lines, hickeys. The crack and the milkiness of the mirror were part of how they looked, somehow, forever framed in its imperfections.

"So—uh," Cookie began after minutes had passed, "when did you find out about Ty and Bri? *How* did you find out?"

"He told me." Rae Jean's voice was flat. It didn't ping against the tiles and porcelain the way voices used to when two sisters were in the bathroom at the same time. "We were in this—this flurry of confessions . . ."

"A flurry. . . !"

". . . and out it came. This was weeks ago. It just never hit me until I saw Sabrina last night. And even then . . . I don't know, I guess I was sort of—repressing how I was feeling. I figured, maybe all cousins have sex. I've never had any. Cousins, I mean. And then when I saw myself at the hairdresser's, when she'd finished, it just hit me."

"Well, I should hope it would hit you, kid. Now here's the tricky part: did they get it on before you started going with Ty or after?"

"Why is it tricky?"

"Huh?"

"Why did you say 'tricky'?"

Their eyes never met in the mirror. The mechanical rhythm of the combing tethered them.

"Because . . ."

"Because if it was before, then maybe Ty is marrying me to be close to Bri, or, because he thinks I'll be like her, right? And if it was after, then Ty is a creep. And I'm a loser both ways, right?" The pinging had begun.

"I think we're done," said Cookie. "I think it's straight enough. Now we have to wash it again and put in this other shit. The neutralizer."

Cookie held Rae Jean's head in the sink and sprayed warm water over it for a long time. The two women said nothing until Cookie had emptied the neutralizer bottle into Rae's hair and had begun the combing again.

Then Rae Jean spoke. "I'm not going to tell you."

"What?"

"When they slept together. I'm still marrying Ty. Are you ever going to get married?"

"I doubt it."

"Why not?"

Cookie took a deep breath, then shrugged. "I don't know. I think it has something to do with crinolines."

"Crinolines?"

"I guess you don't remember. Or maybe you weren't there right then. It was when Monica got married. She had this big bouffant-y sort of dress, you know, with the huge wide puffy skirt and the long train. When the store delivered it, they forgot to send the crinoline along. So Dad had to drive downtown to pick it up. Except that the woman who had fitted Monica wasn't in, and the girl who was there didn't know what kind of crinoline went with the dress. So she gave Dad a whole bunch of different kinds. I just remember Dad coming into the house with his arms full of snow-white crinoline. The *car* must have been full of crinoline. We had a very small car at the time, as I recall. I pictured my father cruising through the city drowning in a sea of mesh and lace and elastic. I felt embarrassed. It all seemed so silly, weddings, marriage . . . crinolines."

Rae Jean's eyes were no longer focused on her reflection. She looked beyond the mirror and hardly seemed to breathe. At last she said, "Have you noticed how being in here, so far away from everything, with the door closed and the fan on, blocks out all other sounds? You can't tell there's anyone else in the house. In the world, even."

Cookie combed through the silence. She could hardly believe no one had knocked. By now the children would be yapping and squabbling in full force.

Finally, "We're done, Rae, except for one more wash."

"Who would have thought you could get rid of a perm with another perm? Like fighting fire with fire. How did you know what to do? You never fuss with your hair."

"Don't tell anyone, but I learned it from a guy I used to live with. He was a rather vain fellow. Fussed with his hair a lot."

"You know, you may feel safe in here now, but the savages are out there. What are you going to tell them?"

Rae Jean said nothing. Cookie bent her over the sink and ran the water.

While towelling Rae Jean's hair, Cookie cleared her throat. "I need a cigarette. When—why did you write that stuff in your wedding notebook?"

"What stuff?"

" 'Coffin board, heavy stone. . . .' "

"I don't know. It was just something I read in one of Mom's poem books. I hardly remember doing it."

"I thought I'd seen it somewhere before. So what does it mean?" Cookie pulled the towel away from her sister's head. At last their eyes met in the clouded, cracked mirror. Cookie ran her fingers through Rae Jean's ravaged tresses and waited for an answer.

But Rae lowered her gaze and said only, "Who knows? Nothing."

"Plug in the blow-dryer, will you? It was probably the same book where Mom got that poem she always recited to us when we were upset about something. Remember that poem?"

"Mom never said any poems to me."

"Aw, she must have."

"Nope. Ag—Agnes Hiebert—she said German verses all the time. Half the time I didn't know what they meant. But they were always about work, I think. About getting work done quickly. She was an enormous woman, and she always sat in the kitchen on a wooden chair—"

"Wearing peas in her panties. . . ."

Rae Jean nodded. "A bag of frozen peas in her pants, and gave us instructions and said those German verses. Sometimes she was peeling potatoes, but we often caught her playing solitaire, too. It will be funny seeing her at the wedding. If they come."

"What about Samantha, Rae?" said Cookie as she gathered up packaging from the vanity and dropped it into the undersized waste basket beside the toilet. "What did you learn from her, do you think?"

"Samantha—well, Dianne once said Samantha was the cold light of morning by which I saw what I could or could not become. She was right. I'll never forget her saying that."

"Good old Dianne."

"Bad old Sabrina."

Cookie stood with the blow-dryer aimed at the side of Rae's head. "Well, the reason Mom never said the box poem to you was because you were never upset. You weren't, you know. Dianne, and Monica, and Wendy, and Sabrina, and me—all of us—we were the upset queens of this neighbourhood when we were growing up, let me tell you. Anyway, this poem was about building a box: '. . . fashion each part with care. . . .' And then it says something like, 'Lock all your heartaches within it, then sit on the lid and laugh.' I forget how many verses there were, but there was always that line. 'Fasten the strong box securely—then sit on the lid and laugh, sit on the lid and laugh.' I think Mom really believed that. I think she's always buried her problems, and wanted us to do that, too. I don't think Monica and Sabrina ever did actually have it out after Sabrina stole Monica's boyfriend. So, Rae Jean, what are *you* going to do?"

"I guess I have exactly five more minutes to figure it out, don't I? Five more minutes to be the only ones in the world." Rae Jean shook her head to loosen the damp strings of hair. "But never mind that. Where is everybloody going to sit at the wedding reception?"

"Every*bloody?*"

"Well, it will be bloody if Ty and Bri start making eyes at each other, or if Monica decides to scratch Sabrina's eyes out. Or if Mom and Samantha and Ag get into a fight about who should sit with us at the head table."

"Don't worry, little sister; we fixed it all. Trust us. It's in the book." With her thumb, Cookie slid the plastic switch on the hair dryer to ON.

Beyond the tumult of the dryer and the fan, beyond the tightly locked door of the remote basement bathroom, children began to seep slowly into the rec room, to play with their mothers' toys, and to bang and chew on the piano. The sun came round to shine briefly through one high, unobstructed window. And above, in the kitchen, amidst the banging of cupboards and the filling of pots, could be heard the rising and falling of voices, the laughter of women.

Karaoke King

It was travellers who entered the motel through the front door, the lobby door. People who'd left the freeway to look for a place to spend the night and found PALOMINO, in neon script, flashing at them through the darkness, or through the thick curtains of snow. Families, usually, with children who believed in the promise of golden horses with white manes and tails. Families who called the clerk around midnight to ask for a quieter room, one where the nightly caterwauling couldn't be heard. The motel was built of flimsy stuff, and the hallways funnelled the noise shamelessly throughout the fifty shabby cubicles.

But most of the patrons of the Palomino Motel slipped in the back door. An orange neon horse head glowed above it. Beside the door, at a jaunty angle, a banner announced KARAOKE TONITE.

And no palominos grazed nearby. No horses of any kind were kept anywhere around the Palomino Motel. No one could remember real horses ever being there.

The weather had been hot and dry for several days. And though it was after nine o'clock by the time he'd finished picking up his new workboots at the saddlery on Main Street, the sun was still bright, the temperature still over ninety when Calvin Carefoot pulled up at the Palomino for the second time that week. And there, like the last time, in the corner booth of the cool Trigger Lounge, sat the woman with the wine-coloured hair and the big wristwatch. And again, she was alone.

Calvin could see that she didn't notice him hesitating in front of the porthole window of the lounge floor. She appeared to be studying her songbook, although Calvin had discovered last time that she knew the songbook backward and forward. He sidled out of her range of vision and approached the bar. A jukebox played tuneless music over the loudspeakers; karaoke was on break or hadn't begun yet.

My sister needs me. My sister—I told you about her—Carlita. She wants me to come back. My mother is dead, my father is dead, and my brothers have gone in with the Zapatistas. Carlita has no one but the babies. I don't know if I'll come back. But it was very fine with you, Calvin. We'll be together in our dreams for a long time. . . . It was very fine with you. . . .

Calvin asked the bartender for a beer. "Real beer tonight. Strong beer." If the young man was surprised, his face didn't show it. Calvin had drunk only non-alcoholic beer the last time.

He eyed the woman in the booth. Tonight she was swathed in something filmy and orange. She stood out among the rest of the bar patrons. Calvin planned to make his move when the DJs did their opening number. That way he wouldn't need to start a conversation with her right away.

"So, Cal, how ya doin'?" The bartender grinned at him over the ice tub. The ice heap rattled as the man gouged it with a tall, thick-bottomed glass.

Calvin lowered his beer can from his mouth. The same bartender, the same greeting. Calving hadn't realized till he got home that everyone in the lounge had known his name because it was embossed on his khaki shirt pocket. His name had been on his shirt for years. He never thought about it any more; the dry-cleaning company had sold him three pairs of khaki pants and a dozen shirts, and they laundered them for him every week at a discount rate. Calvin nodded to the bartender and continued gazing around the room. The woman with the burgundy hair hadn't spotted him yet.

When Calvin had first wandered into the lounge five or six days ago, he hadn't noticed that it was any different from any other drinking place—clumps of people at tables, pairs on the dance floor, single men at the bar, couples nuzzling in dark corners, a large group having a noisy party. The Trigger Lounge was decorated with gold and white horses racing along sand-coloured walls, and white rail fences meandering among the racing horses. A white rail fence formed the front of the bar, and white rail fences sectioned off the dance floor. Fake kerosene lamps cast a sultry amber light that mingled with the light of the TV monitors suspended high above the crowd.

But tonight Calvin could see the signs—heads bent over songbooks, eyes straining to read titles and words, drinks going down in quick, rhythmic sips, nervous pens scratching messages on request cards, the small white cards lying expectantly on the request table beside the stage. And an atmosphere of waiting, misgiving, broken now and then by bursts of bravado from the large noisy group.

"You singin' tonight, Cal?" The bartender again.

The DJs bounded onto the stage. The karaoke machine came to life. The DJs—a young man and woman with perfect teeth and hair and dressed in white—began to sing about Bad Leroy Brown.

Calvin moved toward the booth. "Not likely," he mumbled.

Today he would find out her name. Last time she'd known his immediately. He had not asked hers, and she hadn't told him.

Some of the audience sang along with the DJs. The woman herself was singing as Calvin slid into her booth.

He stared at her giant watch. She reached up with her other hand and with long, shiny, wine-coloured fingernails shaped like miniature eggs traced the lettering on the front of his cap. She'd done that last time, too, except they'd been different letters, because he'd been wearing a different cap.

"D-I-L-L-O-N," she drawled in her keg-shaped voice. " 'Sthat your last name, Calvin? Dillon? Sounds like some kinda pantywaist sheriff from the Old West."

"It's a machine company. Pumps. I'm a pumpman out in St. Claude." He jerked his head towards the west wall of the lounge. "In the hills." There. He'd told her quiet a lot. He had a right to ask her questions.

"Well, Calvin—"

"Carefoot."

"What?"

"Calvin Carefoot."

"Well, Calvin Carefoot the pumpman from the hills, I'm pleased to meet you—again." The woman raised her glass to him. But instead of taking a sip, she continued singing. Her voice had a smoky mellowness that Calvin had warmed to the first time he'd heard it. His father had played alto sax in a barn band when Calvin was a child, and her voice reminded him of his dad practising on the back porch Saturday evenings before the sun went down.

She was a coarse attractive woman: a wide, short face; pale wide-set eyes; thin hair that drifted about her head like tinted dandelion fluff; a large lumpy body; large hands and feet. But her burgundy lips looked like wine-flavoured candy and she'd draped her shoulders and breasts and hips with pumpkin-coloured silk.

"Would you like a drink?" Calvin touched the nearly empty glass. A waiter paused at their table.

The woman smiled. "Soda water—with a lime twist."

Her teeth were bright white. "Don't want to gum up my pipes." She stroked her wattled throat with long fingers. The couple on stage finished up "Leroy Brown" and went into their spiel accompanied by karaoke drums.

Now. "What should I call you?" Calvin said to the wrist-watch.

"What should you call me?" Calvin's question seemed to amuse her. "Well, let's see—how about Desiree? You could call me Desiree."

"Is that you name, then?"

"Let's try it."

The first one to emerge from the crowd of singer-drinkers was a petite Filipino girl Calvin had seen the other time. She was a regular, Desiree had told him. They always called up the regulars first, to give the first-timers courage and inspiration, she said. Words and pictures flashed onto the monitor screens. The girl sang "Killing Me Softly" in breathy tones and swayed ever so slightly. Her sequinned violet dress shimmered in the limelight. A boy, whom Calvin judged to be barely eighteen, sat at her table and watched her with dangerous eyes. The girl herself carried what Desiree called "an aura of gloom, as though she's participating in some kind of ritual of pain." Desiree reminded Calvin of Lucinda when she said things like that, and yet she was distinctly different from Lucinda.

I don't know if I'll come back. But it was very fine with you, Calvin. . . ."

The woman leaned towards him. "How come you're here alone again, Calvin? No girls back where you came from? In the hills?"

"You're here alone, too. Again."

"But I came for something. What'd you come for?"

Calvin tipped back his beer can and let the last third of the liquid wash down his throat. "I had a girl once."

"But not any more?"

Calvin shook his head. "She was young and real beautiful. I'm fifty-two. She was young. And she loved me. It was the craziest thing. . . ."

"She didn't die, did she?" The woman put her hand on his arm.

Calvin shook his head. She took her hand away. He nodded to the waiter and raised the empty can. "She went back to Mexico. Her sister needed her."

"Well, well. She's got her whole life ahead of her." The wine-coloured lips parted in a gentle smile. "She can't see what romance means to us old folks."

Calvin gave a dry laugh and shook his head. "She was younger than I can remember being."

Desiree rubbed the back of his hand with the back of hers. Her skin was as smooth as the look of the silk on her breasts. "Why don't you take off your cap, Calvin?"

Her touch on the brim of the cap electrified him. She laid the cap on the table.

A group of girlfriends went up on the stage next. Three of them stood together and shared a microphone, while the fourth girl, wearing white spandex pants and a red-striped T-shirt that was so short it showed her bare abdomen, took another mike to the front of the stage. They did a number called "Love Shack." The male DJ helped out with the low bass part here and there, and the back-up girls sang mostly off-key. The girl up front didn't sing much. She mostly squirmed and wriggled and tried to look seductive.

"They look desperate, don't they?" Desiree mused. "If only I could tell them what I know. Was your woman like that?"

Calvin shook his head. "Lucinda was a modest girl. I don't know what she would have thought of all this." He stared at the singer in the spandex pants. "She always wore long skirts with flowers all over. The kind of skirt where you twirl and it flares out and you can see bare legs underneath."

"Did she twirl a lot?"

"Not once, that I can remember. . . ."

Two couples sitting together at a table beside the stage started to heckle the singers. On the stage, next to the couples, stood a life-sized cardboard cutout of the two DJs, who by day were celebrities from a city radio station. The cutout was an advertisement for an upcoming karaoke contest. One of the hecklers grabbed hold of the cutout and manipulated it like a huge paper doll, parodying the dancing girl's movements. The whole table began to mimic the whining of the singers. When the song was over, the girls left the stage to polite applause from a few tables and jeering from the hecklers.

A man with a friendly moustache and a corduroy jacket took his place under the spotlights. "That's Bill," murmured Desiree. Then, "Oh-oh," as the music started up. " 'Can't Smile Without You.' Lots of key changes. But he'll pull it off."

"You know him?" Calvin asked, liking the man a little less.

"He lives on my street. Owns a chain of laundromats. He's a laundry king."

"Bill."

"Bill. His wife doesn't know he comes here. Or at least, doesn't know he does karaoke. He's still in the closet. But he's very good."

"Karaoke king."

"Prince, anyway. *If you only knew what I'm going through, I just can't smile. . . .* Dumb song."

Bill was the best singer Calvin had heard at the Trigger Lounge, except maybe for Desiree. A kind of jealousy crawled up the back of his neck. He went to the men's room, and when he came back he sat a little closer to her. Now he could smell her. Two college boys were on stage doing "Life Is a Highway," which Calvin had heard last time. They shouted and swaggered. Most of the audience ignored them, but the hecklers heckled vigorously.

"What do you do, Desiree?" Calvin tried out the name.

"I sing."

"Sing?" He was surprised. He'd thought she worked in or owned a clothing shop, or a hairdressing salon. "Somewhere else besides here?" Maybe she was famous and he didn't know it.

"I do a lot of pretending."

"Pretending."

"I love pretending. Why do you think my hair is purple? Why do you think I dress up this old fat every night? Most of the people here are here because they like to pretend. You know what I like to do?" The yelling on stage intensified. Desiree moved a tiny bit nearer to Calvin and directed her voice towards his ear: "In the evening, when the sun is going down and shining a certain way through my venetians, I put on a costume (I buy costumes at second-hand stores—glittery things and hats and stuff), and I put tapes on my stereo, and I stand in front of a big long mirror, and I sing. Sometimes I'm Cleo Laine, sometimes Ella Fitzgerald, or Sarah Vaughan." She leaned forward so that her lips nearly touched Calvin's cheek. "Sometimes I put on this big tux I found at Glad Rags—this big tux—and I pretend I'm Nat King Cole."

Calvin began to worry that the woman with the burgundy hair was crazy. Lucinda had crazy things about her too, though, and he wondered why women like that attracted him so.

"I especially like live-performance recordings. The applause, you know."

"I don't know. . . ."

"Don't know what? Whether it's all right for me to do that?" She patted his knee. "Don't worry. It's all under control. I run an X-ray machine by day. And I wear a costume for that, too." She fingered his shirtsleeve. "What do you call this? You wore the same thing last time. I'll bet you wear it every day and I'll bet hardly anybody else you know does."

I'll bet if I said to the people in your 'hood, tell me about Calvin Carefoot, they'd say he's the guy who wears the khaki uniform all the time. They might even have a nickname for you: G.I. Joe or Khak-man or something. Why do you do it, Cal?"

The college boys stumbled off the stage and the DJs, in unison, bellowed into their microphones, "And no-o-o-ow, Jumpin' Crosley Javitts!" The crowd came to life.

"Now you'll see," said Desiree.

Calvin expected to see another man like Bill. But the singer crossing the dance floor was in his late sixties and walked with a limp. He supported his game leg with a battered hickory cane. The dancers parted to let him through. Once the man was on stage, facing the crowd, Calvin saw a pocked face partially concealed by a weedy growth of greying beard. The man had a potbelly and wore a tight orlon sweater over a bulky cotton shirt. The folds and puckers of the shirt were clearly outlined by the tight weave of the blue orlon. Some costume, Calvin thought.

"What are you doin' for us tonight, Crosley?" crooned the DJ.

The man put the microphone to his lips. " 'Born to Be Wild,' " he growled.

Calvin looked at the monitor overhead. The words appeared over footage of biker gangs racing along wide concrete highways. Crosley didn't actually sing the words; he merely spoke them, as though reciting a poem. The little finger of one hand, the one clutching the handle of the cane, was raised and curled, as though all the energy of the song was concentrated on it. The finger was like an antenna picking up electrical charges from the atmosphere.

The audience loved Crosley Javitts. The hecklers cheered him on.

Desiree touched Calvin's arm again. "See? He's the best pretender we have."

"Lucinda, she—" Calvin cleared his throat. "She believed in things."

"Yes?"

"She was only part Mexican. Her mother was a Catholic Mexican, and her grandmother was Mexican Indian. But her father—Lucinda's father—was a hippie who moved down to Mexico from the States in '69. She was a mix-up of all kinds of beliefs—Indian beliefs, like that we're all equal with animals, and then peace and free love and truth, and besides that all that Mary-mother-of-Jesus stuff. She prayed a lot, and even when she wasn't praying, she was talking like she was praying. I always felt protected when we were together."

Desiree said, "So maybe that's a kind of pretending, too. Or this is a kind of believing. It's all creating a life for yourself, a life you can live."

At first, Calvin though she'd said 'a lie for yourself.' He caught the *f* in the last part of her sentence.

Then the DJs sang again: "You Don't Bring Me Flowers." Desiree shifted around in her seat and produced a bright pink plastic handbag that had been lying beside her. The handbag looked to Calvin like a schoolgirl's pencil case. She probably got it at one of her second-hand shops for fifty cents, he thought. It bulged with the outlines of tubes and compacts. "It'll be my turn soon," she said. "I've got to go pretty up." She winked at Calvin and sang, "But used-to-be's don't count any more, they just lay on the floor till we sweep them away. . . ."

Calvin reached for the songbook and began turning the dog-eared pages. So many titles he'd never heard of, so many songs he didn't know. And yet all those people—he glanced at their hopeful faces—had these songs echoing, bursting from their hearts.

Calvin continued to thumb through the book. Finally he found what he was looking for: a number his father often used to play on his sax, sort of his signature tune. The song was common; you could hear it almost anywhere on the radio these days. But it had been a piece of his father's soul, and so it was for Calvin. He eyed the square white card resting at the edge of the table. . . .

When Desiree came back, two white-haired ladies were singing an Everly Brothers tune. The women were sisters. The Everly Sisters, the DJs called them. Though their voices were dry and leathery, they sang in perfect harmony, swayed in perfect unison.

Desiree sat very close to Calvin now. "I don't remember you drinking last time, babe."

"I haven't had a drink in five years."

"You better go after her, my friend. Go down to Mexico to be with her."

The waitress set another beer in front of Calvin. He caressed it for a moment and said, "Maybe I don't really fit the part. I'm not much of a pretender. People down there would find these duds pretty funny.

Calvin wasn't paying attention to what was happening up front, hadn't heard the end of the Everly Sisters' dream song. All at once Desiree was skimming dragonfly-like towards the stage. The dancers parted to let her through. They'd introduced her and the song she'd sing, had said her name out loud through the stereo speakers, and he'd missed it all.

As she took her place under the spotlights, he was transfixed by her image, by her smile and her colours. Desiree had painted herself as carefully as an artist composing a scene: the burgundy of her hair and eyes and lips and nails; the burnished orange silk; her earrings made of rhinestones and feathers; even the shade her skin had tanned.

And then she started to sing. Calvin drifted into a dream of his own as the burnished tones fell into the audience like the ripe yellow plums that grew wild in the hills. He heard no words. The colours became the sounds.

When Desiree had finished her song, Calvin heard the DJ,

amid the applause, say into the microphone, "Thank you, Helen."

Helen! Her name wasn't Desiree at all, it was Helen. She smiled a perfect smile as she made her way among the dancers who'd stopped dancing for her song.

Before she'd arranged herself again in the booth, Calvin heard his name called over the speakers. Helen raised her eyebrows at him. The DJs scanned the room looking for someone named Calvin to come forward. He could pretend he'd left, that he'd had to go before his name came up on the cards, that no man named Calvin remained. He knew Desiree would not betray him. Would Helen? But there it was on his shirt for all to see: *Calvin.*

"Whatever you want, baby," she whispered. She put the Dillon cap back on his head.

In his mind she led him to the stage. He followed her courage and grace across the dance floor and stepped into the light.

For a moment, he forgot what to sing. The DJs pointed to the monitor hanging from the ceiling in front of him. They pressed buttons and the machine started over. Piano, saxophone. . . . He stared at the screen. But Calvin did not need to read the words.

At the far side of the room, in the corner, in the darkness of the booth, the face of her big watch flashed in the rhythm of her applause. Calvin didn't hear the applause. He saw the wristwatch, and when he passed the table where the Filipino girl sat with her boyfriend, he saw them looking at him with eyes of coal.

Desiree stroked the back of his neck. "You've made a space for yourself on that stage now. You did it. And it was beautiful." She ran her fingertips across the letters stitched onto the breast of his shirt. "You'll be on that stage forever. It's part of you now. . . ."

"I can't even remember any of it. . . ."

"It'll come back to you in your dreams. . . ."

"My dreams. . . ?"

"You're someone else now, someone a little different than you were before."

"My dreams?"

Bill went up again. The Filipino girl. A nervous bald man sang "King of the Road." Calvin had another beer and the palominos racing around the walls of the lounge ran faster and faster, until they began to blur and stumble. Calvin and Helen-Desiree hardly talked. They watched the singers and rearranged themselves from time to time, their thighs and shoulders and arms, to savour the warmth of each other's bodies.

All night the singers came and went. Helen began drinking margueritas. She and Calvin danced together. The booze finally silenced the hecklers.

The karaoke took its last break. Jukebox music took over.

"Time to hop on one of those horses," said Helen.

"What?"

"Come on, pumpman."

"Where?"

She tugged at his arm. "Have you ever been in one of the rooms here?"

Calvin shook his head. "I'm no Don Juan"—he drew on his beer—"Desiree."

She stood up. He imagined her in her big tuxedo, strutting and cooing in front of her mirror.

"You could always pretend," she whispered. "Pretend you're a great lover, and that this is a castle on a mountain, with a lake of pure, clear water below your window, and a pretty pony drinking from it."

It was very fine with you. We'll be together for a long time, in our dreams. . . .

And then Calvin sadly and slowly and gingerly made love to his Desiree, in a sand-and-white room not too far from the lounge, but it was Lucinda who was on his mind. Jumpin' Crosley Javitts serenaded them with "Folsom Prinson." Once, Calvin thought he heard the sound of his own voice singing "Blueberry Hill," as though still echoing in the hallways from when he'd taken his turn on the karaoke stage. As he sat at the edge of the bed and felt Desiree's burgundy fingernails playing among the hairs on his back, and listened to the rattle of her giant, second-hand wristwatch, he thought only of Lucinda and how he'd lost her.

In the dingy bathroom he drank water from a plastic tumbler to wash away the sweetness of the beer. While Helen-Desiree was in the bathroom, he got dressed and stole out to the parking lot. The warmth of the air surprised him; it was past one a.m.

Calvin became more and more clear-headed as he drove. The open empty highway rolled out steadily beneath his pick-up truck.

He played the radio for a while, but its music got in the way of the songs and the voices and the pictures crowded inside his head like sharp sticks in a gunny sack. "Nearly full moon," he mumbled. Hadn't someone sung "Blue Moon" tonight? He tried to remember. Perhaps it was when he and Desiree had been pressed together in that sweaty motel room, when the rustling of sheets and the friction of their bodies had distorted the distant crooning and crying of the karaoke singers.

Calvin tried to recall the words of each song as it jutted into his memory. He sang snatches here and there and wished he'd taken one of the songbooks home with him. Instead he listened to the song the tires made on the flat highway, accompanied by the monotone of the winds. The hills were still many miles away.

A body hurtled out of a bank of stunted black trees at the

side of the road. A sleek, bounding animal. In a trance of sounds and memories, Calvin imagined first a wild horse racing through the woods, through the broad ditch onto the highway. He could not stop the truck or turn it in time, though he tried, and just before it tossed the creature up and sideways he realized it was a deer.

"No!" he shouted as metal crushed the ribs and shoulders of the leaping animal.

When the truck came to a stop, all Calvin could hear was Lucinda sobbing in the seat beside him. He bowed his head over the steering wheel and put his hand on the nylon surface where she might have been sitting, had often sat, and listened to her gentle weeping. He looked across the passenger seat and saw only the square box that held his workboots, snuggled against the armrest of the door.

He didn't have a rifle with him. The wrench would have to do.

He thought he would find her on the pavement or the gravel shoulder. But she was not visible in the glow of the taillights.

There? That shape in the ditch grasses?

Calvin went back to the truck and turned it so the headlights shone in the ditch. A car passed in the other lane. It did not stop of even slow down. The doe's hind hoofs dug at the tangled plants flattened beneath her. Her front legs were folded beneath her chest.

She's probably got a fawn back there in the bush, Calvin thought. She was probably being chased, by dogs or something. She'd have been leading them away from her baby. The fawn is probably still lying quietly somewhere in a thicket, waiting.

The headlights were too bright for this. He returned to the truck and reached through the window for the switch. The park lights were soft and yellow, good enough for what he had to do.

He stroked the trembling neck of the animal. Funny that her nerve ends could still quiver, even though her spine was broken. He wondered if she could feel his hands.

Do it, or you won't do it at all.

Her body stiffened when he struck her. He only had to do it once.

One time Lucinda had sat with a cat just killed on the highway, sat beside it for a few minutes while its life forces drained away, "to attend its soul to heaven," she'd said, " so that it won't get lost or lonely on the way."

Calving stayed in the ditch with a dead deer until he saw a stream of traffic in the distance. Not wanting to answer questions, he walked to the pick-up without a backward glance and hoisted himself into the cab.

The travellers passed, with rushes of noise, like small tornadoes roaring by.

Calvin turned off the park lights. Then he sat behind the wheel, in the stationary truck, listening to the silence of the fawn and the dead mother. Lucinda was no longer with him. Her space beside him was dark, simply a place to put his new boots.

His shirt was wet. How had it gotten so wet? This strange heat in the middle of the night. . . .

He looked at his plain watch, now well tarnished, which had been his father's. Would Desiree have returned to the lounge to sing again, along with all the others, to pretend she was beautiful, that she was someone else? That her karaoke soul would fly to heaven attended by Bill the Laundry King and Jumpin' Crosley Javitts? He gazed down at his shirt, his costume, the name emblazoned on his pocket.

He got out of the truck. The highway lay empty again, and grasses began to shift restlessly on the slope of the ditch as a fresh breeze crept across the prairie. Alone, in the light of the not-quite-full moon, Calvin threw off his shirt and sang his karaoke song to the heaven-bound soul of the deer:

The moon stood still
On Blueberry Hill,
And lingered until
My dream came true.
The wind in the willow played . . .

Fourth and India

After several morning of playing rummy on the broad
terrace, Selene pointed her bug-black sunglasses at Alex and
said, "Let's find a new game. Something—deeper." She
flipped her mouse-coloured flyaway hair with short fingers
and turned in her chair to stretch her legs. Alex wondered
what had happened to Selene's hair. It used to be shiny and
blondish. Had anxiety changed her body chemistry? Could
fear do that?

"I agree," replied Gradie. "Though maybe not about the
deep part. Games aren't fun if they're worky. I hate chess, hate
people playing chess. I like talky games myself. Or games
where you have to draw things." She leaned forward on the
whitewashed wooden table. "Why do you suppose none of
us has ever been married?" Then, suddenly remembering
about Selene: "I mean, I often wonder that about myself."

But Selene grinned and brushed her shoulder up against
Alex's, and replied, "We've been spoiled, Aunt Gradie. By a
macho young bear we met in the formative years of our
sexuality."

"Yeah—no man's ever measured up since." A joke they shared. Used to share. Hadn't since Woody came into their lives.

The bear was still a presence, still lurked somewhere beneath the plane of their sisterhood—subconscious most of the time, rearing up now and then like guilt, or a mystic power. At the summer cottage they'd been, so long ago now, on the kind of July day that exists only in childhood memory —a day of smothering motherly heat, when the smallest drop of lake spray tingled on the skin like acid; skies that stayed clear and blue from sunrise to bedtime; dappled, dancing leaf shadows; water that enclosed the body like cool silk. Alex was certain the bear had come the same afternoon as the eclipse. The two were entwined in her memory; each had summoned up the other. They'd come to the dock of the cottage as one entity. But Selene remained unconvinced. She scarcely recalled the eclipse, but said she had a *feeling* they had happened on different days, weeks apart.

Where had Mother been? Selene thought she'd just gone inside the cottage to make lemonade. But it sounded too better-homes-and-gardens to Alex. Alex thought their mother had simply abandoned them, bored with sitting on the dock watching her daughters bob about in the green-brown lake water.

Selene had been five the summer of the eclipse bear, Alex two years older. Their cottage hunkered in a forest of birch and spruce at the far end of the lake lots, separated from other cottages by a low spot where no one had wanted to build. Alex was a fair swimmer by the time she was seven. Selene was cautious around water and, after all, only five. She was forced to wear a bright blue life jacket any time she stepped out the cabin door. On that hot July day, Alex wore a too-small bathing suit covered up with one of her father's white T-shirts, Selene a suit that matched her sister's (they often dressed as twins) and the ever-present life jacket.

No one knew why a lone black bear would come out of the underbrush and jump into the lake to bully a couple of little girls. There must have been a cub around, everyone said. But the sisters did not see a cub. The bear had not been very large; they were certain, when shown pictures later, that it was little more than a cub itself.

Neither Alex nor Selene actually saw the bear plunge into the lake. Only seconds before it grabbed the hem of Alex's shirt did they see its sleek head, its teeth, the churning of the silky waters. Alex saw it coming toward her and screamed. Then she felt herself being dragged. As the bear and the girl thrashed in the water, the bear shortened and tightened its hold on the shirt, working its way up to her neck, her face.

And then suddenly the funny twist that so often happens between sisters, one older, the other younger: Alex, the victim, screaming softly, whimpering, trying to swim away from the strong bear, heading for shore, and Selene, all baby fat and puffy blue nylon, enlarged, enraged, growling and shouting in her own bear voice and raising her arms menacingly.

Still Mother had not come. What could she have done?

Alex found footing. Selene lay back and kicked the bear's jaw. The surprised bear let go of Alex. But instead of going after Selene, who kept up her woofing and growling, it swam a little further into the lake, then made a wide circle and struck for shore several yards up from the dock.

Selene pulled herself onto the dock at the ladder. Alex, exhausted, waded onto the narrow strip of sand they called their beach.

And finally, they'd seen Mother, frozen and speechless on the lawn.

She never left their side again at the lake cottage. And before she died, she pleaded with her daughters to forgive her, although it had never occurred to them not to.

How distant that story seemed to Alex, here in California, among palm trees and thick layers of humanity.

And when she had found out about Selene's monster (Selene did not tell her about him for a month or so after he first appeared) she found she had no way of rescuing her. All Alex was able to do was to take this trip to California with her, which was so precious little.

"Mom and Dad must have told you the story about our bear." Alex started into it. Gradie clapped her hands together and cried, "Of course, of course! The bear!" Alex couldn't help but picture a cartoon bear, a Disney bear, jaws dripping one minute, stupid and docile the next, having been kicked in the chin by a superhuman five-year-old.

But even in California, the sisters seemed once again to be cornered. Walking by the open door of Aunt Gradie's apartment earlier that morning, Alex had heard Gradie talking to Selene inside. "There's a wildness in us that takes over when our civility gets stripped away," Gradie had said. "That's what's happening here. All the human conditioning's corroded, just like the shoreline and the beaches and the houses. A wildness is taking over."

Selene was almost obsessed with California violence. Every day the news was all murder and desperation. The daily news back in Winnipeg was rife with reports of violent acts, which were happening more and more in the small towns of the thousand-mile-wide prairie. But the crimes here seemed worse, somehow. Maybe because the names of the streets and malls and suburbs they happened in were unfamiliar. This was foreign violence, and the sisters were its targets, as though, being non-Californians, they stuck out; at any moment someone would notice, and shoot them.

At least, that's how Selene felt, that's how Alex *imagined* Selene felt, that they were hostages. The crime didn't worry Alex, particularly. Strolling on the edge of the cliffs, she did sometimes look back over her shoulder at the solitary figures sitting in cars and pickups parked on India Street, wondering if one of them might slip out and follow her. But Alex was not as protective of herself as Selene was, and Selene had more right to be afraid.

Coming along the second-level exterior walkway of the Rosecrans that morning—the seventh morning, the beginning of the second full week they'd by staying at the Rosecrans—Alex had been brimming with the sensual pleasure of the walk on the cliffs, and had passed Gradie's door because she wanted to sit on the steps at the ocean end of the walkway to watch the rising tide explode the waves against the rocks below. Gradie's words to Selene failed to draw her into the apartment, where Selene spent most mornings watching television—news, on several channels, talk shows, *Flintstones* sometimes. Instead Alex sat on the top step of the staircase that led to the terrace and the pool. The white sea spray made chaotic patterns against the colourless ocean and the chocolate-coloured rocks. Eventually both Gradie and Selene would come out to play rummy beneath a Tuscan-green-and-pink sun umbrella.

Gradie McNeill was not actually Alex and Selene's aunt. She was their father's cousin, and had lived in California for twenty years, most of the time at the Rosecrans on Loma Cliffs. The sisters had never visited her here before, though she came back to Canada every once in a while to see her relatives and old friends. Alex and Selene had not seen her for a long time, because their parents were both dead now, but little about her had changed. All the things the sisters most remembered about her were still there: auburn hair done in a French roll; green eyes set in a tanned, well-lined face; shapely legs; jewellery; the mink-brown tinge in her full lips. The most striking feature about the "aunt," however, was that she was over six feet tall and (their father used to say) *burly*. She reminded the girls, when they were little and she was in her twenties, of the bronze statues in the city park. Selene said she'd always thought of Aunt Gradie as a drill sergeant because of her straight posture, her muscular physique, her square shoulders. Gradie's nature was most un-drill-sergeant-like, though.

The sight of her when she'd met the sisters at the front of her building the evening they'd arrived had soothed them after their long day of travel. ("My meeting might not be over in time for me to pick you up at the airport," she'd told them on the phone. "It isn't terribly far by taxi. Just tell the driver to take you to the corner of Fourth and India. Everyone know where that is. . . .")

On the patio, as the cards leaped from quick fingers into three piles, Selene said suddenly, "None of us married—that's given me an idea for a new game. . . ."

But Selene never did get to propose her new idea. At that moment, they heard screams coming from next door, sounds not unlike seagulls shrieking.

Selene ran to the low brick partition between the terrace and the neighbouring property, which happened to be a small park that sloped to a beach. Between the beach and the cliff on which the Rosecrans perched was a concrete sea wall, which had stairs braced against it, leading to a flat expanse of rock and tidal pools. Alex had noticed people sitting on the rock from time to time, but had not yet been there, and as far as she knew, neither had Selene.

Alex followed her to the partition. The beach and park were almost deserted, but along the steps and down across the table of rock a group of fifteen or twenty Asian children were strung like wooden beads. They rushed in bright colours down the long staircase like a necklace sliding off a dresser, and then snaked across the near edge of the rock. The wave action was heavy, and the spray battered the shoreline with war-like ferocity, though the day was calm and sunny. The children squealed as they were engulfed in the tumult.

Two adults, chaperones, hung back near the bottom of the stairs.

"Exchange students or something," said Gradie, who had come more slowly to the brick fence. "Or a tour group sending the little ones off for a day on their own. I don't know—I've seen Japanese children here before."

"A little young to be exchange students," Alex replied. "You'd think they'd never seen the ocean."

"They may have seen it. Just never been this close before, or never at a place where the waves come over the rocks like this."

A few of the children stayed well up on the steps. Some of them are afraid, Alex thought, scared of getting wet, scared of being washed away. She glanced at Selene, who was bent over with her arms folded on the top of the brick ledge.

But Selene was not looking down. She was gazing into the distance at something—someone—on the beach, at the other end of the beach. Another group of children, a smaller one. A tall man accompanied them, a man wearing a hat. He strolled pensively, like a grandfather, not too near the rolling surf, while the children skittered around him like sandpipers.

"This is the second time I've seen them here," murmured Selene.

Alex didn't know which children she meant. Gradie suggested they drive to Cardiff for lunch. They didn't play rummy on the terrace again.

The Rosecrans Apartment Hotel was pink and green and white, U-shaped, made of stucco and wood. An Englishman named Roger Willis had built it in the mid-fifties after falling in love with California and at the same time a German girl who'd been staying at his lodgings. Roj, as Gradie called him, still owned and managed the hotel. He was eighty-one, but looked and acted more like sixty. Although he spoke fondly and often of his Gisele, Alex had not yet laid eyes on her, and wondered if she was an invalid, or away on a trip. The glamorous photographs of her in his office appeared to have been taken twenty or thirty years ago. Gisele had been a blonde California-look-ing woman, and Roj said she liked to paint. "In fact," he said, "there's probably a painting of hers in your room."

Alex scanned the portraits in Gradie's suite for signa-tures, but she found nothing to identify the artist. Most of the paintings were of similar-looking women. If actually done by Gisele, they could have been self-portraits.

They grounds of the Rosecrans, behind the terrace inside the U, and in the front between the street and the entrance gate, were landscaped with clipped lawns and curving, amorphous plots of decorative plants. Every day Roger put-tered around the lawns and flower gardens and the shrub-bery. He moves like Fred Astaire, Alex thought to herself whenever she caught a glimpse of him from the railing on the second floor.

From up there, Alex also watched Bonita, the Mexican chambermaid, criss-crossing the courtyard with her red plas-tic laundry basket under her arm, moving between the white doors of the ground-floor rooms and the cramped space beneath one of the staircases where she did the wash. Her hair was the same colour as Gradie's. She wore it clipped up away from her face. Sometimes she'd stop at the rabbit cage with a basin of vegetable parings culled from the apartment kitch-ens. She fed the rabbit tenderly, as though it were her child.

The lop-eared rabbit lived in a cage on stilts in a shady corner of the courtyard on a patch of grass. Gradie told the sister, when they arrived and entered the courtyard from the street, that its name was van Gogh. "It belongs to Roj and Gisele. They've had several since I've been here. For the kids that come to stay here, I guess."

Alex noticed that Selene visited the cage often during the course of their long, languid days. She sat on a lawn chair beside the cage so she and the rabbit were eye to eye, and with one finger rubbed its twitchy nose and whiskers through the mesh.

The Rosecrans was an elegant, aging, two-storey structure that dissected two very unlike communities. India Street ran through both neighbourhoods, but Fourth Avenue marked the boundary between Loma Cliffs and Loma Beach. The enclave of Loma Beach was a mixture of commercial and residential. Houses and apartments there looked tired and neglected. They were overgrown with exotic but untended vegetation. Most of the businesses were convenience ventures, Quik-this and Quik-that: all-night liquor stores, fast food, speedy printing, one-hour photo processing, 24-hour groceries, ice-cream parlours, drop-in clinics, shabby boutiques. The people on the streets were surfers, transients, and runaway teens. Electrical wires spanning the streets were draped with running shoes tied together with their laces. Alex pictured brawling mobs of youths roaming the streets, stealing runners from one another and making sport of tossing them up to the wires.

Loma Cliffs, on the other hand, consisted solely of old upper-class homes on a small landscaped properties. The houses—no two alike, in keeping with a fifty-year-old by-law—nestled together along India Street and perched one on top of another up the hillside that overlooked the cliffs and the Pacific. All the homes in Loma Cliffs were protected by high-tech security systems. ARMED RESPONSE!, warned the signs on the fronts of the houses.

Two days after they'd seen the children on the rock, after lunch in her apartment, Alex walked Gradie to work. Gradie wrote articles for a community newspaper in Loma Beach and spent her afternoons at the offices of the *Loma Surf*. Alex and Selene had always assumed Gradie had retired early, living on the inheritance from her parents' farm, passing the time playing bridge and attending flower shows. Odd how they had plugged this person they so seldom saw into stereotypes that had never existed in their own lives.

"I can't keep this up for too long," Alex said as they

started off past India Park. Her voice made a sharp noise in the momentary stillness of India Street concrete as they walked. A haze—upper-level fog, according to Gradie, smog according to Selene—veiled the clean blue of the sky they'd seen the first morning. Most mornings since had started sunny, almost crisp. But mid-morning, the haze crept across the sky, leaving the city and the ocean shadowless and cool and bright.

"What can't you keep up?"

"Doing nothing. I like it here, and I love walking and exploring all the street and everything, and I could watch the ocean forever, but I need a project or something. I feel like a voyeur."

Gradie swept a Mars bar wrapper off the sidewalk and carried it gingerly to a trash can at the corner of the park. "Well, the clinic always needs volunteers to do paperwork and screen patients and such. Or maybe you could check at the day-cares. There are two nearby."

"I don't think they take just anybody to volunteer at day-cares." Alex had hoped she would tell her there was work at her newspaper.

"Maybe you could help Bonita. I feel the poor woman is over-worked, and probably gets a pittance for it. It isn't glamorous work, though, if that's what you're looking for."

Suddenly Gradie clutched Alex's arm. "Listen—we have to do something about Selene. After all, Woody Gold is dead."

A seagull landed on the grass beside the walk and picked up a piece of popcorn. The bird waddled onto the sidewalk in front of Gradie and Alex and then strutted and fluttered ahead as though leading them somewhere.

Woody Gold had been Selene's stalker. He'd been a constant sinister presence in her life for five years, and now he was dead, found drowned in the Red River during spring break-up. He wasn't anyone Selene had known, not an ex-boyfriend or ex-husband, or someone she worked with. Woody Gold had simply picked Selene out of a group of women from her office who ate their lunches on the boulevard every day in summer. Woody Gold. His name had invoked fear and loathing for what seemed a lifetime. The way Gradie said it now, here in California, it sounded to Alex like the name of a puppet or a children's party clown.

"She doesn't do anything except play games and watch TV," Gradie continued. "She never goes anywhere. Has she left the hotel at all since you've come? Besides going to Cardiff with us the other day?"

Alex shrugged. "She walked a little way on the cliffs with me yesterday." *And she's started talking about the bear again.*

"Well, it's something. Maybe she's making a start. She needs counselling, therapy. I know someone . . ."

"Selene's been in therapy for years, Gradie."

"But you'd think she'd be relieved and—well, happy, on top of the world, that she doesn't have to worry about him any more."

Where the park ended, India Street turned slightly inland. It was at this angling of the street that Loma Beach really began. Despite its seedy appearance, Mercedes were common. The women passed several as they made their way along the street.

Woody Gold had slashed Selene's tires and set fire to the elevator in her apartment block. Alex couldn't remember how many times Selene had woken in the night to the sickening tapping of her door-knocker, to the telephone ringing and the sound of his voice on her answering machine, how many times she'd had a gun pointed at her head. "It's hard for us to understand, Gradie, but—Woody Gold told Selene almost every day for the last five years that they would die together, that he would kill both her and himself if she didn't—cooperate. She really believed that's what would happen. She didn't give in, ever. But no matter how hard she worked to survive, to escape every day from his spying and his threats, I think she believed deep down, way deep down, that eventually he would kill her."

"Exactly! And now he's out of her life!"

"No, he isn't. He never will be."

Selene felt guilty, or maybe cheated, which sometimes has the same effect on people. Woody had gone and died without telling her, without leaving a note. It made her think he'd had something else going on in his life that she didn't know about, that he'd been killed, or had killed himself, *over something, or somebody, else.* The ending to her years of terror had been too abrupt. His stalking had become a routine in her existence, and should have ended with the process of justice. It should have been an orderly closure. Not merely a body spinning and bobbing in the spring current one day. And if he had to die, Selene would have like to be there. She would probably have liked to be the one to kill him.

Alex put her hand on Gradie's arm. "What I'm saying is, Selene doesn't know what real life is any more. She plays games and watches television because for so long now she's had no control over anything. She can't take charge. She can't even participate in our realities. It's just—damn screwed up."

The seagull lifted from the pavement and flew sideways across an empty lot, towards the ocean. As they got deeper into Loma Beach the sounds of the quarrelling gulls faded. A man in a rumpled sports jacket appeared around a corner and came toward them. He carried an attaché case in one hand, and in the other hand, which he held high and away from his lumpy body, were two ice cream cones. Alex stole a glance at him as they passed on the sidewalk. His hair was shoulder-length and grey, and he wore thick glasses. The ice cream was beginning to run down his wrist. Alex thought she saw him nod slightly at Gradie, thought she caught an answering but ever-so-slight nod from her. "Do you know him?" Alex asked.

"Not really."

Alex turned to see where he was going. As she watched, he stopped alongside the bird-of-paradise shrubs edging India Park and flung the ice cream cones into them. Then he continued on, licking his wrist.

Alex couldn't imagine where he'd been taking them. He didn't look like he belonged to the houses in Loma Cliffs, and if he'd been headed toward the park in the first place, he wouldn't have thrown the ice cream away when he got there. He must have been going to one of the classy homes. Who was waiting for him there? Who was the second cone for? A child? A lover? What kind of lover would Willy Loman have in a fancy suburb in California?

"Not really?" Alex echoed Gradie's reply.

"I've seen him before, that's all. What do you plan to do about Selene, then?"

"It's not what will I do with Selene here in California. It's what will I do with her when we get home again."

It had been Selene's idea to escape to California. While Woody Gold had been alive, she hadn't once attempted to run away, even if just temporarily, hadn't taken a single vacation away from home. She had been tethered to him, like a poodle on a thick chain.

"I don't know," Alex continued. "I'm hoping she'll make some kind of move on her own. Some small move, a lead we can follow."

Aunt Gradie nodded slowly, thoughtfully. Alex had no inkling, then, just what kind of move Selene would make, though she had already been given her first clue.

Gradie's office was nearer to the water than Alex had expected. The building itself was disappointing, a box on a corner. But the beach and a quarter-mile-long fishing pier were in view, and the street was lively. After Gradie had introduced her to the few staff members who were in at the moment, Alex stepped into the comings and going of surfers and drifters and took a stroll to the shore. She sat on the sand for a long time. This beach was much wider and longer than the one in India Park beside the Rosecrans. As the cloud that had dulled the morning shredded away, and the sun lit up the waves, people appeared on the sand and in the water like communal birds. Alex watched them for a long time, her thoughts bobbing aimlessly along with the young men in wet-suits astride their boards on the ocean swells.

She remembered how Selene had described the discovery of Woody Gold's body. Selene had not been there. As far as Alex knew, Selene had never talked to anyone who had been there. The police who had been involved with her case had told her that Woody was dead and how he'd died, and that was all.

"Someone saw him from the Osborne Street Bridge" was how she'd begun, sitting in the hedged yard of Alex's townhouse. "Someone saw a lump of something in the water. The water was running fast and there were still ice chunks coming down the river. At first, it was hard to tell if the lump was ice or a log or something else. If the sun had been shining, the body might never had been seen, because you know how the light and shadows can play tricks on you." She was referring to the time at the lake when they thought they'd seen a Loch Ness monster swimming under the trees that arched out over the water. The day had been hot and bright. The monster disappeared and reappeared and changed shape and size as it drifted along the dappled shoreline. It turned out in the end to be a beaver pulling a dead tree limb. Their mother said later, "The light and shadows can really play tricks on days like this."

"But the day Woody died was a grey day and once he got near the bridge the people walking across it could see that the shape among the ice chunks was a person. He was spinning and dancing on the rough water like a bug. Just before he went under the bridge the people saw that he was face up and his eyes were open and some thought he was still alive. And maybe he was—then. He was probably looking for me." Selene's apartment faced that river. She often sat on her balcony and watched it flowing past. But she'd been at work when Woody's body had happened by.

Alex became drowsy and dozed for a while in the sunshine, thinking, no matter how long I sit on this beach, I will see no one I know, and no one will know me.

As she passed India Park on her way back, Alex remembered the ice cream cones lying behind the shrubs, and the man who had thrown them there. She didn't actually part the foliage, but glanced at the spot where he'd flung them and imagined how they looked, lying there like wasted lovers.

And then Alex saw the same man and children who had been walking on the beach the day the Japanese children had visited the shore. This time they were on the lawn of the park, near the street. Some of the children were dispersed among the flowers and palm trees, doing cartwheels and playing tag. Two lay on the grass reading books. The father—Alex recognized him only by his hat—sat with his back to her on a bench under a cluster of palms. His voice mingled with the wind-like voice of the waves rolling up the beach. She couldn't hear all the words, but could tell he was warning the younger children not to go to the water without him. Alex couldn't see the beach or those children, because the park rose to a hump from the street, then swept gently downward to the water's edge. The father called to the youngsters in short phrases. He said their names. He warned and scolded.

Then Alex recalled what Selene had said at the terrace wall: *this is the second time I've seen them here.* Could she have meant this man and his family. It occurred to her that they might be staying at the Rosecrans. Alex had never noticed them there, but she had seen precious few of the tenants since they'd arrived. Where was the mother? Sleeping, perhaps, taking a rest while her husband watched the kids.

Alex had just decided to start up one of the paths that entered the park when the man stood and turned to speak to two of the children quarrelling behind the bench. Alex froze at the verge of the cedar-chip path. The straight, thin, tall body, the moustache, the long graceful arms—not exactly like, but so like another man Alex knew, had know well. It was as if their talking about him, Gradie and Alex, had conjured him up.

Alex hurried along the sidewalk towards the Rosecrans, which was just a block from where she'd stood. Out of the corner of her eye she caught the movements of the father of the six children. Selene must have realized. But she had been almost smiling when she'd seen him on the beach from the terrace. She had not seemed afraid at all.

The next morning was calm, the skies clean and blue. Selene and Gradie and Alex took muffins and strawberries and coffee out to the terrace. Gradie spread an emerald green cloth over one of the wooden tables and they sat and ate their breakfast while looking at invisible lands across the ocean, with the warm sun caressing the backs of their heads. White fishing boats and pleasure craft skimmmed past the Rosecrans, and Alex wondered how the pink and green of the hotel looked from out there. Alex and Gradie talked of taking a daylong or overnight cruise to Mexico.

Alex poured cream over her strawberries and moved her chair a little farther into the shade of the sun umbrella. Then she said, "What's with this Gisele?"

"Gisele?" echoed Selene.

"Roger's wife," Alex reminded her.

"Oh. . . ."

Gradie dabbed the corners of her mouth with a green cotton napkin. "What *with* her?"

"What I mean is, we never see her. Is she dead?"

"Well," Gradie began. She started folding her napkin into

a fan. "I've lived here for nearly fifteen years and I've never seen her, either."

"*What?*"

"She's dead," said Selene flatly.

"Doesn't Roger realize she's dead? He acts like she's always just in the next room when I go into his office."

Gradie laughed. A seagull mimicked her laugh from a jutting rock beneath the sea wall. "I don't know that she's dead, exactly. She may be in a nursing home, or maybe they're divorced. She might have gone back to Germany. . . ."

"Or all of the above," said Selene.

Alex tapped her finger on the table and watched Gradie's face, to see if she were playing a joke on them. "I can't believe you've never spoken to anyone who knows what happened to her. Somebody must know."

Gradie shrugged but kept her eyes on her back-and-forth folding. "I suppose somebody does. I've never asked Roj. It's always seemed too indelicate a thing to do. Doesn't Roj strike you as being a sensitive man, sort of—delicate?"

"He was in the Second World War. How delicate can he be?"

Gradie looked into Alex's eyes. "The most delicate of all, I should think, Alexandra."

"You make him sound like a Victorian lady."

"It's a mystery, isn't it?"

Selene and Alex glanced at each other. Mystery, indeed— but both of them were thinking more about the mystery that was Gradie McNeill than the fate of the phantom wife.

When Alex had returned from India Park yesterday afternoon, Selene had been lying peacefully on a chaise longue, her bare legs slightly bent and golden, her eyes shielded as always by the black sunglasses. One of Gradie's sun-hats lay on the patio floor beside her. Alex had sat down at a table next to her and browsed through the newspaper she'd picked up in the apartment. But the umbrella was furled and the sun was too bright for her to read. She went over to Selene and lifted her glasses. Her eyes were wide open.

"What?"

"Are that guy and his kids staying here?"

"What guy?" Selene pulled the glasses back over her eyes.

"The one we saw on the beach the other day."

"What beach?"

"The beach next door."

"I haven't seen them here. They'd be kind of hard to miss, don't you think? How many kids are there? Six or seven?"

Without changing the position of her body, Selene picked up the hat and covered her face with it.

Alex looked in the direction of India Park, though she could not see it because of the brick partition. "I saw them there again just now. On the beach." Selene's breathing didn't change. Alex studied her sister's body. Ever since she could remember, their shapes, their skin, their postures had been dissimilar. Old photos showed the sisters frolicking in swimsuits, on the lawn, at the lake, beside motel pools. And they were different even then, Alex square and sturdy and sallow-skinned, Selene slender and graceful, with paler, more transparent skin that turned golden in one afternoon of sunshine. But now, lately, Alex had seen Selene's body slowly begin to conform to hers. Selene was still slimmer and more willowy, but Alex could see her chin beginning to double, and her spine begin to curve just ever so slightly beneath the neck. And her jaw was more square and jowly on both sides of her coral-painted mouth. "What did you do this afternoon?"

"I went through Gradie' drawers."

"Selene!"

"Oh Alexandra. I didn't really. I saw her photo albums in the hall closet the first night we were here and she said I could look at them any time. It was interesting."

Alex was glad. It was a change from the television.

They had spent last evening downtown, walking by the harbour. Gradie had taken them to the forty-fifth floor of the Armstrong Hotel for a drink. Alex had stayed away from the tall windows, but Selene had pressed her body against them and gazed calmly at the tiny world below. When Gradie had suggested a walk along the streets, Selene had tightened her grasp on her handbag and said loudly, "It's time to go back. It's time to go back, Alex."

And for a moment, Alex thought she meant home, back to Canada. But she didn't. She only wanted the old chair in front of Gradie's TV.

Now Gradie smoothed the strip of green napkin with a firm hand and smiled at them. "I have to do the weekend shopping. I'll be back in time for lunch. I have a favourite spot right in Loma Beach I'd like to take you to."

They watched her labour up the steps with the tray. They could tell by the way she didn't look at them that she was not open to either of them spying on her Saturday.

Two women who were also sisters, but younger than Alex and Selene, came down to the terrace with coffee. Alex and Selene had met them before and didn't like them. They sat at the next table and opened up some chit-chat about the thinness of the bathroom towels. How dare they talk to my sister, who has suffered so, about thin towels, Alex thought to herself. Selene put on her sunglasses and pretended to listen while Alex folded the emerald cloth Gradie had left behind.

"Roj?"

The office was empty. Photographs of Gisele stared at Alex across the silence. Behind the desk, in a corner of the room, was a door leading to the Willises' private quarters. The door was closed.

Alex sat on the leather sofa beside the magazine rack for a moment and listened. She thought she could hear soft bumping noises—drawers and cabinets opening and closing. But they could have been coming from an upstairs apartment. The corner door remained closed.

Gisele in a ruffled playsuit, perched on a patio table. Gisele in a feathered hat and green silk dress, holding a Pekingese to her breast. Gisele posing with a woman who looked like Lauren Bacall.

A newspaper lay still folded on the coffee table in front of the sofa. ASIAN STUDENTS ASSAULTED IN MALL PARKING LOT. Alex picked it up and skimmed the front-page article. The victims had been Japanese, studying at a California college. One had died of his injuries. Witnesses said the attack had been unprovoked. Some said it had been a Filipino gang, others said Latino, a clerk in a store facing the parking lot was certain the assailants had been neo-Nazis. The families in Japan and the Japanese government were demanding answers and formal apologies from the President. As the California shoreline and economy crumbled, enemies were everywhere and everyone.

The noises stopped. Alex went to the desk and scanned its surface. She folded her hands behind her back and tried to keep a third eye on both the private door and the public entrance through which she'd just come. The desktop was neat. A notepad with careful numbers penned in columns, a pen, ruler, a bowl of Russian mints, telephone, telephone book, a list of names and addresses taped to the front of the telephone book, paper clips in a dish, two staplers, a chunk of pink onyx. Alex began to read the names on the front of the phone book. The top one was not a person's name. *Rancho Cabrillo, Encinitas.* The other names were of men and women, and the addresses were all local.

Alex walked behind the desk and picked up some of the photos. But she concentrated on the private door. Wouldn't guests, or friends coming to call, or delivery people, sometimes knock on the door? What could possibly be wrong with that? A movement on the street, which she could see through a window behind Roger's desk, caught her attention—Roger, getting into his car. He pulled away from the curb.

Alex crept up to the door. Was that music? A radio? A stereo?

She knocked. After waiting a minute or two, she knocked again.

Her hand went to the knob. The door was not locked. She pushed it. Now there was a crack through which she saw white walls and a mirror. Because of its position, Alex could not see herself in the mirror, but it did reflect another room. A small part of another room. And in the reflection she saw someone sitting in a chair. That was all. Not even the whole person—just the back half of him. His body twitched from time to time, as though he were doing something with his arms. But Alex could not see more of him without stepping across the threshold. Baroque music filled the rooms. If the man in the chair were to turn, would he see her in the mirror? If she could see him, could he see her?

The music stopped. The man leaned back and laughed, and she saw his face.

Alex closed the door. She hadn't knocked very loudly. They wouldn't have heard her above the music.

Alex went back to the sofa. She had heard no voices, only the music. The man sitting in the chair was the man who'd thrown the melting ice cream cones into the shrubbery beside India Park the previous day. He was dressed much the same. The long grey hair and the cut of his sports coat could not be mistaken. The ice cream must have been for someone in Roger Willis's apartment. But for whom?

After a while, Alex left the office and went back to the patio. Selene was not there, nor was she in Gradie's suite. The television was off, the only sounds the constant swish and sigh of the surf, and the seagulls' cries as they drifted over the rocks and the tidal pools below the terrace.

Alex did see Roger later that day. While swimming in the
Rosecrans pool at sunset, she noticed him crouching in a patch
of portulaca near the rabbit cage. He looked like a rabbit
himself, with his soft white hair and his hunched back. As she
pulled herself out of the slippery chlorine-smelling water, he
straightened up and sat back on his haunches, and watched
her wrap herself in one of the thin towels Bonita laundered
every day in the little room beneath the stairs. Alex had felt
all day since she'd been in his office that he knew she'd spied
through his private door. That someone had seen her and told
him, or that he'd seen her himself from some secret watching
place. Now, when he turned his eyes toward her, she shrivelled a little, as though he could see something *inside* her.

But she crossed the terrace and spoke to him. "Are they
blooming?"

He squinted at her against the sun. "Alex, yes?"

"Yes."

"Not quite blooming. I'm trying to get the sprinkler set
right. Damned thing's practically a computer. Look at all the
adjustments you can make on it." He lifted the sprinkler head
out of the fleshy mass of portulaca.

"Well, how about if we just fiddle till it's the way you
want it? You turn on the tap, and I'll run back and forth
adjusting until you have it the way you want it. I'm dressed
for it." Alex flung her towel back onto a chair near the pool.
"It's a new sprinkler, I gather?"

"Yes, a gift," he said wryly.

"I'm surprised you don't have an automatic sprinkling
system, with all the shrubbery and flower beds you have
around the place."

He laughed. "You may have realized by now that we
haven't changed much at the Rosecrans since we built it. I
rather like the old ways. Even a sprinkler is to me inferior to
a hose with a nozzle."

The furnishings in all the apartments were still the originals—wide-slat window blinds, chiffon flounces over the bedroom windows, a huge Norge range in the kitchen, a chrome suite with red-vinyl-covered chairs, flamboyant double-tiered lampshades in the living room, kitschy knick-knacks on the bathroom walls. He'd said we. "I've noticed you're pulling a lot of plants out of the flower beds," said Alex.

"Ah, you've seen me thrashing about in the bushes, have you?" Roger straightened up. "There, we'll try that one now. Yes, that's something that has begun to look a bit sad—the perennials and so on. We're going to start a re-landscaping scheme this spring. I'll go turn on the tap. Ready?"

And so Alex began her temporary position as an assistant to Fred Astaire in his garden. Somehow, somewhere, he would have to mention Gisele, and somehow, somewhere, if she was alive, Alex would surely get a chance to see her, or perhaps uncover her fate.

Gradie arranged four Porterhouse steaks on the barbecue grill. They began to hiss at once. Alex laid the green cloth and three place settings on the patio table. From the apartment door Selene emerged carrying a large earthenware bowl of salad.

"Four steaks?" Alex exclaimed. "I don't think I can eat even one, and I hate to tell you, but Selene hardly ever touches red meat."

"A friend is dropping by for supper," Gradie replied. "He'll be here any minute. And Selene doesn't have to touch the meat. All she needs to do is chew it and swallow it, or starve."

Alex recognized a testiness in Gradie that she recalled from some of the long-ago visits. She had no patience with pettiness. "Who's the guest, then?"

Selene put the salad in the middle of the table and said, "I've got a job."

Alex stared at her sister. She had not yet told Selene and Gradie about *her* job.

Gradie froze in front of the barbecue, holding a pair of giant tongs in the air.

"A job?" repeated Alex.

Selene stretched out in a chaise longue between the barbecue and the pool. "I'm sort of a nanny, I guess you could say. For that man with all the children. His wife died a year and a half ago, and he came here to get away from her ghost. He said he wanted to find the edge of the earth, and this is it." She frowned at the meat on the grill. "Steak?"

The man who looked like Woody Gold. Alex felt as though a piano wire were being twisted around her neck.

"I talked to him on the beach next door today," Selene continued. "He's staying at a place on the other side of the park." She waved her hand in the direction of Loma Beach.

"Probably the Breakers Guest House," Gradie murmured.

"Kind of odd, isn't it?" said Alex. "That he would take his children out of school? That he would take them with him at all?"

"He's a teacher. They all do lessons every morning. I told him I'd watch the kids a few hours every day, so he can have some time to himself. The guy at his motel knows Roger, so he's going to check my credentials with him." Selene put on her sunglasses and grinned at Gradie. "I mean, anybody's who related to Gradie McNeill has got to be trustworthy, right?" She put her head back and faced the setting sun.

Alex had not told Gradie about the resemblance between the two men. The wire tightened.

Gradie grasped a steak with the tongs and turned it. "What's his name?" she asked.

"Eli. Eli-something."

"I'll go and get another place setting." Alex walked past Selene to the staircase.

"Don't take the mushrooms and bread out of the oven until Ford gets here," Gradie called after her. "He's late."

Ford Lorenzo Claybourn turned out to be a giant dressed in white. He appeared older than Gradie, but he was suave and dark skinned, part Spanish perhaps, and his body matched Gradie's perfectly. He ate the part of Selene's steak she didn't want, and drank a lot of wine. They all drank a lot of wine that night.

As the sisters drew back the sea-coloured covers on their twin beds in the room next to Gradie's and slid their panties down their thighs, Alex whispered, "You don't know anything about that man with the children. You're always going on about moral decadence here—how do you know you can trust him? You, of all people . . ." The wine had drained away her discretion.

Selene propped her pillow against the wall and reached for a paperback book on the nightstand. "Sometimes it's easy to tell, that's all."

"Sometimes as in, depending what frame of mind *you're* in?"

"Sometimes as in, I talked to his kids. I could tell by the kids. And I could see in his eyes he trusted me right away. We both trusted each other right away."

But could her perception be trusted, after Woody Gold? Alex wondered.

"You're right, though," Selene went on. "I mean, right to be cautious. He isn't really like his children. He's sort of a closed-up kind of person. Shy, you might say. I wish we could get a better reading lamp in here."

The sheets were cool against Alex's skin. She threw her pillow on the floor next to her panties. "Don't go in too deep, little sister. You haven't got your life jacket any more."

Selene looked past her book to the dresser mirror that faced her form the opposite wall. "Don't forget, by nature I'm a risk-taker. What's been happening to me—what happened to me—the last while—isn't really who I am." She rolled onto her side to face Alex's bed. "Imagine Gradie coming all the way to California to find a man her size to love."

"I'd like to see them naked together."

"Just look through her photo album sometime."

"Really?"

Selene shifted restlessly under her cover. "I'm too drunk to read."

"Turn out the light," Alex mumbled, as she had always done when they were children sharing a room.

She never did mention her job to Selene and Gradie. She just did it. They caught on, eventually.

Ford showed up often after the barbecue. He came with them on their excursions and telephoned on the days he wasn't with them. Quite regularly now, he and Gradie went off on their own in his black Jaguar. One day, the four of them took a leisurely ride to L.A. Alex and Ford and Gradie wanted to spend the evening nightclubbing and stay the night in some funky motel, but Selene clenched up at the idea. She said she needed to babysit for Eli in the morning, but Alex and Gradie recognized the little signs of anxiety in her—the way she pressed her handbag to her breast with stiff fingers, the way she seemed to breathe in sharp quiet gasps, the way her voice went low and flat. Ford paid for their dinner and they drove home listening to Gradie's recording of Leonard Cohen.

Alex tried to work out in her mind, as she squatted and dug and raked in the perennial beds, how Selene could be so afraid of new places, of unidentifiable violence, and yet so eager to get involved with a stranger walking on a beach. For four hours every day, Selene played with the six children. Much of the time they were in the park. But Eli had given Selene an extra key to his rooms at the Breakers, and sometimes when Alex went to the terrace wall she could not see or hear any sign of her sister kicking through the surf with the bright, noisy brood. Of course, Eli was not really a stranger. He was in some ways quite familiar to Selene.

The sun got warmer day by day; the brown earth Roger and Alex pampered with their old tools turned rich and mellow. She went with him to a nursery miles away at the edge of the city to buy new plants. The old ones were hauled away by a stocky young man with a rusty truck. The *we* was rampant in Roger's conversation, but there was still no clue as to Gisele's whereabouts. Alex tried to think of strategies for getting into his apartment.

They took siestas every day from 11:30 till two in the afternoon. Alex and Selene and Gradie lunched together at various places, and then seldom saw one another until six or so. The three of them would swim together, Alex would shower, and then they spent the rest of the evening dining, taking drives, talking, reading the newspapers. Occasionally they would rent a movie. Alex found herself glad for the routine they established, though she had never before realized how much she liked routine.

Selene still passed the mornings watching news magazines and talk shows and cartoons on television.

One afternoon, just before two, Alex went looking for Bonita, to ask for an extra blanket. Gradie's suite had begun to heat up during the day, and Gradie had turned on her air conditioner. Selene seemed to have no problem with the cold air pumping into the apartment, but Alex found the nights chilly.

She heard the motors of the washing machine and dryer blathering away, and crossed the patio to see if Bonita was working in the laundry room under the stairs. The door was closed. It was hardly ever closed during the day. Again, Alex felt some hesitation about opening the door with the peeling paint, but she saw a dim outline of someone through the small window beside the door, and decided to go in. Alex wasn't certain Bonita would understand *blanket*. But more than likely, one would be lying folded somewhere in the tiny room, and she would be able to convey her request with gestures. The door opened out. It wasn't on its latch. Alex pulled on it and peered into the gloomy interior. She was just about to call Bonita's name when she saw, in a corner near a storage rack of folded bedding, two figures in an embrace. The noise of the machines had drowned out the little sound Alex had made, and the couple did not notice her right away. Bonita's blouse was bunched up above her breasts. Her face was raised to his. Roger was kissing her forehead and running his hands up and down her bare back. Both Roger's and Bonita's eyes were closed, but within a second of Alex entering, Bonita's opened lazily, and Alex stepped back, out the door. She was sure Bonita had sensed that someone had come in, but Alex did not know if she had slipped out quickly enough not to be recognized.

She lowered herself into the swimming pool and began to cruise slowly along its length on her back. A few minutes later Roger appeared at the laundry room door. He and Alex greeted each other in their usual way. There was no sign of Bonita. I'll get the extra blanket later, thought Alex, now that I know where to find one.

While planting pansies in a shaded corner near the entrance to the Rosecrans, Alex listened to Roger describing the rolling fields of ranunculus flowers near Cardiff and realized that his fluent patter and elegant posture and natty clothes had taken on a new meaning. No longer a measure of the man, they now seemed more of a disguise, a deception. Her Fred Astaire had been diminished. Holding a saffron-coloured pansy at the end of her trowel, she hesitated before lowering it into one of the holes Roger was digging in a careful pattern in the triangular bed. Could it be that she really believed Gisele lay serenely somewhere inside the Willises' suite, surrounded by pillows and shawls, nibbling on bon-bons and laughing melodically with loving friends who came to call, while her husband cavorted with the chambermaid behind her back? All at once Alex became aware that though on an intellectual level she believed Gisele to be dead, some part of her harboured a secret desire for Gisele to be alive and beautiful and devoted to Roger.

"Something wrong with my excavations, Alex?" inquired Roger, who, having finished the holes, was now helping Alex put the flowers in.

"No, of course not. So if these ranunculuses are so special, how come we don't have any?"

"They grow from bulbs. I'll put in all the bulb flowers in the fall. You'll have to come back in October." He laughed and scooped soil around the stem of the tiny plant he'd just set in. "Look over there across the street." He pointed with his trowel. "See the arrangement in front of that house? Those are ranunculi."

"I've often wondered what those are. They look like roses on steroids. We don't have them in Canada."

"Too short a growing season. They're very sensitive to frost."

Alex buried roots with her gloved hands. "I've looked at the pictures of your wife in your office quite often. I'd like to meet her sometime." There. What more could she do?

Roger got to his feet. He scanned the flower bed. Alex looked up at him. "I'll get the water hose," he said.

Through the arch of the gate, Alex noticed Selene curled up on the grass near the rabbit cage. She had her arms akimbo on the seat of the chair next to it, and appeared to be nearly asleep, drowsing in the shadow of the hotel wall. Van Gogh preened with his pointed front paws, oblivious to Selene, who normally talked to him and scratched his ear through the mesh with her index finger. Selene had been preoccupied lately. Alex wondered and feared what was happening within her.

Roger, dragging the hose, blocked Selene from Alex's view. He did not make eye contact with Alex as he approached, yanking on the limp, warm hosing, but Alex intended to press on. "Is your wife at home today?"

Roger knelt and smoothed the soil as though it were an expensive carpet. He picked up a handful. "No," he replied. "She's not." The dry soil ran through his fingers. "Go turn on the spigot, will you, dear?"

Men, women, children, staring with those gaunt eyes, their lips pursed; clusters of men in dark suits and bow ties; women posed in complacent rows on kitchen chairs set out in the garden. Most of the photographs in the first album were black and white, a bit faded, cracked like old mirrors. Alex recognized some of them; her parents had kept the same family portraits in their albums. Many more in Gradie's first album were of her own parents, Alex's great-aunt Justina and great-uncle John. Gradie took after her father in every way except for the eyes, which were very much Aunt Justy's. The photographs were labelled, but except for family members, the names meant nothing to Alex. Gradie's family had lived in Saskatchewan.

The second album showed Gradie as a child on a stark and dusty prairie farm. To her surprise, Alex found pictures of Selene and herself, most of them in their home in Winnipeg. But one, according to the caption, had been taken at the farm. Alex and Selene's family had gone on many car trips during the girls' childhood. Alex could not remember ever being at her great-uncle's farm—near Saskatoon it had been. The picture showed two shy, solemn little girls standing next to their beautiful older cousin, who smiled brightly and towered over them.

The third and fourth albums covered Gradie's travels and her life in California, and it was near the end of the fourth album that Alex, impatient for something revealing, discovered the photos Selene had talked about: Gradie and Ford clutching white towels to their bronzed bodies and laughing. They stood on a strip of sand. The ocean surged behind them. More photographs of stranger sitting at a table, surrounded by trees and flowers and shadows. The table was spread with a magnificent luncheon. The guests were naked—at least, naked from the waist up. Alex could not find Gradie among them, but she thought she spotted Ford at the end of one side of the table. Gradie must have snapped the picture. Most of the fourth album was unlabelled.

Alex returned to the beginning of the third album, to the part of Gradie's life that, for the sister, had been the adventure—a life in California. But time and again, she found herself drawn to the fourth and last album, which lay open beside her on the sofa.

Browsing around Loma Beach one morning (Roger Willis had gone away for the day), Alex found a small sports shop and, in it, a pair of lavender running shoes. The proprietor, seeing her fondle the soft leather, persuaded her to "jump in."

"Jump on in, girl!" he commanded in a falsetto voice. "Just do it! Get into those shoes and run like the wind!"

Alex had always meant to take up jogging. "I guess they'll be my main souvenir," she told him. "I've never seen shoes like this back home."

"Wave when you go by my window!" he replied.

The shoes were expensive, and, having made the purchase, Alex decided she'd better use them. She began jogging in the evenings, usually just before supper if they were eating late, mid-evening if they dined early. Sometimes she ran along the cliffs, sometimes through Loma Beach, lengthening her course a little every day. And whenever she jogged past the sports shop where she'd bought the shoes, she waved into the window, without checking first to see if the proprietor was even looking.

About the third evening of jogging, Gradie watched Alex lace up the purple runners and said, "This Sunday Ford and I are going to Black's Beach. We were wondering if you and Selene would like to come along. It's out near Torrey Pines."
Alex glanced at Selene, who had just come into the living room dressed in her swimsuit. "Sure, why not," said Alex.
But Selene said, "I don't know. Eli might need me this Sunday."
"Well, we won't leave until about five. The cliffs there are four hundred feet high. At sunset you can watch the hang-gliders soaring off the edges." Gradie paused. "I hope you won't mind—it's a clothing-optional beach. Mostly optional."
"A nude beach!" Selene crowed. "I've never been to one of those!"
"There's a lot of walking involved," Gradie continued. "You can only get there by way of trails leading down from the tops of the cliffs. They're steep and, well, treacherous. But there is one trail that begins at a lower spot. It's not as steep. We'll take that one this time."
Alex finished tying her laces and stood up. She gazed at her shoes and said, "Go there often, Gradie?"
Gradie, too, looked at the shoes. "It's where Ford and I met. But to answer your question, no, not very often." Her eyes slid up to Alex's. "Ford and I belong to an organization called Nu Integral."
"You're nudists."
"That's right. There are a bunch of camps around here. The one we usually go to is in Arriz Desert Park. I'm on the executive. That's where I was the night you arrived—at a meeting."
Selene arranged a loud beach towel on her shoulders. "What do you have meetings—about?"
"Fund-raising, mostly. Member's dues cover our costs, but we raise money to donate to environmental groups, like the Sierra Club, Save-the-Whales. . . ."

"We've seen your albums. . . ," Alex began.

"I know. I thought you might have questions about some of the pictures."

"What I wanted to ask was, you've travelled a lot. Did you visit nudist—colonies—in other countries?"

Gradie threw back her head and laughed. "Oh, yes, Alex—always. Nu Integral has gotten lots of good ideas from foreign groups.'

What kind of ideas? wondered Alex.

"Anyway, come with us to Black's on Sunday. You might even decide to join."

Selene walked out with Alex. "Looks like you'll get your wish," she breathed into Alex's ear as they made their way towards the setting sun.

"As far as we know, poor Gradie has had her clothes on the whole time we've been here." They descended the stairs in unison. "Poor, poor girl."

Mid-afternoon Sunday the skies thickened and turned dark. The plans to go to Black's Beach were put on hold, and, by six, rain fell like the sisters had never seen rain fall before. Lightning danced above the lead-coloured ocean, thunder enclosed the Rosecrans. "We'll try again next Sunday" were the last words Gradie said before she and Ford disappeared for the rest of the evening.

In a week and a half Alex and Selene would be home, gone from California, gone from the sea and the palms and the cliffs, back to the river where Woody Gold had died.

The next day, Alex woke up from a nap under one of the sun umbrellas. She and Roger had worked hard that morning, digging into grass on the street side of the hotel, working the soil, fertilizing it, and struggling with the nursery trees Roger wanted to plant there. Alex worried about him, straining with the heavy pots, but he always seemed to have more stamina than she did. Having slept deeply after a swim in the pool, Alex found herself listless and somewhat disoriented, as though drunk. Her vision still clotted with the residue of fleeting dreams and hallucinations, she turned her head to the door of the laundry room. It was closed. The machines chugged and blared inside.

Alex roused herself and pattered across the empty patio to the terrace wall. She rubbed her face and her eyes and squinted in the light.

There was Selene, below, on the giant slab of rock that separated the terrace from the Loma Park beach. The tide was out, small waves clawed feebly at the stone edge. Selene, without her sunglasses for a change, and wearing a bright shirt and shorts, was leaning against a twisted pillar of rock that was about her height. Her hands were folded behind her, one knee was bent. Her eyes were closed. She could have been asleep. Gulls swirled around her.

Alex put on her own sunglasses and had just decided to join her sister when she saw movements she had not noticed in the glare of the sun: the children—at least, some of the six children—lolling on the bit of Loma Park lawn visible from the terrace; and closer to Alex, much closer, their father, descending the steps that led to the table of rock. He was dressed in white.

Alex caught her breath. So familiar, so terrifying in his resemblance to Selene's monster. He walked slowly and carefully, like someone stalking a wild animal. Once he was directly below Alex, his hat hid his face.

Alex wanted to shout down to Selene, to warn her. She opened her mouth to call her sister, but did not call, mesmerized by the motions of the tall, thin man prowling along the pocked surface of the stone slab.

Selene faced the ocean. She was invisible except to anyone standing at the terrace wall of the Rosecrans—or anyone passing by in a boat. But Eli knew she was there. He must have been watching. He made a wide circle around the pillar and then stood and observed her for a few seconds. The tide, beginning to move in now, pushed the scrabbling waves further up the rock. Water collected around his deck shoes. He inched forward, his body straight, silent, clothed in white.

Only a couple of feet away from Selene, whose eyes, Alex could see, were still closed, he raised his hand. Alex again nearly cried out. But he simply removed his hat. Slow currents of drifting tidal air played in his dark curls. Alex's lips moved: *She must know someone's there!*

He paused only inches away from Selene. Then, he bent forward and, without touching any other part of her body, put his lips on hers, and kissed her, deeply, as deeply as Alex had been sleeping only moments earlier.

Selene did not open her eyes. She did not move. But Alex could feel her respond to the kiss.

It lasted only seconds—maybe five—but to Alex the kiss was five years long, the span of time that Selene had been kissless because of Woody Gold.

And then he drew away from her and walked slowly back across the expanse of rock, to the steps cut into the sea wall. Alex watched Selene. She did not open her eyes. She might have been inside a dream.

The last Alex saw of Eli that day was him strolling on the Loma Park beach with his hands folded behind him, and his children skittering along like sandpipers.

How many times had he and Selene played out that fantasy? Or was it the first time? Did she need to be rescued?

Alex ran her fingertips across the skin of her neck and chest. The sun was making her sweat and burn. With great strides she covered the width of the patio and dove into the deep end of the pool. When she surfaced at the other end, Roger was smiling down at her like Fred Astaire.

"Oh yes. She is gone, I'm afraid. Yes, dead. Many years already." The man with the glasses and the silver hair clutched his knee and rocked back and forth in the leather sofa. "There'd never been an undertow there before. Roj and Gisele often swam off the cliffs right at that spot. Of course, it was always risky. Always risky. But that's what they were like. They liked a bit of danger. Both in exceptional physical condition, you see . . . . That's what made Gisele's illness so ironic, so bitter."

Alex let her breath out slowly. The office and the apartment beyond were quite still. At first, she'd worried that Roger would appear at any moment, and that she would not be able to ask the Ice Cream Man her questions. She had seen him slipping into the office and had run to intercept him before he went inside Roger's quarters. "Are you going to see Gisele?" she'd flung out before she'd had time to think of more discreet wording.

"Illness?" she echoed.

"Some sort of mental state. Poor girl was a bit mad towards the end. In and out of Rancho Cabrillo—that's a hospital near Arriz Park. But she seemed to be getting better. It was her idea to go swimming that day, like they used to. They found her body a day later." The man looked down at his lap and sighed. "More often than not they don't. She was so very lovely."

"Doesn't it seem," said Alex, "that Roger still speaks about her as if she's alive?"

The man shook his head, but answered, "Yes, yes, yes. To tell you the truth, I think—I think it's possible that there was no undertow. That the accident had a somewhat different nature than Roger described. Or, more likely, Gisele swam out beyond their relatively safe zone on purpose, with no intention of ever returning alive. That could explain why Roger hasn't been able to deal with the whole thing."

The man got up from the sofa and peered through the Venetian window blinds into the courtyard. "Her ashes are spread throughout the flower beds here. She loved gardening."

Alex recalled Roger sifting the dirt through his elegant fingers when she'd asked him if Gisele were at home. "Are you his lawyer then?" she asked, nodding towards the briefcase on the floor beside the sofa.

"Dear lord, no. Do I look like one? I'm Henry Champagne." He stuck out his hand to her. "I come here to play Gisele's harpsichord. She has—had—one of the finest harpsichords in the city. Roj had it made for her. I play one in a church just the other side of Loma Beach, but every Thursday afternoon while Roj is up at Rancho he lets me play here. My music is in that attaché case, you see." Henry Champagne went over to the table with the photographs. He picked one up and drew it close to his thick lenses. "I taught her to play. She claimed to be a relative of Amadeus Mozart. Played quite well. Though I must say I enjoyed her piano more. I dearly loved to listen to her piano." He caressed the photograph near his face, almost touching it with his cheek. Finally he lowered it to the table as if he did not want to let it go, as if he would never get another chance to hold it again.

Then he looked at his watch. "And, there's a young girl from Sunset Cliff—just over there—who comes for a half-hour lesson on Thursdays. She may very well be waiting for me as we speak."

The two ice creams. "I've been here several weeks and I've never seen a girl," commented Alex.

"There's another entrance to Roj's apartment than through this office. It's on the Cliffs side over there, sort of hidden among the underbrush. He leaves the door open and she lets herself in. Coming from Loma Beach, I usually go in through the office; if it's unlocked, that is."

"Why does Roger still go to Rancho?"

The man picked up his briefcase. "He does gardening for them. Donates his time. There are others who do so. Together they keep the grounds nice." He glanced outside to the courtyard once more. "I see this rabbit is managing to survive. There have been almost dozens, I think. Every one called van Gogh. Did you know Gisele was a painter?"

"Yes. . . ."

"She named the first rabbit just before she died. Roj is the one who keeps calling them van Gogh. Of course, he has put all her early works in the guest rooms. You should see the ones she did while at Rancho. Beautiful. Horribly beautiful."

He started for the apartment door. "Where are they?" Alex called after him. "The Rancho paintings?"

Henry Champagne opened the door. "In here. His place is full of them. Why don't you come in and browse? He won't be back for hours."

Alex hesitated. "No," she said. "I'll ask him to show me himself sometime."

But Alex lingered in the office after the man had shut the door. A short time later she heard a whisper of the harpsichord through the walls. She could not tell who was playing, Henry Champagne or the student. As she gazed at the photographs, she could almost imagine it was Gisele herself who sat at the keyboard, her body arched towards the perfect instrument, stylish fingertips roaming the wooden keys like sandpipers.

The man with the two ice cream cones had been in love with Gisele. Still was.

Alex did not get to see the horribly beautiful paintings. Two days later, she came face to face with the mean side of California, with the *wildness* that was taking over.

They spent Saturday in Tijuana. The sisters, Ford, and Gradie. Alex learned not to say TI-AH-WAH-NAH, the way everybody back home did. "It's TI-HWANAH," Selene told her.

By the time they returned to the Rosecrans, the sun had set and the light was beginning to fade. Ford stayed in the courtyard to fire up the barbecue, Gradie went to check on the steaks she'd put in to marinate before they'd left that morning. Selene mumbled something about needing a swim after sitting in the car for so long. "Good idea," Alex said to the empty living room. She called into the kitchen, "Gradie, do I have time for a twenty-minute run?"

After changing into her jogging clothes, Alex set out. If the sun had not gone down, she would have chosen to run along the cliffs. But now they were dark, the trail along the top too uneven for night running.

She turned left, past Loma Park, into Loma Beach.

Alex had never jogged on a Saturday night before. She was surprised at the number of people on the streets. They were of all types and ages, but most of them were thin-legged boys, adolescents, looking for a good Saturday-night time. This may not last even twenty minutes, Alex thought as she dodged around the pedestrians on the sidewalks.

She'd summoned up the courage at last to talk to Selene about Eli. The sister had been on the cliff walk one morning after an early breakfast. A night fog was just beginning to lift, or burn off. They strolled more slowly than they sometimes did, looking carefully at each wildflower they passed, tossing toast pieces to gulls and pigeons.

Alex said, "Are you going to be able to leave the children easily?"

Selene cocked her head and quickened the pace a bit. "No. Not easily."

Alex waited for more. Nothing more came. "You never talk about their father. What's he like? I mean, it isn't just you and the children all the time, is it?"

Selene looked at Alex sharply.

"I've seen you occasionally," Alex continued. "With him."

"Eli and I," breathed Selene, "were two caged people. He,

not so much by the death of his wife, but by having to deal for the past year and a half with his children's loss. And I—well, you know what caged me."

First Woody himself, and then his unexpected drowning.

"We—we released each other—in small ways. I knew as soon as I saw him, and then talked to him, that through him I could re-create Woody Gold. *Re-do* him, shape him into something that was not a monster. It was the most amazing thing to have happened, Alexandra. Like something in a fairy tale. . . ."

One kiss.

"But now, you have to tear yourself away from him. You'll be in mourning again."

"Maybe not," answered Selene. "Maybe not."

Selene had changed the subject after that, chattering about the children. Alex tried to pay attention, but became consumed with a worry that Selene might not return home with her.

Looking for a less crowded route and a shortcut back to the Rosecrans, Alex turned into an alley that would lead her to Loma Park. They had only a few more days in California. Long ago she and Selene had talked about taking an overnight cruise to Ensenada. Perhaps they should skip Black's Beach and go tomorrow. Gradie would understand.

Deep in thought and aware only of the sounds of her own feet slapping the uneven asphalt in the lonely, narrow alley, Alex missed the rhythm of other feet matching hers and then speeding up and coming nearer.

All at once she felt two strong hands, on in each of her armpits. She felt herself lifted off her feet. But her captors kept on running, holding her between them like a trophy.

Alex twisted her head and saw they were only boys, really—strong, laughing boys wearing baseball caps. They appeared to be joyful, delighted to have found her. She writhed and screamed. "No! No! Please—I have nothing. . . !"

But they tossed her into a black passageway between two decrepit buildings and began to pull on her feet.

"No!" she shouted, thinking, with all the people on the street someone would surely hear her. But would they come? She tried to get up.

They boys said nothing. One of them pushed her roughly back to the cluttered, weedy ground.

Her head struck something hard, a cement curb or a rock of some sort. "Selene. . . ."

The air roared, the wooden buildings tipped away, the passageway washed over her like black water. And swirling in it, a fleeting vision of a chubby foot, kicking that clenched, hairy jaw.

"They stole my shoes."

"But that's all?"

"They were expensive. And I really liked them, Selene."

"Teach you to stay out of alleys."

"Don't you mean out of California?"

Ford had spent the bulk of the late evening on the phone with the police. She could hear him in the kitchen, trying to keep his voice low, but erupting into indignation every so often. "We don't care about getting the running shoes back!" he hissed into the receiver. "She was assaulted! They knocked her unconscious! The kids are wild on the streets around here!"

But Alex had no descriptions to give, because of the twilight and the boys' hats, and her panic. Even the young woman who had seen the boys follow her into the alley, and through the gloom had watched them chuck her between the buildings, could not say anything more than that they looked like all the young surfers in Loma Beach.

The woman who found Alex was dressed like a sixties hippie and smelled musty, a little mothball-y. Alex took great comfort in the aromas given off by her rescuer, who was kind to her and matter-of-fact about a teenage prank gone slightly amiss. "They might not have realized they knocked you out," she said as she escorted Alex to the walk-in clinic only a block away. "They beat it up the other end of the alley, but they didn't seem scared. They were laughin' and swingin' yer runners. When I seen you didn't come out right away, I checked. Lots of kids are doped up around here. They wouldn't've noticed a little detail like unconsciousness. Me—I wear sandals. Nobody never steals sandals."

Alex said nothing on the ways to the clinic. The woman did not seem to expect her to talk.

"I had just started to stop," Selene said to Alex as they lay in their beds that night.

"Started to stop what?"

"Worrying. About this place. About California. About the ugliness hiding inside the bird-of-paradise flowers, under the palms, along the shoreline."

But Alex heard in Selene's tone and saw in the way she moved, in her bed and on the terrace and on the beach, that California was no longer the monster it had been when they'd first come to Fourth and India.

The kiss, granted like a wish by the Woody-Gold-looking man who had strolled so self-absorbed on the sands of Loma Park, had kicked Selene's monsters in the chin.

"What happened to me wasn't so bad," Alex said. "I got mugged. I'm okay." At least now Selene would go home with her.

And yet, Alex couldn't sleep. Her head hurt, despite the painkillers the intern at the clinic had given her. But it wasn't only the discomfort of the abrasion on the back of her skull that kept her awake. ("A great huge chunk of cement in the weeds!" the hippie-woman had told her. "You go look at it sometime when you're feeling up to it!") The adrenalin was high. Alex was still afraid.

At about one o'clock she got up and thought of waking Selene. But instead she slipped into a pair of shorts and a

T-shirt and tiptoed out of the apartment. Moon-washed, the terrace was gun-metal blue. Points of light bobbed on the restless ocean waters. Alex sat on the top step of the staircase leading down to the patio. Somewhere in the hotel, someone else was still awake, listening to Spanish guitar music.

When will it be my turn? she wondered. All these different kinds of love she'd uncovered at the edge of the continent had made her realize she had none. All her recent glimpses of tender moments and glorious past loves had created a desire in her, a long-suppressed need for someone to hold her, to kiss her deeply. But all she had gotten for herself here was the salt-scented embrace of two pimple-faced surfers who wanted nothing but her shoes. The bear had paralyzed her emotionally, and then, Selene's stalker. Where would she find her healing?

Suddenly Alex heard voices on the rock table below the terrace wall. Low murmurs that she could just make out above the swish and slap of the tide. Instead of being curious, Alex felt her skin go clammy with fear. The guitar music drifted softly across the courtyard as she moved along the walkway. Before entering Gradie's apartment, Alex glanced up at the moon. It was supposed to be full. She remembered talking about it the night before with Selene. "Tomorrow's full moon—the crazies will be out," Alex had said, reciting a saying of their mother's.

It was not full now, though. A large, perfect curve cut into the side of it, like the overlapping bite of a cookie-cutter. Alex had seen it many times before—a lunar eclipse, the end of a lunar eclipse. It would have been just beginning when she turned into the alley in Loma Beach earlier that evening.

Gradie insisted they cancel Black's Beach so Alex could recover on a chaise longue on the patio. And Alex did spend most of the morning and early afternoon drowsing beneath one of the pink and green umbrellas. Selene stayed with her the whole time. "You might have a concussion. You could lapse into a coma." (After the bear attack, their mother had taken them to a doctor every time they bumped their heads.)

But later Alex insisted that the beach was just what she needed.

She sat huddled under a towel while Ford and Gradie and Selene disappeared and reappeared among giant friendly swells of ocean. Gradie had chosen a secluded part of the beach, where the surf was gentle and the rocks few.

Selene wore her nakedness gracefully. Ford and Gradie looked like large, bronze sculptures.

Alex did not take off her swimsuit. She found herself glancing over her shoulder every few minutes, as though worried someone was sneaking up on her. *When will this go away?*

Monday afternoon, Alex began to pack. Their plane would be leaving early the next morning, and they were all going out for dinner later. She'd gone to look for Roger in the morning, to finish up the borders. But she found no sign of him anywhere on the grounds. In his office, a man named Chuck, who was probably around the same age as Roger, told her he was "holding down the fort," and that Roger had gone up north to visit Gisele's sister. He didn't say how far up north, or when he'd be back.

Gisele's sister. Henry Champagne hadn't mentioned a sister. Alex felt as though another huge mystery lay unfathomed at the centre of the Rosecrans Hotel.

"But he left you a note. You're Alex, I know. I've seen you working around the place. Here."

Pressed flowers in a card. "Come back again, Alex. Next year. We'll put bird-of-paradise flowers all along the front of the hotel, and you can see the ranunculi in full glory."

She found Bonita feeding van Gogh and bade both of them farewell. In Bonita's eyes, Alex was certain she saw a kind of defiance, a claim of rights to Roger's passion.

Selene came in at four and found Alex hunting around the apartment for small things left lying about and easily left behind.

Selene put on her bathing suit. "I haven't had a swim today. We went fishing on the pier."

When she came back, she put on a bathrobe and flopped into a deep sofa in front of the TV.

Alex started throwing things into one of her suitcases in the bedroom.

Finally she went to the living room. She stood in the entrance and glared at Selene.

"What's wrong, Alex?"

"Why aren't you packing? Have you decided to stay in California forever?"

"Alex . . ."

"Fine."

Alex went back to the bedroom. She emptied her bags onto her bed and began repacking everything.

Selene came to the door. "Did you think I wasn't going home with you?"

"You led me to believe . . ."

"Whoa. I'm going home. Maybe not to my old place on the river. I think I need to be done with that. But I'm going home."

"What about Eli, then, and the kids. . . ?"

"We know where to find each other if we need to. I've got to try on my new life first."

They heard the front door. Gradie came in and sagged onto the bed. "I'm going to miss you," she said.

At dawn, Gradie drove the sisters to the airport in her Mustang. As they glided along India Street for the first time since she had been violated in the alley, Alex looked down each side street as they passed, wondering where the hippie-woman who smelled of mothballs might have spent the night, where she might be sleeping. No one was in the streets at this time of morning. Loma Beach was quiet as a tomb.

Then Alex shouted, "My runners! There! There!" She pointed up and Gradie slammed on the brakes.

The three women got out of the Mustang and stood in the empty street gazing at the lavender runners slung by their laces over the wires that crossed the street about twenty feet above their heads. "My beautiful, beautiful shoes," whispered Alex. "They didn't steal them, it was an initiation. . . ."

"We'll get them down and mail them to you," said Gradie.

"No. No. Please—take a picture and send it to me. It will be a better souvenir. I'll put it in my photo album."

As they continued along the old pavement in Gradie's car, hitting green lights at every intersection, Alex watched through the rear window, watched Loma Beach slide away. No wind funnelled along India Street. The runners hung perfectly still in the centre of the span, suspended forever above Alex and Selene's small corner of California.

Jumpers

Dave and Irene live in the bush right next to the Rat River Good Neighbour Centre. Their driveway curves through a stubby woodlot just off a dirt road that runs parallel to the river. Finding their place is harder than we thought it would be; we haven't been to the village for a couple of years. On the phone earlier, Irene reminded me about the sign on the main road pointing to the community hall. But the sign isn't visible in the dark. And I realize we've always come here in summer, always arrived in daylight; we've never called on Dave and Irene at the end of October. So we pass the sign the first time. But after that, it's easier. Soon, landmarks show themselves, though they are only silhouettes of landmarks. Just the curve of the trees and the shapes of the houses, and I recall that there are houses only on the left side of the dirt road, until you get to Dave and Irene's driveway, which juts off to the right. I remember, too, that the U.S. border is just half a mile beyond their yard. A ditch and a dike mark the boundary. The official crossing is seven miles away.

As soon as we get around the first curve in the driveway,

we see signs—highway signs. They are planted in the grassy shoulders. All of them are the same: STOP. "Dave's the last person to obey rules," says Walter. "Funny he's got traffic laws on his own driveway."

"It isn't really funny when you think of it. He's exactly the one who would steal the rules. I mean, it's not funny that he would *steal* them, anyway. I guess it is sort of weird that he would put them up on his property."

"Course, if he puts them up just out of sight of the cops going by on the road," says Walter, "he's sort of thumbing his nose at the law."

I count nine stop signs in total.

We turn another curve in the driveway, a sharp right-angle one, and the house lights appear. "Do you think Dave's ever done anything really illegal?" I ask Walter.

"What do you call stealing highway signs?"

"That's harmless stuff. I mean something nasty, that hurt somebody."

Walter stops the car in front of the house. "Naw. He's a pussy-cat."

The house used to be ramshackle and unpainted. It's a very old house and has historical value in the community. Dave and Irene have always been proud of it, despite its bent floors and crumbling foundation. But now, even in the dark, we can see that the wood siding had been painted white and the windows have new aluminum frames. A cat with half a tail slinks around the corner of the drooping front porch and stands in the light of a yellow bulb hanging over the front door. She glares a warning at us and blocks our entrance for a moment, then zips away with a whispery cry.

Dave flings open the door before we knock. He is tall and thin as usual in the inner doorway. Irene wriggles like a kitten through the space between him and the frame. We all say long-time-no-see, and the next thing we do is admire Dave's collection of caps, which hang on hundreds of pegs throughout the rooms on the main floor. The caps say things like POOL SEED, RAT RIVER REUNION '87, HAPPINESS IS FARMING, NOTHING RUNS LIKE A DEERE, PRAISE THE LORD REVIVAL JUNE 1979. Then of course we have to look at the kid, who was kind of a surprise for Dave and Irene. We haven't seen her since she was a newborn. She's a tall toddler now. We watch her tear pages out of a book a while and then Dave says, "Let's play crib."

Irene gets the cards and clears the table, and Dave pulls beer and Baby Duck out of the fridge and we ask him about the stop signs on the driveway.

"Darn jumpers," he tells us. "It's getting scary. And us with a kid?"

He's told us before about the jumpers—mostly dare-devils who want to sneak across the border for the fun of it. Sometimes older folks have bought something in the States they don't want to pay duty on and they decide to jump. Tracks are worn into the ditch and the dike straight south of Dave and Irene's.

"I walk over there sometimes," says Dave. "The tracks are always fresh. Weeds don't get a chance to even think of taking hold. Lately we've been getting a lot of scummy types showing up at our door asking for directions in the middle of the night, or asking for a lift to town. One time a guy got stuck out there with his Jeep on a rainy night. Expected me to help him out. Well, hell, he looked mean, so I went, but Irene called the RC's, and they showed up in ten minutes. There's nothing the RC's like better than catching jumpers, especially if they got drugs on them."

I'm thinking, this is so typical of Dave and Irene. They have little dangerous parts to their lives that other people we know don't have. That's the reason Walter and I were attracted to them from the beginning, when we met them at a steak house in Grafton, North Dakota, during a curling bonspiel. A drunk American was hassling Irene, and Dave heaved the man out without asking the manager first. Dave has a brother who seems perfectly normal to us, but a few years ago got it into his head that Dave had cheated him out of some farm pay, and started threatening to burn down their house. And one time while Irene was in the back lean-to doing laundry and making crab-apple jelly on the summer stove, Dave came off the field, drove himself to the hospital in Altona and had his appendix removed. The nurse phoned Irene to tell her that her husband was doing well after his surgery, and Irene hadn't even known he was sick. Things like that just never happen to Walter and me. What's so interesting about Dave and Irene is that none of those things bother them too much. Dave actually gets a twinkle in his eye when he tells us his brother nearly killed his grandfather once. Dave and Irene enjoy life.

Walter says, "Dave, you don't really think nine stop signs are going to stop drug-runners from coming into your yard?"

For god's sake, Walter, I'm thinking, it's symbolic. . . .

"Well," says Dave, "I had a few beers last May, after the guy got stuck in the Jeep, and I went on a little spree around the countryside stomping down those signs. I was just mad."

Then I ask Irene if she still goes to the Grace Church a mile up the road next to the Rat River Good Neighbour Centre.

"I take Raina every Sunday. Dave comes occasionally." I like imagining Irene and the baby sitting in the sun on a pew in that little village church Sunday mornings. Maybe I feel they'll stay safe that way.

While we play cribbage, we listen to Elvis records played out of a genuine cafe jukebox Dave got somewhere, and I look at the kitchen walls. They are crowded with things: framed blow-ups of Raina, calendars featuring fifties cars, Bible verses burned into wood plaques, scribbled drawings of sunshine done in crayon, cartoons cut out of the newspaper. They're all hung at different levels, some with tape.

Walter shuffles the cards, hoping to get past the skunk line, and I say, "This window wasn't here last time." I'm talking about a bay window beside the dinette table we're playing on. The window looks out over a backyard we've never seen before. It's too dark to tell what's in the yard, though when I cup my hands around my eyes I see a swing set near the back door. "You've fixed the place up quite a bit."

"Dave's grandpa died. He left his estate to his grandchildren instead of his own kids."

"He didn't like 'em," says Dave.

"He couldn't have liked your brother too much, either," says Walter as he deals the cards.

"My brother got the same amount as everybody."

Nobody comments about that. I'm thinking, maybe the grandfather beat somebody up when he was young. Dave does not elaborate.

We drink lots of beer and Baby Duck, and the time goes by pretty fast. After crib, we play hearts and black-out, and about two-thirty a.m. Dave says, "Irene, get the kid. Let's go have breakfast in Hallock." As usual, although he has drunk the most, he is the most lively and clear-headed.

Irene sags to the table and says into the woolly sleeve of her right arm, "Dave, forget it."

But my Walter, who is mellow, goes along with it. Hallock is about ten miles the other side of the border. It has a truck stop that serves good food. Walter and I have been there, though never with Dave and Irene.

Just as I'm about to say what a dumb idea it is, Irene looks up from her sweater sleeve and smiles, and jumps up and runs upstairs to get the sleeping kid. "We'll take my car," says Dave. And he's gone.

I go to the can, and when I come out I hear a rumbling sound at the front of the house. "What's that?" I ask Walter.

"Pick-up truck," he shrugs.

Irene comes down with a groggy child in a snowsuit. They're out the door before Walter and I even have our jackets on. On the driveway beside our Mazda is a shiny

white car with Dave at the wheel. Irene and the baby sit in
the front with him, and Walter and I almost have enough
room in the back to dance, should we get the urge. Dave tells
us it's a '77 Chrysler he got in trade on a load of seed peas
last spring. "Irene loves the Thrush," he says as he guns it.
We roar down the lane surrounded by stop signs.

"Faster," says Raina softly. Dave guns it again. Irene and
the kid giggle in the front seat.

Without a moon the fields and woods around us are
simply black spaces with changing textures. We race along
smooth dirt roads through the empty darkness towards the
highway that leads to the customs at Emerson. Bright orange
lights blaze seven miles away at the crossing. I haven't ever
approached the customs from this angle, and I'm surprised
at how those orange lights shine across those seven miles.
The baby watches Walter and me over Irene's shoulder. She's
wearing a pink cap with kitten ears. Her thumb is resting
loosely in her mouth.

After turning onto the highway, the Chrysler rumbles
once more as Dave floors it, and in a flash we are at the
customs. No other vehicles are anywhere around. The buildings glow orange and silent. We glide past the Canadian
building and purr up to the U.S. gate.

The guard is a woman without a hat. She smiles at us
when she says hello into the window. Maybe they had a big
drug bust earlier tonight. After a few questions, she cheer-
fully tells Dave to open the trunk. "Damn" he says as he gets
out of the car.

"Problem?" I ask Irene.

"Well, I don't know," she says. "He can't get the trunk
open. Never has. We're lucky we haven't had a flat yet. It's
just that we don't use this car that much, except to joyride."

We listen to Dave explaining to the guard that the lock is
either rusted shut or jammed with dirt. She looks at his
driver's license and some other stuff from his wallet, and

finally lets us through, and even though I can't see her face, I know she isn't smiling any more.

The highway is four-lane now so Dave really floors it, and while we speed towards the Hallock exit I ask him to tell us again about the time the flying saucer came to their bush one summer a few years back. "A bright greenish-white light, right?" I say, to get him started.

"Yep, right about this time, too. All we saw was the light. It was like a searchlight, the way it moved through the trees. Right, Irene?"

"And the humming," Irene says. "It hummed real low and loud."

"We turned on some lights in the house and then the humming got higher and as it got higher the lights got dimmer and dimmer until they were just faint brown glows. And at the same time as the humming got higher, it also got quieter, and the searchlight got fainter."

"I would have been afraid," I say.

Irene says, "We weren't scared. We were just sorry we didn't see what it was all coming from."

Anne Murray is singing on the radio and Dave turns up the volume a little. "So spread your tiny wings and fly away," Irene sings sweetly into Raina's ear. We hear no more about the UFO.

Walter falls asleep. I think he's already regretting we came along on this joyride. I shake him when we see Hallock in the distance.

The truck stop has ten gas pumps and a huge parking lot for the big rigs that stop there. The cafe part is a white bungalow attached to a square, flat service station. The place is busy, though not with truckers. All kinds of people are in the cafe, and it's noisy with talking and dishes and the jukebox. Dave saunters ahead of us to a large booth in a corner. He settles in so that he has a view of the whole cafe. "Chips," says the baby.

We have to raise our voices to tell the waitress what we want to eat. We all order the same thing: eggs and Canadian bacon and hash browns and Texas toast. And coffee. While we wait, Dave starts wiggling in his seat in time to the music. None of us is as talkative as the other customers in the joint, and that seems to irk him. So to make up for it, he sings along with the jukebox. Pretty soon Raina is dancing and la-la-ing, too.

Then I notice that four burly men in the booth next to ours, behind Irene and the baby, are giving Dave dark looks. I jostle Walter's arm and roll my eyes in their direction. Walter clears his throat loudly and stares at Dave until Dave gets the message. But Dave has connected with his kid and he is not interested in humouring strangers in a truck stop.

One of the strangers stretches his neck in our direction and says, "You geeks from across the line?"

The word *geeks* makes me laugh. Walter frowns, probably wondering if he should clobber the guy. Irene elbows Dave, but Dave is now singing louder as well as shimmying in his seat.

All of a sudden the guy sitting behind Irene and Raina grabs hold of the baby's pink kitten ears and pulls the little cap off with a quick jerk. The cap goes flying off to another booth somewhere. Like lightning Dave is spread across our table and has his hands around the American's throat, between Irene's and Raina's heads. I'm thinking, lucky our eggs weren't on the table yet. And then I'm thinking, that was the meanest thing I've ever seen, a punk like that grabbing a baby's soft, pink little cap right off her head.

Next there's bumping and crashing as Dave and the American get into position. All sorts of things drop and break. The kid is crying, the other customers are silent. Irene finally makes a break for it with the baby, just around the same moment that Water, who is trying to pull Dave away from the molester, slips on something that's spilled and lands on his butt on a large piece of glass that's got pointy edges curving upwards. I pause on my way to the door and gape at the chunks of sugar dispenser scattered on the floor. Walter carefully gets to his feet. The piece of glass is caught there, partially in his skin, partially in his jeans. And I can't decide what to do: I want to help Walter get the sugar dispenser out of his butt, but I also want to make sure Irene and the baby are all right, even though I know they're out in the parking lot. I have to tell Irene how outrageous I think it is for that guy to pick on a baby.

And then the manager is out on the floor, a small, sad-looking man with a grim pack of bigger friends looming behind him. Walter yanks the piece of glass out of his jeans and I start looking for the blood. He straightens up and tries to walk normal to the men's room.

Irene and the baby are not in the car, or anywhere in sight. My throat gets tight, and I'm afraid to call because I'm afraid there'll be no answer. I am also afraid to walk just anywhere in the dark in the middle of the night on a truck-stop parking lot. But Irene must be out there somewhere. I begin strolling around the pavement and listening for voices or footsteps. I'm not dressed really warm, since I didn't know ahead of time that I'd be spending time in the open air. No cars go by on the street, and even the highway half a block away is silent. It's three-thirty. When I look into the cafe window I can see Dave and the punks arguing with the manager, probably about who should be evicted. Dave's arms are like octopus tentacles, the way they wave around.

As I come up to the glass door of the service station attached to the cafe I see the back of Irene. She is staring at a rack of junk food displayed against the far wall. Raina is in her arms, and Irene is swaying back and forth, probably humming "Snowbird."

I go inside and take a drink out of a cooler. "You missed the good part," I tell Irene. "Walter got a big hunk of glass in his cheek." I slap my butt and try to laugh. My voice gets snagged in my throat and I take a quick swig of Dr. Pepper.

"We better get him to Emergency," she replies without smiling or even looking at me. "He might need stitches or something. I hope he doesn't have a scar. It'd be Dave's fault."

She didn't get it; she thinks the cut is on his face.

Even though Irene's face is buried in the hood of Raina's snowsuit I can tell that her eyes are wet. "Don't worry," I say. "The worst that can happen to Dave is that he'll get beat up. No big deal, right?" It would be a very big deal to me. But I'm assuming Dave and Irene are emotionally equipped for things like that.

Then Irene whispers into the hood, "One of these days she's gonna be the one who's in his way. I can feel it coming." The kid wiggles down and Irene sets her loose.

I clear my throat and take another pull of the Dr. Pepper. "What do you mean?" I begin, not sure I've understood her correctly. "This wasn't Dave's fault. Those other guys started it."

Her voice is soft and tense. "He's nearly killed people sometimes."

She's still not looking at me. Her attention is fixed on a bag of Cheezies. Raina is babbling in front of an assortment of magazines.

"Irene, listen to me: does he hit you?" I didn't start this, either. But someone has to ask the question.

"Pardon?" Her body is rigid.

"I just want to know if Dave ever hits you."

"Does Walter ever hit you?" She's still stuck on the Cheezies.

"No, of course not."

"Well, Dave doesn't hit me, either."

I shouldn't have said *of course not.*

Her arm jerks up from her side and she plucks a bag from the rack. I keep staring at her face, and she finally turns to me. "Why should you worry?" She is smiling now. "You aren't . . ."

Dave walks in. The baby toddles up to him and hands him what looks like a wrestling magazine. Dave doesn't look ruffled at all. His hat is back on his head. "We're going," he barks.

What had Irene started to say? That I wasn't a close enough friend for her to confide in? I wasn't. That I would understand? Maybe I wouldn't. But I needed to finish this.

She slips away to pay the attendant for her snack. I notice as I pass her on the way to the door that it isn't the Cheezies that she took off the shelf; it's a bag of jalapeño potato chips.

"Where's Walter?" I ask.

"At the car," growls Dave. "Says his butt's numb. He's worried that a nerve's been damaged."

Irene picks up the kid. "Numbness is normal after traumatization," she says. "He'll feel the pain tomorrow."

I leave the service station to find Walter.

"Traumatization?" I hear Dave saying behind me.

Walter is standing slightly bent over beside the Chrysler.

"Get kicked out?" I say. I need to keep talking to hold off the thoughts about what Irene said.

"Dave's a jerk," says Walter through clenched lips.

"Worse than a geek."

"He took a swipe at the manager."

All of a sudden I don't know the family lingering in the service station. They've taken on frightening proportions.

Yet, when the three of them at last come through the glass door onto the parking lot and just saunter towards us in the blue light of mercury vapour, and a little bit of jukebox leaks out of the cafe as another customer goes in, everything seems the way it's always been.

We're about to get into the Chrysler when Irene says, "Dave? Raina's cap."

"I'll get it," I say before Dave has a chance.

I hold my head high as I go back into the truck stop to find the pink kitten-ears cap. I notice the manager watching me as I search the booths and the floor. The cap does not seem to be anywhere, and I ask the waitress instead of the manger if someone put it behind the counter or something. She can't find it, and I have to leave without it.

Then we have a big blow-up about that. We have to make all kinds of threats to keep Dave from going back in. "I'll call them tomorrow," says Irene. "I'll ask them to put it aside and we'll pick it up next week. In the daytime."

Walter sits tilted to keep his weight off his injured cheek. "Don't hit any bumps," he warns Dave.

"Aw, come on, Walter," says Dave. "Don't be so half-assed about it. Scrapping with the Americans is a tradition among the towns along the border. You should be proud of your battle scars."

"I'll be proud next week," Walter mumbles.

Once we're back on the highway and Dave can push the Chrysler to one-ten, he relaxes and jokes some more. On the four-lane he starts to sing again. The baby is asleep.

A mile before we get to the customs, Dave slows down as we near an exit.

"What are you doing?" says Irene.

"Taking a little detour."

We exit onto a narrow asphalt road and go west. Walter leans forward and says, "Dave, I'm in no mood for a joyride. I'd like to get home to clean up this cut."

"Hey, this is a shortcut to cleaning up your cut!" Dave chuckles.

"Oh geez, he's gonna jump," says Irene.

I lean forward and say into Dave's ear, "Is this safe? I mean, could we get caught?"

Dave doesn't answer. We slow down and the car swerves onto a side road. The headlights show that we are among dense trees. The road is only a trail. Walter has one hand braced on the backrest and the other on the seat in front of him, to keep himself raised off his bum, because the trail is full of ruts and dead branches and clumps of dry mud.

"Dave, not with the kid!" says Irene.

"Look," says Dave. "Chances are only about one in a hundred that the RCMP will be nearby, or that anybody'll be around to notice, at this time of night. And even with the sensors, it takes at least ten minutes for the cruiser car to get there. By that time, we're long home."

"Censors?" I say.

"Heat sensors, or maybe they work by the weight of a body or a car. I don't know, I've just heard about them. . . ."

"Oh my god. . . ."

The bush comes to an end and we're in an open field. Dave turns off the headlights. "There's more woods on the other side of this field. We have to find the opening without light."

I say, "How come you know how to do all this?"

The Chrysler starts across the black space. Dave drives very slowly. "I used to come here when I was younger. You were with me once, weren't you, Walt?"

Walter does not answer.

"We never crossed, though. Just looked at the place where other people crossed. I think this field is about half a mile wide." He speeds up a bit.

Looking around, I can see the orange lights of the customs way off to the right. At the moment, they are like a haven.

Just as Dave slows down in anticipation of the next bush, the trees are suddenly in front of us, and Walter and Irene and I all yell together, "DAVE!"

Despite the brakes we hit a tree. Not very hard, but we all lurch forward and Raina wakes up. At the same time as we hear the crunch at the front of the car, there is a THUNK at the back.

"Dave. . . !" wails Walter.

"SHUT UP!" Dave yells back. He turns the headlights back

on and gets out of the car and inspects the grille. Then he walks to the back of the car. Apparently the trunk is open. Dave tries to shut it several times, and the Chrysler rocks.

"Ha!" he exclaims as he gets back into the front seat. "Knocked the trunk open. It's empty. No dead bodies. Can't close it, though. The rest of the trail is to the left, I think." Dave turns up the music.

We drive through another stretch of bush, and then another stretch of open field, but this time we keep the headlights on because we are down low now, approaching the dike that was built to keep the Rat River out in spring.

"Do you think we've set off the sensors yet?" I ask as we see the rise of the dike ahead.

"I doubt it," says Dave. Then, "Ready?" And he cranks up Hank Snow singing "I've Been Everywhere, Man."

Off go the headlights. Up we go, and then down again. I remember how my father used to fly us over dips in the country dirt roads in his '59 Pontiac. Prairie roller-coaster, he called it. We are on grass and ruts.

And then up again and down. Except that on the second up there is a very loud THUNK! from the back of the car and a soft slap on the grass.

"That's it!" yells Dave above the radio. "Now let's boogie on home!"

"Dave," says Walter, "you left your trunk lid back there in the gully."

"Serious?" Dave hits the brakes. "Damn!"

Irene says, "There's car lights way over there."

"Forget the trunk!" I shout. "Let's get out of here!"

Dave hesitates for a moment. Then he kills the headlights and says, "Come on, Walter. Help me get it."

"I shouldn't have told you," says Walter. "Dave, if I get out of this car it will be to make a run for it to your yard."

Dave stands outside the Chrysler and looks back at the crossing. Irene and Raina look up at him from the passenger's seat. Irene turns off the radio. "Get in and close the door, Dave," she says quietly. "They'll see the interior lights."

"I can't leave my lid out there for them to find," says Dave, but he gets into the car and we start inching into the darkness. Up ahead we can see the yard light and brief glimpses of the porch light, like a firefly in the trees. Dave manages to keep on the road, but he has to drive slowly. "We didn't even smuggle anything," he grumbles. "Makes the whole thing kinda useless."

We are all quiet as we steal along that endless half-mile, except for Dave, who says "Damn" once, softly.

We did smuggle something across the border, though. Walter has a wound from Dave's war with the American punks. And I've brought back a secret fear of the little dangerous parts in Dave and Irene's life. They're not so little. Irene is afraid of crossing Dave's dangerous borders.

"Where's that other car?" Dave asks as we get near the driveway.

"I've lost track of it in the trees," says Irene. "It could be anywhere."

Dave makes the turn onto his driveway. The stop signs are invisible as we slink along the dark path to Dave and Irene's old house with new windows and new paint. It's not quite four-thirty in the morning.

"You better stay till sunrise," Dave advises when we pull up in front of the house.

"Not a chance!" bellows Walter. "We'll wait a few minutes to make sure the cops aren't around. That's it."

Irene puts coffee on before she takes Raina up to bed. In the slanty bathroom at the back of the house, I take a look at Walter's cut. He's got a wad of Kleenex in his pants to keep the blood from staining his clothes, but there isn't much blood. I put peroxide on it and bandage it with gauze and white tape. "It's starting to hurt," he says.

"I think that's a good sign," I tell him.

"Guy's crazy."

I find Irene in the kitchen cleaning up the mess we left at the table earlier in the evening, when we'd been having simple fun, the old kind of fun. I spend a few seconds just gazing at the drawings taped to the walls while she glides back and forth between the table and the sink. Dave is nowhere around.

I pick up the white paper napkins we'd used as coasters. "Irene . . ."

Walter's voice behind me: "C'mon."

"Thanks for coming," Irene says in a polite tone. "We'll do it again."

As Walter tugs me to the door, she keeps on with polite chatter, and I am forced to face the facts: she and I are not close. Never have been. We are two couples who get together once or twice a year to play cards. Walter and I are allowed in only so far. My feelings this particular night, as we take our ritual leave, don't matter.

We drive away with our headlights on. When we leave the yard, Dave is staring at the trunk of his Chrysler, wondering how he can reclaim the lid the border stole from him. Maybe he's even planning to go back there tonight before the sun comes up.

I can see a lamp on in Dave and Irene's upstairs bedroom window. I wonder how old Raina will be when we see her again. I don't think we'll see Dave and Irene for a while. But there is always that little church just up the road, where Irene and the baby sit on their sunlit pew every Sunday morning, trying to keep safe.

When we turn onto the road that leads back to town and away from the American border, I see a dead cat curled up at the grassy edge. I don't recall it being there when we arrived. I turn my eyes away from it, in case it's the half-tailed one that spoke to us on Dave and Irene's porch.

"Faster," I say.

The Middle Sisters' Secret

"Lie down, Mother."

"On the floor? Can't we do it on the bed?"

"What kind of job would that make? All lumpy."

"We could put a board on it."

I remember stroking Mother's frayed collar with the stubby chalkstick Lilah had brought home from school. Had stolen from the music room while Mr. Cook played "Church in the Wildwood" on Harriet Fielding's knuckles. "It was difficult enough finding a piece of paper that size," I told my mother, "never mind a sheet of plywood." I slid my hand under her armpit and felt a gape in the seam there, like a tiny mouth gnawing at the tender flesh of her hairless underarm. "Besides, it would be just as hard as the floor."

My mother stayed firm in her chair. "It's not the hard I'm worried about. It's getting down there."

"I'll lower you in, like when we go to the pool."

She spread out her hands and smoothed the wide lap of her dress. "It's not really the getting down, it's the getting up again."

"Mother you're not crippled, for goodness' sake! Now, just get down. Please."

That's how the day began, in our square kitchen, seven years ago. Funny how it's come back to me, here on a wooden bench polished smooth over the years by thousands of clenched buttocks. I've kept that day, enshrined it, in some compartment of my daughter-brain, and now, with nothing to look at, no one to talk to while I wait for the police to finish with my Lilah, it soaks into my consciousness like warm oil.

Air as light as flower petals blew over us through the window I'd opened early that morning. I'd had to sweat to get it open. The frame had been stuck shut; I'd never thought of opening that particular window, since it faced the Fielding's frosted bathroom pane. But today spring had looked different through it, somehow. Maybe because the window was clean for a change. And I'd gotten used to the idea of the Fieldings.

Mother got up and stood at the bottom of the paper strip. I put both my hands under her arms and eased her down. "Where'd you get the paper, anyway?" Her voice was disguised now, coming from the back of her throat as her head settled on the paper.

My mother spoke a mixture of English and German. She'd spent most of her life on the fringe of an English community in a large town a hundred miles or so from the city, and she still jumbled her languages. I spoke only English to her.

"You don't want to know." With the chalk, I began to trace around my mother on the brown kraft Lilah had snitched from the Fieldings' garage after dark yesterday. She said their new sofa had been wrapped in it. "But they'd unwrapped it already, hadn't they?" I'd asked her in the night cool of the back porch. Lilah had let go of the flattened roll of paper and run out into the dark beyond the porch where I could hear scuffles and smothered giggles, and where whites of eyes glinted in the light spilling from the doorway.

"I hope this turns out better than the brassiere you made last time I was here."

"What was wrong with it?" I asked, although I knew perfectly well.

"Ha! You had all that material left in the tips. Remember? Long pointy tips on the cups. If you could call them cups. I looked like I had monster nipples."

She'd given me her old bra to use as a pattern. I'd had to take the whole thing apart to get the exact shapes of all the pieces. She couldn't recall where she'd gotten it—at a store (which she would have if she'd been at Myra's), or if one of the other daughters had made it for her. It had looked home-made to me—flat and plain, like it had been cut from a bedsheet. In the end, I had to make her new one out of a bedsheet, too, but I had so wanted it to have proper cups. For three days she'd had to go braless while I cut and re-cut pieces of cloth. But no one seemed to notice. "Well, I do believe you fixed it yourself, didn't you? Just ran them under the sewing machine and tucked them away? You're still wearing it, I bet."

"Those fat seams are uncomfortable." (*Unbehaglich,* she said.) "Make my tits itch."

When I got to her shoulders, my body was opposite hers, and I found myself looking at her face upside down. It looked like a stranger's face. I would never recognize my mother upside down, I realized. She closed her eyes. She was prob-ably thinking the same about me. "Spread out your arms," I directed.

Someone came in the front door. We never used the front door.

At the same time as I heard the door open and close, my mother said, "This reminds me of the time Mr. Duguid raped me."

Already frozen on a fours like a mongrel in a rainstorm,

I hardly knew where to look or what to listen to. "Shhh! There's someone in the front room!"

"Wunderbar," she muttered.

"Mr. Duguid raped you?" I whispered, so softly it was nearly only a thought.

"Sonja? Mama?"

"Shit! It's Myra."

"Wunderbar."

But the front door clicked shut again. Then we heard only silence. Neither of us breathed.

Finally, I put my mouth to my mother's ear and asked again, slowly, "What do you mean, *raped?*"

"Spread out on the floor, just like this." The upside-down eye of my mother winked at me. "Don't worry, I spit in his cough syrup."

"He raped you. You spit—spat—in his cough syrup. He drank it."

"Not on the same day. Where did Myra go? Should I get up?"

Myra's spring hat cruised past the open window. I felt an urge to wait for her to pass again and then snatch the brilliant poppy from her brim. Once more she had to steal my moment. "I think she's going to the backyard. Must think we're out there."

But then my sister Myra's face appeared at the rectangle of fresh air between the window frame and the sill. "There you are!" she chirped from her tippy-toes.

Mother and I blinked at her politely. " 'Lo, My," I chirped back.

"What are you doing?" She stared at Mother on the brown paper.

"Why didn't you come through the living room? Weren't you just in there?" Sneaking around in my front room.

"It looked like you'd just finished waxing the floor. I noticed you still don't have a television set. A television would be good for Mother. She like television, don't you, Mother? 'Life with Riley.' Remember?"

"We spring-cleaned yesterday. And we're waiting for the price to come down. Jack says the price always comes down on things like that. Come on in. Through the front or the back." I finished outlining my mother's bundle shape. For the fun of it, I ran the chalk around her head as well.

"Does this dress have a hood or something?"

"Maybe."

My sister's eyes when she entered the kitchen were full of bewilderment, round and fearful, and her mouth was sort of puckered, with a little hole in the middle. I couldn't help but think of the doll I'd given Lilah for her sixth birthday, the one that had a hole between its sweetly pursed lips, where you could stick the nipple of the miniature baby bottle that came in the box with the doll. My sister Susie would have come in with a wisecrack ready and a slightly evil glint in her eye. But not Myra, not The Chosen One. She'd been uppity ever since her daughter Beth had been appointed to live with Mother after the doctor had told us about Mother's angina. Well, Beth had gotten married and moved to the coast only a few months later, but Myra was still uppity. In fact, both the older sisters—and both the younger ones, too, come to think of it—were uppity about Mother.

I ran the chalk along Mother's waistline once more, just to make sure the dress wouldn't hang like a bag when it was finished. I also thought it might flatter her to know I was paying attention to her figure. Without looking at Myra, I said, "What are you doing here?" She lived practically in the opposite corner of the city.

Mother said in her funny back-of-the-throat voice, "Don't make it tight in the waist. I like it loose."

Beside the stove Myra stood with her open-toes shoes clamped together and her clutchbag pressed against her bust. "I—came to take Mother shopping. And you, too, Sonja."

"Ever hear of phoning first? How did you get here?"

"Well, I took a cab. I had a sudden attack of—spring fever, I guess you might say. Just felt like doing something—crazy."

I could feel her eyes following my chalk. The orange poppy bobbed as she spoke. How would I get her to leave? I needed to find out about this rape. I was sure none of the other sisters knew about it. It would have been mentioned somewhere along the line. I would tell Susie. It would be the middle sisters' secret.

My mother sat up and slid her calves under her rump. Once she had raised herself to her knees, I grabbed her under her arms again and hoisted her to her feet. I was proud of how strong I was. I didn't believe any of the others would have been able to do that. "Shopping for what?"

"Mother needs some new dresses. There's a sale at Kresge's." Myra would never shop for herself at Kresge's. She was going to spring for a cheap dress for her mother.

"I'll pay the cab fare," she added.

I lifted the sheet of paper form the floor and hung it from a nail sticking out of the frame above the open window, where it wafted in the morning breeze that funnelled between the Fieldings' house and ours. Myra had come all the way across town in a taxi. I couldn't just send her away. "I'm making her a dress. Why don't we just visit for a bit? Besides, Mother and I were planning on going to the pool later, over on Sherbrook." When Mother is with me, it's her and me. When she's with you, you can do whatever you like.

We heard noise coming from the Fielding's backyard. Penelope Fielding giving instructions to the gardener. He wasn't a real gardener, just some derelict named Wiggers. Piggly Wiggers, the kids called him. Penelope had given him a pair of overalls and pruning shears and made him into a silk purse. She seemed annoyed with him this morning. He'd probably pruned a weed and uprooted a crocus.

The Fieldings and I were not on good terms. "Just because they own and we rent," I'd explained to Mother the first time she'd come to visit after Jack and I moved to Balmoral Street. "Just because Mr. Fielding's a vice-president and calls himself Boswell Q. Their children study music. Ours take piano lessons. Used to take piano lessons. Those are the reasons they look down their pointy noses at us."

Myra sat down on a chair at the table, across from Mother. She held herself in a stiff sort of way, as though the chair might collapse underneath her fat ass. She didn't rest her arms on the table. "Don't worry, I wiped the jam off," I said, and then I filled the kettle and put it on to boil."

"Well," Myra began, and I could see she wasn't going along with the plan, "you can still make your dress. Mother needs more than one. It won't hurt her to have two. Why don't we just ask her what she wants?"

Through the silence that followed, I kept my back turned to them. But I pictured the two of them sitting there, perhaps sharing a secret look between them, maybe even mouthing messages to each other. But I didn't let on. "We can still have coffee," I said.

In the end, Mother never really said anything. We drank the coffee, Myra asked about Jack, when he'd be home from the job up north, about Lilah and Jack Jr., and about Susie, whom the other sisters hadn't seen much since she'd walked out on the Italian, her third husband. And then she got Mother's coat from the hook at the back porch and draped it over Mother's shoulders. "Would you like to change your shoes?" Myra asked in a sugary voice.

Mother shot me a glance, which I answered with a wink, and shook her head. Myra would have to suffer the humiliation of her mother wearing felt morning slippers in public. The coat, on the other hand, was very classy (Greta? Doris?), making the slippers even more embarrassing.

"So, you're going to Kresge's," I said, to let them know I

wouldn't be part of Myra's cozy threesome. After all, she didn't know about the rape.

I'd always known about the two things that had taken the wind out of my mother's sails. According to her, all these years, two things: one was being cheated out of her education. She started ninth grade, all eager, dressed in new hand-me-downs, but late fall of that year her father, my grandfather, loaded his whole family into an old bus and trundled them all down to South America—Bolivia, it was—to investigate the possibility of farming there. When they returned home early in January, my mother and a couple of her older sisters tried to return to school. But the principal met them at the front door, as though he'd been lying in wait for them, and told them they'd missed too many classes to catch up, and they were to go home. "And don't bother to come back, any of you," Mother mimicked whenever she told that story. In those days, no one paid much attention to rights and laws, and my mother and her sisters meekly trudged home. No one fought for them, no one even took their side. Hardly any of the immigrant kids went past eighth grade; secondary education was for the snotty English brats. But my mother said she'd never realized how badly she'd wanted to go to school until the principal had rejected her at the door. She said it seemed as though he'd planned it all, so triumphant he'd been, towering over them on the front steps of the high school, strutting, pointing at the street from which they'd come.

The second thing was the premature death of her husband, my father. It wasn't only that she loved him and missed him. His dying left her penniless and, in the man-driven world outside our four walls, powerless. After he went, there was a flurry of marriages among the older sisters, the middle ones found full-time jobs—telephone operators, store clerks, maids—and together we all managed to support our mother and the younger sisters. Her bitterness about losing her husband didn't show until after I was married. She became moody, nasty sometimes, and talked for hours about how she hadn't gotten a proper chance in life, about how far she could have gone if she'd been allowed to finish school. She'd been good in art, she told us. She could have been great.

Mother didn't get into snits like that any more. Not since her heart problem, not since she'd had to start relying on us for her maintenance. Not since she'd had to learn to hold her tongue in front of grandchildren. My children did not know her. She hardly spoke when they were around.

The two things that had robbed her of greatness, of validity, even, were known to all of us. They were part of her legend. And now, a third: being molested by Mr. Duguid.

My mother and her sister Dora worked as *au pair* girls for the Duguids after the school doors clanged shut, though they weren't called *au pairs* then. I don't know what the Duguids would have called them. But I suppose the two girls looked after the babies and cleaned house and made lunch. I don't know. And I don't know how long they worked there. I remember Mother saying something about Mrs. Duguid being sickly after the last baby.

Who were the Duguids? Dead now, of course. Where had Mr. Duguid violated my mother? And where had Mrs. Duguid been all the while?

Lilah and Jack Jr. came home for lunch. We ate together, hardly talking at all. They said nothing about the huge paper doll hanging by the window, didn't ask about the empty chair.

I remember how quiet mealtimes were when Jack worked up north those three years. Noon was a pensive time for me, it seemed. I don't think I paid much attention to Jack Jr. and Lilah. I never looked them up and down or asked them questions, never imagined that anything might terrify them.

I don't think I ever warned them. We drowsed over our hot dogs, never dreaming that Herman Cook the music teacher, who coddled Harriet Fielding because she practised her scales every day, secretly lusted after Lilah.

And seven year later would lie in wait for her as she took a familiar back lane home from her evening shift at Kresge's.

We were nearly done lunch when we heard someone hammering at the back door. We just looked at one another, my children and I. And then the someone shouted, "Are your kids in there with you? I want to talk to them about my sofa!"

Penelope Fielding.

Both Lilah and Jack, mouths full of dry bun ends, leaped from the table and bounded through the freshly waxed living room. The front door closed softly.

I stayed at the table, sipping my coffee, while Mrs. Fielding pounded at the rear, yelling threats. The door wasn't locked. I half expected her to walk right in.

After her nap, Mother wandered into the front room, still in her old dress (the new one, as far as I knew, was still in the bag), and sank into her favourite chair. I followed her and sat across from her on the hard chair no one liked.

"Do you have the cloth?" she said.

"The cloth?"

"For my dress."

"Of course I have the cloth." I didn't have the cloth. Jack would be home on the weekend, and I had intended to go out with him Saturday afternoon, to shop and maybe have a drink at the Occidental. By now I'd lost interest in the dress, though.

"I should have picked some I liked at Kresge's," Mother continued as if she hadn't heard me, or as if she knew I was lying. "I saw some nice cloth on sale." Punishment for the lie.

Then she just sat there, her face slack and sleepy, contented, I thought.

"How can you be so calm?" It was a shout in that colourless room.

"What?"

"You told me this morning you were raped! How can you be so calm?"

"I wasn't raped this morning."

"Who have you told about this?" I demanded. "Who did you tell *then?*"

"It was more than sixty years ago."

She looked, at that moment, like someone done with the past, someone who'd closed several doors behind her and was glad of it, glad they were closed, finally, glad she didn't need to reopen them and review just how she'd made out. Her inner eye was sealed shut.

And right then I could have left it alone, left it concealed in an era I'd never been part of. But I felt the need to know her last secret, so her whole story could be told someday. And I wanted her to give me something. Me. Sonja. Something of hers no one else had.

"Mother—did that man. . . ?"

She stared at the thin drape forming a huge square of light in front of the windows. A knot formed on her profile, just above her nose, between her eyes. But all she did was wave her hand, as though a fly had buzzed near her ear.

"Mother. Tell me."

"It happened more often in those day. To girls like us."

Girls like *you?*

"You worked for a couple, probably sometime the man would take you. Most girls just quit then. Some got treats or even money. Not us. We did what Lilah always says."

"What Lilah always says?"

"We got even."

"Did Mrs. Duguid know?"

"He only got me once. Dora I think never. He wasn't a big scary monster, Sonja. He was just a silly pig.

"It happened when I was there alone. After that Dora and I agreed—never alone. If one was too sick to go to work, we were both too sick." She wagged her finger in front of her nose, reminding her sister of the rules. "And if we were separated by many rooms while we worked, or one was upstairs and one was downstairs, we sang. We were good singers. If one stopped singing, the other went to check on her. Of course, he wasn't always home. Vice-president of something. But the day Mr. Duguid got me, he was home, and I was at the house alone. Except for Mrs. Duguid and the children."

"Where were they? Didn't they hear?"

"To tell you the truth, I don't know where they were. Probably upstairs in their rooms." My mother smoothed her lap with the palms of her hands. She did that so often. Like there was something there she wanted to brush off. Or like there was a flaw in the pattern she needed to fix.

"Where did he—do it?"

"The usual place!"

"I mean—what part of the house? What kind of house was it?"

"In the kitchen. At the back, away from the main part. It wasn't a mansion. It was a stone house beside other stone houses. Not a big house. Lots of little stuffy rooms. Velvet drapes and wood in the nice rooms. Some rooms were very plain. The kitchen was very plain. He got me in a plain room." Then her eyes brightened a bit and she looked straight at me and said, as if she had just remembered, "He came at me like an ape. The reason he looked like an ape was because he was waving his arms over his head like an ape. And he had something in one of his hands—maybe a banana. I thought he was going to hit me with it at first. And then when he pushed me down on the floor I thought he was going to use it between my legs. Dora and I always joked that he was . . ."

Again the racket at the back door. Mrs. Fielding ranting and raving about her sofa. I did wonder what Lilah had done to that sofa. I had assumed she'd just taken the paper wrapper. All at once it occurred to me that, were Mrs. Fielding to walk along the side of the house, along the cement walk connecting the front yard to the back, she would see her missing paper wrapper blowing in the breeze inside my kitchen.

Mother kept her eyes glued to me while we listened to Mrs. Fielding's tantrum. I crossed my right knee over my left and watched my shoe bouncing at the end of a fidgety leg.

Before the pounding stopped, but when I recognized the tantrum weakening, I raised my eyes to my mother's and said, "So. It's all a joke. You're playing a joke on me."

"What?" She cocked her head and ran her eyes along the curtain rod and then along the wall until they met mine. "Would I joke about such a thing? They carried their noses in the air, those Duguids, which was lucky for us, or we would not have had work. Impudent."

That's what I though I heard her say. "Impudent?" I said.

"IM-PO-TENT!" She twirled her index finger beside her temple, the way Lilah did to indicate that someone was cuckoo. I didn't know whether Mother meant me or Mr. Duguid.

I thought I could tell if she was making fun of me. She appeared to be completely earnest. She was looking at the sunlit white curtain again—a movie screen where she could watch scenes from her past.

"He could have been impotent," I said. "His wife had just had a baby, hadn't she? How do you know he was impotent?"

Mother shrugged. "I said, it's just something Dora and I joked about. Pay attention."

So they had despised him even before the rape.

"I couldn't scream," she continued. "Well, I didn't want to scream. Because of the children. I was only—so angry.

Because of the children being in the house. And because he caught me. I remember . . ." She searched for a word. "*Krächzen.*"

"Croaking?"

"My throat was so dry. All I could do was make noises like a frog. I was trying to tell him to stop. He had to work hard at those buttons on his fly. But he still held me down at the same time. As though he'd had practice, Sonja. As though he'd had practice. And it was him that went inside me." Even though the uproar at the back had stopped, she added, "Not really a lady at all, is she? Not a *gnädige Frau*, Mrs. Boswell Q. Fielding." Mother let her head fall back against the plump curve of the easy chair.

Worried that her story was done, I leaned forward and said, "I don't understand how a thing like that went—well, that it wasn't dealt with. He was a *criminal*, Mother." Such hollow words. As if we could fix it now. As if anything we could do now would fix it for her.

She sat so still then, unblinking, unbreathing, un-anything, I wondered if she'd had a stroke or a heart attack. But I wondered that almost every day, when in another room she wouldn't answer a call, or when she didn't get up at her usual time in the morning, or she took a longer-than-normal nap. And I began to think about what I would do if she really died there, like that. About whether I would try to revive her or not. Whether I would call the ambulance right away or just sit and hold her hand for a while, staring up into her cold face. About whether or not I would be scared to be in the presence of the death of the person who had given me my life. About how I would feel about the easy chair when everything was over. And just as I was about to struggle on my knees across the hard wax to her side, she spoke. Perhaps I should have struggled on my knees across the hard wax either way. As it turned out, I merely remained sitting in the chair no one liked and waited for further events to unfold, because my mother had come to life again, and it turned out that while I was thinking she'd died, rage had begun to boil inside her.

"Don't you know yet," she said in a voice so taut, so unwilling to come out, it sounded like a man's—low, gritty, monstrous. "Don't you know yet what we were in those days? Who we were?"

I didn't want to hear, although I already knew.

"I've told you what it was like in that crowded boarding house. Seven of us in three rooms no bigger than clothes cupboards, my brothers taking turns sleeping on the one bed they had to share. We never picked through the trash behind the grocery store, the way some of the others did. Dora and I would always knock at the back door and ask politely if they had anything to give us. We brought our own bags. Some days the boy working back there would give us rubbery carrots and dried-out grapefruits and blue chickens, if we were lucky. Some boys filled out bags with the most rotten *Schund* they could find. But it was always Dora and me who were sent begging; people were more likely to give to girls. We had two dresses, the boys had two shirts. When our week-dresses were being scrubbed, we had to sit and wait for them wearing our Sunday ones. We'd get excited when somebody in the neighbourhood died, because maybe it would be our turn to get the dead person's clothes. Then my mother spent days tearing and cutting and re-sewing so she could replace our worn-out things."

I thought about the brassiere; we had not come so far after all.

"If the boys needed new shirts, and it was a lady who died, then they had to go around town wearing the dead lady's dresses or nightgowns neatly sewn by Mother into shirts. You never saw such shirts. My brothers looked like gypsies."

The gypsy-shirts story. Yes, yes, we'd heard it all before.

"Do you think those things weren't noticed by the *Engländers* who ran the town? And I've told you what happened at school. That's how our whole life was."

I marvelled at how still my mother sat as she hurled those words into the listless, uncaring front room of my city house. How still she sat as the words bounced off the walls like sponge balls.

"And it was no different for the men. For my father and our father. They were called names, got the worst jobs. And Sonja—they were good people. We were all good people. What did they want from us? What more could we have done? I don't know what more any of us could have done. They wanted us to disappear, and that's the one thing we could not do. It's because I could not make myself disappear that Mr. Duguid caught me and punished me for it. But what difference do you think that would have made to the police? All that would have happened is that Dora and I would have lost our jobs. The only thing we could do was get even."

"By spitting into cough syrup."

"He called it cough syrup. It was some kind of liquor he drank from a little crystal glass." She raised her hand and measured the size of the little crystal glass between her thumb and index finger. "That isn't all we did. We put lye on his shaving brush. And one Sunday we saw his long car at the church. We crouched beside the line of cars and crept into the driver's seat of his car and pulled down our underpants and peed on it. Both of us. We soaked it good. But we like spitting into the cough syrup the best, because we were putting something of ourselves inside him, inside his body. And he never knew."

"But . . ." I wanted to tell her that it isn't getting even if the person you're getting even with doesn't know you got even. I didn't say it, though. In her mind, she'd had her revenge. "How could you even face him after that?" I asked her.

Again the hands stroking the skirt of the old dress. "Face

him! I had to bring him his cigars and slippers. In the parlour with the velvet drapes. He didn't rape me in there. He did it in the kitchen." She sighed. Her hands became dormant in her lap. "It was how things were then. That's all."

That's all. The sun had slipped over to the corner of the house. The square of curtain was dull now, except along one side, where a thin beam of light squeezed between the drape and the window frame. Soon Lilah and Jack Jr., coming from the street down the sidewalk that connected the front yard with the back, would cast momentary shadows on that sliver of light, and then soon after that no sun at all would come through the front window.

As I looked at the doomed sliver of sunshine, I remembered how this had all started: Mother lying on her back on a sheet of brown wrapping paper in *my* plain room, her face upside down. *This reminds me of the time Mr. Duguid raped me.*

"Are we going swimming?"

In my mind I took my mother's face in my hands and kissed her pale brown lips. In reality I said, "Yes, yes. We will go right now so I can have supper ready on time. You know how hungry the kids get." I could hardly wait to lower my mother into the clear water of the pool. Only I could do it. Myra could never do it. She wasn't nearly strong enough.

I didn't buy the cloth for the dress on Saturday. I'd almost stopped thinking about the dress by then. We took the new store-bought one out of the bag after swimming, and Mother started to wear it. Jack and I did have a drink at the Occidental. A couple, actually, while Mother napped. I can't think why I didn't tell him about the rape. Every time I was about to start, I decided to wait just a little longer, and before I knew it the weekend was over and Jack was gone again. The sofa-wrapper stayed up on its nail by the window.

The following week, Mother moved to a different daughter's house, and not long after that she did have a stroke. Not at my house, as I had hoped and feared, but at the home of the youngest daughter, my youngest sister, which, I suppose, was fitting. My youngest sister still lived in the town where we'd all been born.

Mother didn't die of that stroke. Once in the hospital, she had more strokes, and never stayed with any of the daughters again. We city sisters visited her as often as we could, watched her eyes move from one face to another, listened to her silence, yearned for some gesture from her paralyzed arms.

After she died, we shared our stories, answered the questions our children asked, preserved her legend. I sat alone with Susie many times, many times started to tell her the secret of the rape.

But the time was never right. I think, deep down, I wasn't certain that the secret was true. I sometimes think Mother made it up to make me feel better about being a middle sister. But could she have known my private need, have sensed my desire to have a unique piece of her for myself? The secret became a sort of terrible thing, something I could scarcely keep, scarcely tell.

My daughter appears at last at the darkish end of the long police station corridor. As she comes to me, her face is white, she is tired, drained empty. And I wonder if this is the right time to share my mother's secret, true or untrue, whether the story would console her somehow, would convince her that what she is doing is the right thing, the right kind of revenge. I must decide, as she emerges from what is surely a very plain room, if the terrible gift my mother gave me will become a good gift, a connection with the grandmother she's never thought much about. Lilah could not make herself disappear, either, and she'd been punished for it.

My mother's outline hung by the window even after she left my house. The top corners curled over. The new shape reminded me of a nun's habit. Just before she had the first stroke, I unhooked it, finally, and folded it and put it into a closet. I don't know if it came along with us when we moved away from Balmoral Street, into our own house. It may still be in some closet, just like the day itself. I do remember Piggly Wigger's hungry, hollow eyes, when I lowered the sofa-wrapping from the nail, staring up into mine from the sidewalk between the Fieldings' house and ours.

And yet the paper outline still flutters in front of the open windows. I won't ever forget the shape my mother's body made when I ran the stolen chalk around her. And now, I must teach my daughter that shape. I must make very sure she will remember it forever.

Colours of the Moon

"Wendell?"

She doesn't knock. The opening of two doors, the sounds their hinges make, the latches as they separate and join again, will be warning enough. Knocking would be too formal, too much the politeness of a stranger.

A familiar reek of damp cellar and ferrets permeates the dark of the entrance landing. Geraldine has not often been inside the house, but she remembers the entry of it well, and can tell from the darkness that the third door, the one that leads to the kitchen, is closed. By instinct she takes the three steps up to the third door. Voices stub against it from the other side.

"Wendell?" again softly, as she pushes into the dim light.

He is nearly only a silhouette, standing there in the middle of the room. A bulb over the sink back-lights the thin, gentle curve of him, but in the glow of a TV set squatting on the counter-top she sees the white of his eyes, because he is looking at her.

"I walked over. The moon is so bright, I didn't need a flashlight."

Wendell doesn't move, except for the turning of his head, the focusing of his eyes on the TV screen. He says nothing.

Geraldine doesn't need to ask what he's doing. She's witnessed it once before, the way he watches *Star Trek* late in the evening. The picture on the screen is fuzzy, but the sound is perfectly clear. It balloons from an AM-FM receiver on a shelf above the TV. In his hand, Wendell holds a rabbit-ear antenna, and it is only if he stands in that particular spot with the antenna in his hand that he can pick up the signal.

For a moment neither of them speaks. Starship *Enterprise* is in trouble. Commands snap at them from two speakers on the shelf.

"Why aren't you at the party?" Wendell and Geraldine say in unison. But the *Enterprise* begins to lurch about in the electronic blizzard on the screen, and neither answers.

Geraldine puts her hip to the kitchen counter and slides along it, touching canisters, a honey jar, drinking glasses etched with a Coca-Cola logo, a stack of fertilizer bills, stuffed olives shrivelling in a chipped pickle dish, a threadbare towel hanging from a faux-silver ring beside the sink, a tableknife with cheese-spread on its tip, oranges clustered in a basket, an unopened bag of roasted sunflower seeds. She has noticed a nearly empty bag of seeds on the table.

"Wendell—this . . ." Geraldine picks up a green, saucer-shaped candleholder, its rim almost overflowing with congealed wax. A bit of white candle and black wick remain in the centre.

"It's the same one, Geraldine, if that's what you're asking. Not the only thing in this house that hasn't moved in four years. Don't read anything into it." With that, Wendell turns down the volume of the TV, and Geraldine fears that she must read something into it.

The first blue-moon party had been six years ago, early in July. Not the first blue moon, of course. But the first party

Geraldine's parents, or perhaps anyone, had ever thrown to celebrate it.

The night was warm and dry and clear. The moon rose, for the second time that month, into an unblemished sky the colour of blueberry tea.

The blue-moon guests lolled on the grass around the gazebo, under the canopy of one of the elm trees that sheltered the inner yard. A few sat at wood tables. The younger ones, further away, under a different elm, had made a fire with deadfall and old newspapers. A stereo played moon songs that the whole family and their friends had collected for weeks and taped. Many guests had already gone home. Some who were still there had drunk too much blue champagne and would end up spending the night in their cars, or even under shrubs near the patio. Geraldine's father would take their car keys and hide them in the house until morning.

The smell from the fire, the smoke floating past the moon, the bass tones from the tape player, the softness of the grass, the warmth of the air drugged the moon watchers. And that was when Geraldine talked to Wendell for the first time, as a woman. That was how she found out about his turtle. She was nineteen.

Wendell guzzled ginger ale and popped sunflower seeds under the celebrity moon, and stroked the head of his springer spaniel, Emmett, who went everywhere with him. "A few years ago I was a drinker," Wendell told Geraldine. "Hardly a night of the week that I wasn't tight. No matter how busy I was. Always fit it in. And I drank in a lot of places, including the fields here about. Used to have a Merc. Now, one night— do you remember?—I ripped across that field there" (he pointed with the ginger ale can) "between my place and yours, and your mom and dad were barbecuing pickerel or something for some old relatives they hadn't seen for years who were visiting here from—where was it?—California somewhere, I think.

"So there they were, around sunset, sitting on the lawn. After sunset? Maybe they'd already eaten the pickerel. It was August, and we'd just harvested some wheat, and I'd been out doin' my Saturday drinking, and when I was just about home I decided to pay my neighbours a call. So I turn off the road close to my place and gun the Merc through the ditch and rip off over the stubble to your place here, right between those granaries. See? Around the lilacs—or maybe I clipped 'em a little—and up onto the lawn."

Geraldine listened out of politeness. Wendell Isaac always wore a cap, and a khaki shirt and pants, but she liked his face and the way his eyes looked so deeply into hers and, when he walked, the way he kept his back so straight and proud. And he liked animals. She'd heard he had ferrets for pets.

"Then I see that your folks are having a sort of elegant straight-laced kind of evening, and I don't want to embarrass them, so I lean out my electric window and call, 'You got time to harvest my peas next week, Frank?' as though I came tearing between his granaries regularly to talk business.

"And he nods, slow, like this, and I do a one-eighty on the lawn, leaving grass-burns, and rip back around the lilacs and between the granaries and head home.

"Thing is, the space between those granaries isn't hardly wide enough to let a vehicle through. But I did it twice that night, totally pie-eyed. Not a scratch on the Merc. And you know, I didn't have any field peas that year, either . . .

"And that's the same night I met the turtle."

"The turtle?"

He nodded. "An important turtle. Changed my life."

As Geraldine searches drawers and shelves in Wendell's kitchen, other sounds come through the open windows: slithering and rustling from the ferret cage under the trees near the back door, and the *peent* of nighthawks as they hunt near the tall yardlight. Soft, warm noises that can smooth away little fears. Her home, straight to the west, is too far away for her to hear the stereo playing moon music again, at the second blue-moon party of the decade, only this time it is September.

"So? Are you going?" says Wendell at last.

Geraldine finds the matches and lights the candle, just as she did the night she came to tell Wendell she was expecting their child. As she did then, she places the candle on the small table in the middle of the kitchen.

Then she sits down in one of the two vinyl-bottomed chairs and says, "Yes. I am going with him."

Wendell blows out a puff of air between his lips. "Then clear out of here!"

"Wendell, this has all been over for so long. And yet you've clung to some sort of illusion, some sort of fantasy that you and me and Jem are a family. I guess in one small way we are; you and I are the biological parents of a child—"

"More than biological! More than biological, Geraldine. I have been a father to him."

"Not really, Wendell. You've visited and played with him, but you don't get close to him. There's more of a bond between you and the turtle than between you and Jem. You're scared of him."

Using his one free hand, Wendell begins to eat sunflower seeds. Though he still faces the television, Geraldine can tell by the way he looks through it, beyond it, that he is not paying attention to the dialogue.

"Wendell, sit down."

"I suppose you were going to leave without letting me say goodbye to him!"

"Wendell, sit. Please."

Static replaces the crooning of Mr. Spock. Bodies shift behind the bright curtain of snow on the television screen.

"He's dead," he croaks. "That's why this is happening. He's dead."

"What?"

"The turtle. I found him. Been dead a while, I think. A week or so. Weighed just a feather."

"What turtle, Mr. Isaac? Are there turtles around here?" Geraldine leaned toward him. They faced each other across the picnic table.

"After I leave your place that night," Wendell continued, patio lanterns dancing in his glistening eyes, "I don't go home right away. I drive around some more, by myself, having a few more snorts now and then. And for the first time in my life I'm feeling lonely and useless and sorry for myself. No family, all my friends are married and have kids. And I'm almost home and dreading arriving there, when all of a sudden I see this big rock in the middle of the road. Looks like a big rock. I swerve the Merc to miss it, even though I'm almost blind drunk by now, and the Merc"—Wendell bent even closer to Geraldine so the brim of his hat touched her forehead—"my Merc flies over the deep ditch that runs alongside the road. You know how deep that ditch is. And I mean, the car actually flies. Slow. In sloooow motion. Lands like a feather.

"And I get out and inspect that rock, and it's a turtle. Sticks out its head and says, 'HELP.' Not in a voice, exactly, but I could read its lips. And again it says, 'HELP.'

"I can tell it needs water. What else would a turtle want? So I carry it to my pond, even though it's a huge son-of-a-gun, and go back to the house and can't get the thing off my mind. And all of a sudden I'm clear-headed. And I decide that night that I will stop drinking if I am seeing turtles on the road and floating through the air in my Merc. Because turtles don't live around these parts. Especially giant-sized ones. It must have been a hallucination, I'm thinking.

"Next morning, I find the Merc in perfect condition on the other side of the ditch, and I see the turtle sunning itself on a piece of old raft beside the pond.

"So I quit drinking, because the turtle was a sign. He was only going to save me once, I reckoned. And I've never seen it since. But I know it still lives in my pond. I can, like, feel it living there."

Wendell looked around at all the people standing and sitting and lying in different positions under the blue moon, and then back at Geraldine. "You believe that? The turtle was a sign?"

Geraldine had a seashell she'd brought home from a vacation on Vancouver Island. Every night she whispered her hopes and dreams and worries into it. She believed that there were as many shells in the ocean as there were stars in the heavens, and that every seashell was connected with a star.

She leaned towards Wendell. "Let's go look for it. Take me to the pond."

Around the lilac hedge they walked together, Wendell and Geraldine and Emmett, between the two granaries, into the pale dark of the field between Wendell's farm and Geraldine's. Once they had moved away from the trees, the sky expanded and turned a brighter blue, and the distances and the uncut wheat turned grey-blue, like tarnished steel.

And though they circled the pond several times, stepping soundlessly on the weed mat, parting the willow bushes every few feet, they did not discover the turtle that night. Nor any other night, though they searched for it together many times.

"Where did you find it, Wendell?"

"I was driving along the border between my sunflowers and your wheat. Just over there. And all of a sudden it was in front of me, in the quackgrass. Almost hit it with my truck. I never thought it would die out of the pond, did you? It may have died at the side of the pond, and maybe some dog or a fox managed to drag it further away. I don't know. Emmett couldn't have done it." Wendell fingers the pile of empty sunflower seeds. "There were flies in the openings where its head and legs and tail used to be."

Wendell stares into the candle flame for a moment. "I don't know what happened first. Did the turtle die before we stopped believing in it? Or did our doubts kill it off? Maybe it slowly started dying when we stopped looking for it. I've been drinking again, and coveting what you have with another man. And you're getting ready to take my boy away."

"I'll make sure you get to see him often. He'll spend the summers with you and my mom and dad. Half of Christmas, too." Geraldine tugs at Wendell's fingers and places them, with hers, around the candle so that their hands encircle it.

"You're going," he mutters. Shards of sunflower shell cling to his bottom lip and his bristled chin. "You're going and you're taking Jem away with you."

"Tread softly, Wendell. . . ."

"Geraldine . . ."

"Let go. I'm not going with Tony because I think he'll be a better father. I'm going because I love him."

"To northern Alberta. Seems so far."

"Lots of work for a bush pilot, up there and in the Territories," Geraldine replies.

Wendell squeezes her hand suddenly. "That's not all. I killed Emmett."

Geraldine searches Wendell's downcast eyes and sees the flicker of the candle flame.

"He just lay in the middle of the yard," Wendell continues. "Couldn't hardly get up at all. He was miserable. Miserable. I wouldn't have shot him if I hadn't been so miserable myself. But it was time."

"Oh Wendell . . ." Geraldine tightens the circle of their hands around the ebbing candle light.

"That's why you're not at the party." Geraldine rises from her chair. "Wendell, let's go out to the pond now. I feel hemmed in here, for some reason."

Later that summer, the summer of the first blue moon, Geraldine slipped between the two granaries and followed the grass strip that separated Wendell's field from her dad's. She'd done so almost every Saturday since the party. August had been full of dog days and thunder and night rains, but that evening the air and the land had finally dried up, and the quackgrass did not soak her moccasins as it sometimes did.

Wendell always waited for her around sundown, on a milking stool he kept beside his back door. From the milking stool he could see Geraldine through a gap in the maples. He told her he could see the top half of her body bobbing above the grain. If the sun was behind her, she was usually just a shape against it, he said, but if clouds were moving in from the west, her white shirt stood out clearly above the barley beards. Then he and Emmett would start towards the pond, and there they would meet her to wait for the turtle.

Geraldine sat on one of the logs they'd dragged over from the shelterbelt and rubbed dirt and grass off the bottoms of her moccasins. "I got asked out on a date tonight, Wendell. Somebody wanted to take me out to a show."

"Well, why didn't you go? You should've. About time boys ask you out."

"I don't want boys. Anyway, this wasn't a boy. Do you want to know who it was?"

"Doesn't matter. Why didn't you go?"

Geraldine stood up and looked into the pond, at the edges, trying to see a snake-like head somewhere among the weeds. "Because he kills things for a living. And because I'd rather be here. I think we'll see it tonight, Wendell. Because something tried to stop me from being here."

Wendell nodded. "Don't go too close, he'll go back under. What do you mean, he kills things for a living?"

"Tony Peters."

"The crop-duster? Solo Peters?" Wendell snorted. Geraldine retreated from the pond bank and sat back down on the log. A scuffle behind them caught their attention. Emmett, who'd been trotting around a cluster of rusted implements under the maples, startled himself by actually finding the rabbit he'd smelled as soon as he and Wendell had passed the trees. The rabbit darted out from behind a wagon wheel, and Emmett gave chase.

"Well, he's too old for you, anyway," said Wendell.

"I told you," Geraldine replied, "I don't want boys. But he spreads poison over everything, including your pond. It's killing the turtle. It's killing us."

At that very moment, Wendell and Geraldine could hear two or three small planes humming in the twilight like dragonflies. One of them might have been Solo Peters. Their lights glittered and winked against the coral-coloured horizon. Other things glittered: the town lights stretched beneath the coral sunset, first stars, a yellow crescent moon chasing the sun down its western path.

"Listen to this poem," said Geraldine. "It's by William Butler Yeats. I found it in an old book in Dad's den:

> Had I the heavens' embroidered cloths,
> Enwrought with golden and silver light,
> The blue and the dim and the dark cloths
> Of night and light and the half-light,
> I would spread the cloths under your feet:
> But I, being poor, have only my dreams;
> I have spread my dreams under your feet;
> Tread softly because you tread on my dreams.

Wendell took off his cap and waved away a cloud of mosquitoes. "I suppose it means something. It's your dad's book, you say?"

Geraldine cocked her head at him and smiled crookedly. "What's wrong?" he asked.

"It's just that I've never seen you without your hat, Wendell."

And then they didn't talk for a long time. Killdeers lamented in the summerfallow. Emmett fell asleep with his head on a thin log a few feet away from them. A strip of black appeared above the town lights as Wendell and Geraldine sat together beside Wendell's dugout—clouds moving in from the west, causing full darkness to come earlier than usual. Leopard frogs and salamanders called from their rain-fresh pond jungle. An August chill fell over the land, forcing the mosquitoes into the grass and the warm soil. But the air felt dry. They didn't expect rain.

Crossing the yard with Wendell, beneath the darting nighthawks, Geraldine senses the history of his farm, of Wendell's grandparents' farm, in the decaying maple trees, the bent willows, sway-backed barns and granaries. But mostly in the old perennial garden near the house, where his grandmother's sorrel and onions and lily-of-the-valley have gone wild among stalwart peonies and tiger lilies and columbine. She glances at the lackadaisical pigpen that leans into the maples halfway between the house and the pond. Though the pigs are asleep, the pen has a liveliness to it, mottled as it is in moonlight passing through shivering leaves. "I'm sorry you got the pigs, Wendell. I can't help but feel an ache for them."

"I don't understand your ache," says Wendell. "Never did. That trailer you live in isn't much better than their coop."

"But my mind can fly out of there, and I know nobody is fattening me up for a slaughter."

"What makes you think pigs don't have imaginations and dreams, Geraldine? And they don't know they're being fattened for slaughter. They're happier than . . . happier than we are, I think."

"That's just it, Wendell. We're villains. We're cruel and deceptive."

"How come you never talk that way about the ferrets? Tell me that."

"Because you're not planning to slit their throats."

The pond is quiet. It is too late in the year for the mating songs of frogs or the muttering of mother ducks or the hysterical shrieking of killdeers. The willows haven't been pruned, the matted grass hasn't been burned off for years. The pond is nearly invisible, except at the end where a drainage ditch runs into it. From there, Geraldine and Wendell watch the heavens dance in the wakes and ripples of insects trying to fly to reflected stars, to the very moon itself.

"Take off your cap again." That's how it had really begun, with the cap.

"What? Why?"

Wendell had gone to the house to get root beer. When he came back, Geraldine was sitting cross-legged at the edge of the pond, facing him. She shone the flashlight at the top of his head. "I want to see you uncovered. Please take it off."

The flashlight beam did not shine directly in his eyes. The lower rim of its circle of light grazed the top of his red fertilizer company cap. "Well . . ."

Wendell's slow hand went to the centre of the very top of the cap. He gave it a twist as he pulled it up. His sparse hairs lifted and then lay back down on his skull. "There," he said. "Not much to look at. I'm losin' it, as you can see."

The beam crossed his face and he closed his eyes against its brightness.

"Undo that top button of your shirt."

"What?"

"Is there something about your body you're ashamed of?"

Wendell remained standing as he took a swig of root beer. "My body is perfect."

"Undo the button," Geraldine repeated.

And Wendell opened two of the buttons at the top of his shirt.

Geraldine moved the flashlight beam along the row of buttons that sealed the khaki. "I've never seen a man's body live," she said.

Still tipping the bottle from time to time, Wendell opened the remaining buttons. Under the khaki was a white T-shirt. "This body ain't too live no more," he said. "Have a beer?"

"Lay your shirt on that log."

"I want to tell you something about turtles in Africa." Wendell draped the crisp khaki shirt on the log and with a flourish removed the undershirt as well.

"What beautiful fur you have on your body," Geraldine murmured. "It's shining like gold! Do other men . . ? You're not ashamed of it, are you?"

"There's these certain turtles—I forget what they're called—they lay their eggs on the riverbanks, in the sand . . ."

Geraldine lowered the beam to the John Deere buckle and Wendell's hands followed.

". . . but the crocodiles, they lay eggs there too, and all summer the crocodile eggs and the turtle eggs incubate in the African sunshine. The crocodile mothers, they wait for the young to hatch . . ."

The ends of the belt dangled at his hips. Without waiting for her directions, Wendell's fingers slid the tab of his fly zipper down, and he nudged his trousers below his hips. ". . . but the female turtles bugger off. After a while, I don't know how long, the crocodile embryos, inside their shells, start to call their mothers to come dig 'em up. They cry out from their shells."

Immersed in his story now, Wendell scarcely seemed to realize what he was doing.

"I saw it on TV. Each croc recognizes the sounds of her own babies, and up she slithers to set them free."

Geraldine said, "I thought this was about turtles." She waddled up to Wendell on her knees and untied his shoe-laces. Again she returned to her spot, again the light clung to his body like a swatch of damp silk.

"It is, in the end," Wendell replied. He kicked his high-tops towards Emmett, who still slumbered beside the log. The dog did not respond to the shoes brushing his tail. "It takes her awhile to dig all that sand off the eggs, but the moment they're exposed, the baby crocodiles burst out of their shells like jack-in-the-boxes. Then you know what the mother does?" Wendell pulled at the bottom of one pant leg, then the other, and laid his trousers on top of his shirt.

Geraldine's voice glowed. "It's on your legs, too . . !"

"She takes the little crocklings in her mouth, twenty or so at a time, and carries them down into the river. Just opens her mouth and in they scuttle. And she doesn't hurt a one of them. Crocodiles have special nerves under each tooth that tell them exactly how hard they're biting. In the river, she shakes her head and washes the babies into the water. . . . There isn't much left, Geraldine."

"Get to the turtle." She switched off the flashlight.

"When the *turtles* hatch, they have to make it across the beach to the river on their own. I forgot to tell you that there are all kinds of predators hanging around, just waiting for eggs to pop—lizards and eagles and so on . . ."

He was naked. An outline against the lights of his farm.

"But sometimes . . . sometimes, the mother crocodile no-tices the little turtle babies running past in the soft sand, and she doesn't eat them, like you think she would."

With the flashlight in her hand, Geraldine rose from the coarse, August-long grasses and came to stand face to face with him. She put her hand on his chest. "It's soft."

"No, she just picks up the little tyke, like one of her own, with those gentle teeth, and holds him on her tongue . . ."

Geraldine began to touch all the places on his body where the hair was thick.

". . . and carries him to the river and shakes him out into the water, and doesn't hurt him, because she's got these sensors under her teeth, and because she thinks he's one of the little baby crocodiles that needs help in getting to the safety of the river . . . just carries him to the river. . . ."

At the scent of human sweat and flesh, mosquitoes emerged from the warmish soil and began to hum again the sweetening night air around the pond. Emmett awoke and snapped at his stung shoulders and at the empty space above the tips of his ears.

And though Wendell and Geraldine made love more times that fall, always on the bank of the pond, she told him, when she found out that she was expecting his child, that she didn't love him, and did not want him to try to marry her out of duty.

"At midnight Dad's setting off fireworks he got in the States." Geraldine surveys the sky. "Look up, Wendell," she says. "Remember the poem? The one I hung over Jem's crib even before he was born?

> Had I the heavens' embroidered cloths,
> Enwrought with golden and silver light . . .

You were worried I'd try to make him memorize it before he was two."

"Well, did you?"

A fox barks on the other side of the old pasture next to the pond. All around, the landscape sleeps in a bath of blue light.

"You know," says Geraldine as she lowers herself to the flat, tangled grass at the edge of the drain, "I always thought I understood what Yeats meant about dreams, about giving those you love only your dreams because you're too poor to give them the stars. I thought dreams were a much better thing to spread beneath your lover's feet, sweeter, more noble than even the gold and silver light of heavenly bodies."

Wendell remains standing, staring into the water the way he'd stared at the square television screen in his square kitchen.

"And I thought about how we do tread on one another's dreams. We don't care enough, or we don't understand them, don't even recognize them most of the time.

"But now I see something else in those lines—how our dreams are often dangerous illusions. And passing them on, laying them at the feet of our loved ones, is after all a poor gift. And still we don't want anyone to tread on them. The reality is too painful, just like heaven would be too bright for us if it wasn't covered with 'the blue and the dim and the dark cloths.' "

Something drops into the water at the far side of the pond. Both Geraldine and Wendell turn to the sound. All they've heard is a *plunk*, probably a frog or a muskrat. But neither forgets how they watched, listened, in those days before Jeremy, before Geraldine moved away from the farm to live on her own, for signs of the turtle.

All at once Geraldine begins to weep. Wendell kneels beside her and takes her hand.

"Where's Emmett?" she whispers. "Is he here, close by? He should be here, with us, sleeping up on the rise, or sniffing around in the pasture. Tell me where he is, Wendell."

"He's nearby, sweetheart. He's nearby." Wendell strokes her dark hair with one hand and gestures towards the field with the other. "The turtle, though. He died. . . ."

"I know. . . .

"The spirit of the turtle died for you a long time ago, didn't it?"

After Geraldine had Jem, the two of them moved to a trailer park at the west edge of town, a place full of colour and breezes and noise. At night, the huddled commune of tin-can houses became silent. Winds racing across the fields rested for awhile, until the warming of the earth in the morning invigorated them again for another day of blowing. Then the tin houses would begin a quiet clattering, and the plastic pop-bottle whirligigs built by old folks in the trailer park—Alfred and Tina and Ben and Marie—would begin their spinning and clicking.

But every night around midnight, long after Jem was asleep and Geraldine had put all the fragments of his lively day into a basket that fit under her bed, she would go out and sit in the silence in front of her trailer. She'd put her feet up on the seat of Jem's tricycle and slap mosquitoes away from her ankles, and listen to invisible nighthawks hunting above the streetlights, and gaze up beyond them at the patterns the stars made in the silk of the sky.

And then she would go back inside to light a candle and listen to the seashell. In those days, she still believed in her seashell and the turtle. She talked to Jeremy about them, about stars, and read poetry to him before he went to sleep. She would read and read, in a hushed low voice, and when she closed the book, he would pull at her sleeve and say, "What? What, Mama?"

Every night after snuffing out the candle, Geraldine pushed a bookcase in front of the door that led out into the small yard in front of the trailer. Not a large bookcase, just one that was tall enough to cover the latch. The cupboard had stood in her own bedroom on the farm while she was growing up, and Geraldine had passed her collection of childhood books on to her son. The door it barricaded every night could lock out anyone testing the handle from the outside, but it could easily be opened from the inside. Geraldine did not take any chances with Jeremy.

But the moment came at last when Jem found exactly the right combination of courage and strength and stealth to shoulder the bookcase silently away from that door, to move it only as far as necessary to get at the latch and slip outside. Alone in the dark of night, in his pyjamas, he'd mounted his bright blue tricycle and pedalled away into the Lilliputian bays and crescents of the tin-can community. And then, into the very streets of the town. Geraldine slept through it all.

She awoke to the clicking of Tina's whirligig around two A.M. A wind had come up from the south during the night. Perhaps it was not the clicking that woke her; it might have been the wind itself, or the movement of the thin curtains above her bed. And when Geraldine twisted away from the wall and faced into the room, faced Jeremy's bed against the other wall, under the other bedroom window, which was now whistling gently with the wind passing through it, she saw his covers thrown back and his mattress empty.

He's just playing with his Fisher-Price men in the front room, she thought, and she hobbled half-asleep along the tight hallway, only to discover another, more terrible emptiness at the other end.

The bookcase was ajar, only enough to allow a small body to pass between it and the doorframe.

And then she thought he might be just outside, sitting on the bit of grass where the lawn chairs were, driving his trucks, or in the sandbox.

But the trucks were idle in the sand. They gleamed peacefully in the light from the bulb above the kitchenette window.

And for the first time in her life, Geraldine felt dread, a cold, merciless fear that stopped her heart like a vise and stuck in her throat, so that she could neither move nor call out. The clicking of the whirligigs, the scarcely audible breeze, were too loud. Any small noise he might make would be drowned out.

And then all at once she could move again. Geraldine ran along the crescents and bays like the wind itself. Her cotton shirt blew this way and that as she took the curves with her long stride. She called his name softly as she ran.

Past the hundred mobile homes she flew. Everywhere the spinning pop-bottle windmills clattered, no, roared, like hundreds of airplanes revving their engines on a runway. *Answer louder, Jeremy, I can't hear you. Answer me!*

Geraldine stopped at the entrance to the street, across from the park where she often took him to play. *He's in there,* she thought, *he's in there swinging on the new swings.*

The cloth of her nightshirt glowed white as if caught in the beam of a suddenly bright star and she froze in the middle of the asphalt street. A pair of headlights came towards her, then turned into the trailer park, and Geraldine could see that it was the cruiser car belonging to the town police.

"My boy! My son!" she cried, grabbing a half-rolled-down window even before the car had come to a full stop. "He's gone. . . ."

"No, there he is," said the officer.

In the back seat. Jeremy.

"What, Mama?"

"Hop in," the officer barked. "Somebody reported him cruisin' down Center Avenue on his trike. Trike's in the trunk."

She had not noticed that his trike had been missing, too. "I put furniture in front of the door every night, and the door is locked, but . . . I'll have to get bigger furniture or a different kind of lock, I guess." She pointed the way to her trailer.

"It's dangerous for a kid his age to be out on our streets in the middle of the night. I don't think he'd realized yet that he was lost. Most kids are afraid of being outside in the dark alone."

Why wasn't he scared? Geraldine wondered. Was it because he'd been conceived outside in the dark, in the light of stars and a dim crescent moon?

"Lucky he knew enough to say *trailer* when I asked him where he lived. I thought he might have wandered away during a party or something. I was hoping to find a house here with a lot of lights on or people partying on the lawn. Just cruisin' along Center, he was. . . ."

So far away!

". . . I asked him what his name was and he said *Yates*. 'Yates, yates, yates,' he kept saying. Your name isn't Yates, is it?"

"Yeats," said Jem.

"No," replied Geraldine. "It isn't."

"You'll need to teach him some rules."

The next day she called the hardware store and a man came to install a bolt on the inside of the door, at the very top of it. She had to believe that her son would be safe now, locked in, and the world locked out. She never told Wendell what had happened.

Rules. She had taught her son the rules. Confide in the seashell, live by the stars, honour the turtle. In the wake of the horror of his disappearance, her soul-wrenching fear, the weight of her duty as his guardian and protector, those things seemed childish and flimsy.

As the weeks passed and summer faded, Geraldine's seashell drifted about the trailer in neglect, until one day she tossed it absent-mindedly into Jem's basket, where he found it from time to time and whispered cautiously into its invisible spiralled chamber.

"What did you do with the turtle, Wendell? I think I should finally get to look at it, even though it's dead."

Wendell spreads his arms wide, embracing the pond. "I threw him in there. I held him high over my head, like this, and I threw him as hard as I could, so that he would land in the middle. Hundreds of years from now someone will drain this waterhole and find a perfect turtle shell at the bottom. And they'll wonder at the size of it."

"Maybe I did stop believing, Wendell," says Geraldine. "But I'll never forget the reason for Jeremy being . . ."

Wendell leaps to his feet. "Look! Look-look!"

They watch it, a long, slow, graceful arc in the western sky, pulling a long streamer of brilliant light through the lustre beneath the champagne-coloured moon. How close or how far it is cannot be told, whether it is as large as the earth or as small as a Roman candle. Geraldine and Wendell are paralyzed by its glory. Time ceases to pass. Silence wraps the fields. The stars disappear.

And then the vision itself disappears, well above the horizon, as though it has slipped through an invisible opening in the fabric of the firmament.

"That wasn't fireworks, Geraldine! It didn't come out of your goddamn blue-moon party, I could see that. It was way too high, and over Bill Martens' mustard field."

Geraldine waits, for more fireworks to flash and explode above the farmyard.

"It was a comet!" Wendell breathes. "A comet, for sure. Or a spaceship from another galaxy. Geraldine, it's . . ."

"Wendell, don't you think it could have been a meteor? A falling star?"

"That was no lost hunk of rock," Wendell replies, "accidentally wandering into earth's territory and disintegrating into a ball of flame. I've seen lots of those. This one went so slooow, Geraldine."

She sees again the white of his eyes as he gazes at her, then past her, into the pond, into the pasture. "The turtle didn't ask you for help that night you say your car flew and you quit drinking," she tells him at last. "Turtles don't die out of water the way fish do. And your turtle would have found a pond sooner or later, if it had wanted to."

But Wendell does not hear. "It—it must be a sign of some sort," he says. "For me, or for you, or for anyone who saw it. It might have been the soul of the turtle himself. . . ."

"Going where, I wonder. . . ."

"Right there, it was." With his index fingers and his thumbs, Wendell frames a bit of sky over the mustard field. "Maybe we get more than one chance."

Geraldine gets up slowly. "I'll go now."

"What?"

"Look! Look-look!" Reds and silvers rupture above the clump of trees that shape her parents' farm. At the same time, they hear the drone of an airplane, and then the pop-pop-pop of the blue-moon fireworks. Solo Peters soars high above the fireworks, circling, dipping his wings.

Geraldine begins to run. She races along the path between the harvested fields, and as she runs, she thinks, I'm treading on Emmett's grave. "Goodbye, old dog," she croons. "Goodbye, Emmett." Then, more softly, "Goodbye, Wendell." But she keeps her eyes on the fire-blossoms bursting low in the heavens beyond the levelled grain.

Until she is nearly there, nearly at the edge of the trees. Then Geraldine glances sharply to her right and sees the eyes of the fox, red in the reflected radiance of Roman candles and the moon. The fox, watching her across the brittle stubble of recently gathered wheat, watching her running, running, running.

About the artist

Rae Harris was born in Winnipeg and attended school in Brandon, Manitoba, where she obtained degrees in arts and in education from Brandon University. She later moved to Winnipeg and studied Fine Arts at the University of Manitoba.

She is an educator and an artist and is currently working on a number of large-scale, coloured pencil drawings as part of a series entitled "Waiting Women." Her works are in a number of private collections.